ITHACA

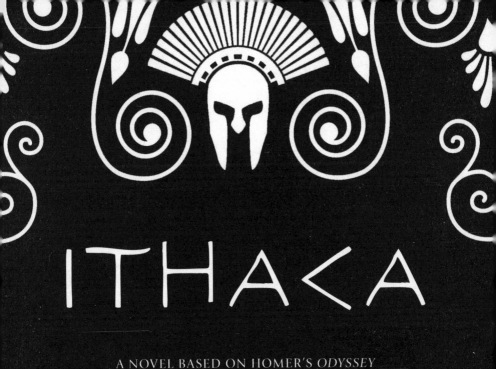

ITHACA

A NOVEL BASED ON HOMER'S *ODYSSEY*

PATRICK DILLON

PEGASUS BOOKS

NEW YORK LONDON

ITHACA

Pegasus Books Ltd.
148 W 37th Street, 13th Floor
New York, NY 10018

First Pegasus Books edition July 2016

Interior design by Maria Fernandez

Library of Congress Cataloging-in-Publication Data is available.

ISBN: 978-1-68177-155-7

10 9 8 7 6 5 4 3 2 1

Printed in the United States of America
Distributed by W. W. Norton & Company

For Catherine, Victor, Marina, and Maria

PART ONE

TELEMACHUS

When I was younger my mother used to tell me stories. Always about my father.

The time they met—already knowing they were to be married—and spent the night on the mountain above her father's home, and Odysseus cut a sprig of laurel leaves that they swore to keep forever. The first boar he killed, aged sixteen—the age I am now. His friends had been left behind in a frantic chase through the forests. In its first charge, the beast, a monster, gored Odysseus's thigh, but he ignored the pain and hurled himself on the animal with a spear. His friends found him that evening, lying bloodied but alive across the boar's carcass.

My mother took me out for picnics. Three, four years ago things were different in the big house. Everything was calm and orderly. Melanthius, the cook, would have a basket ready for us, full of fresh bread and olives, honey cakes in a linen cloth, salty little cheeses wrapped in vine leaves. Eurycleia, my nurse, would fuss around, warning of hornets and snakes. Medon, the steward, would snap at servants who disturbed the perfectly raked gravel. My mother, Penelope, was only sixteen when I was born, the year my father went away to the war. When I was growing up, she seemed more like a girl than a grown woman. Everyone loved her. She laughed at Eurycleia, bewitched Melanthius with a smile, and the two of us would be gone, up through the olive groves behind the house, past the rocks and little temple, to a high promontory above the sea, where we could eat our picnic and she could tell me stories about Odysseus, the father I'd never met, while we gazed at the far-off, misty horizon beyond which he'd vanished.

"And then," her stories always ended, "Odysseus sailed home to Ithaca, and we all lived happily ever after."

I know her stories were true. The sprig of laurel leaves and the boar's tusk, roughly sawn off at the root, are both kept in the little temple on the mountainside. I went up there yesterday, along the weed-choked path that skirts the cliffs then climbs steeply through oak forests to an overgrown valley where a cave was faced, years ago, with a portico of rough wooden columns twined in ivy. Behind a curtain of sacking the cave is stiflingly hot, its air thick with the stench of rancid fat and rotting meat. Rows of oil lamps flicker on every ledge. Smoke coils from a brazier on the altar step. It always takes time to adjust from the sun's glare outside. Only slowly do one's eyes take in the fantastical array of objects that crowd the wooden shelves stapled to the cave's walls: jars of wine and bunches of fading flowers, silver goblets and enameled dishes, rings and bangles. Everyone on the island comes here to make offerings to the goddess to win her help. Farmers leave dishes of grain for a good harvest. The sick leave clay hearts, hands, or feet. Hung from the ceiling is the entire prow of a boat, the thank-offering of some fishermen who survived a wreck. Some of the offerings are encrusted with jewels, others as humble as a comb carved from bone, the love-pledge of a girl trying to capture some boy from the town.

The goddess's statue, a blackened thing of silver and wood, watches over everything through white enameled eyes. The altar step below her is black with spilled oil. As always, lining the step are rows of silver dishes piled with feast-day sacrifices of thigh bones wrapped in yellowing fat. Their putrefying reek makes the air in the cavern almost unbreathable.

Yesterday the priest, a slovenly old man in a wine-stained robe, was filling oil lamps when I came in.

"Telemachus." He nodded curtly to me, then went on with his task. I reached into my satchel, drew out a silver cup, and placed it on the altar.

"To bring your father back?" His voice was sarcastic, as always.

"Yes."

"Light a candle."

We all hate the priest, but no one on Ithaca challenges him. People say he talks directly to the goddess, just as I might talk to my mother or Eurycleia.

"Is there something else?" His white robe was dirty at the sleeves. A single yellow tooth jutted at an angle from his lower lip.

"I want to see my father's offerings."

"You know where to find them."

Among the hundreds of offerings in the cavern are four that my father dedicated before he disappeared. They're kept together on a felt-lined tray next to the altar: the boar's tusk, the sprig of laurel, so faded it's almost grey, and two others.

One is a bronze sword, a wedding gift from my grandfather. Odysseus dedicated it the day he announced he was leaving for the war. Yesterday I picked it up and weighed it in my hand. Boys my age should know how to fight, but with my father gone, there was no one at home to teach me. The sword's hilt sat awkwardly in my hand. Its cold bulk dragged at my arm. I found myself wondering, for the thousandth time, what kind of man could fight all day with a sword like that, stabbing, thrusting, never tiring? A man like my father, Odysseus.

I laid the sword back in the tray and picked up the fourth offering, a tiny, carved owl. My mother told me stories about the laurel, the sword, and the boar's tusk, but she never talked about the owl. I held it closer to a lamp. The carving is crude, the eyes roughly scratched with a pin. The priest told me Odysseus came at dawn on the day he sailed, ordered him out of the cave, and went in alone. He found my father's other offerings on the altar step, but the little owl stood apart—he didn't know why.

"The owl is the symbol of the goddess. Maybe Odysseus left it as an offering to her. To protect him in war. To make sure he came home."

"So why did he set it apart?"

The priest could only ever shrug.

Yesterday, when I put the little carving back in the tray, he put down his jar of oil. "Eurycleia was here yesterday. Sent by your mother. Another gift. *To bring him back.* A bracelet, solid gold—over there."

His voice was mocking. I turned to look. The sight never failed to break my heart. A whole alcove is filled with wooden cases. My mother had them made by the island's best carpenter, to hold her offerings. Sixteen years since he sailed away. Sixteen years of offerings to bring him back: enameled brooches, gold bangles and ingots of pure silver, rings and hairpins. Some were treasures Penelope must have bought from traders in the harbor—blown ostrich's eggs, and turtle shells waxed to shine like brass. Others were embroideries she sewed herself in tiny stitches, whose colors glowed in the candlelight: Ithaca's mountain and the sea under moonlight, a battle scene, ships returning home.

In the beginning, she left offerings to keep Odysseus safe in war. Then, when news came that the war had ended, eight years ago, she left offerings to bring him back. To preserve him from shipwreck and pirates, from storms and whirlpools, currents and sea-monsters—from everything and anything that might keep a good man from his family and island home.

I ran my eyes over them. The new gold bracelet shone on the top shelf. Sixteen years of faith, those offerings represented. Sixteen years of waiting. A small fortune in jewels, precious metal, and hope.

And that's the only fortune my father has left.

I'm in my bedroom thinking about my father when I hear a commotion outside. A man shouting, a girl's high-pitched scream. I pull on a shirt and hurry out onto the gallery. Below, in the shantytown of tents that fills the courtyard, two men are circling, knives in their hands. Agelaus I know; the other is a newcomer. Agelaus's torso is bare, his hair unbrushed. It looks like he's only just woken up. Melantho, my mother's maid, tugs at one arm, sobbing and pleading. The other man, slim and youthful-looking, shifts his weight nervously from one leg to the other as he clutches his knife. I'm guessing he's Melantho's new lover.

The fight doesn't last long. Agelaus rubs his hand over his eyes, like Melantho's voice is giving him a headache, then shoves her aside and in one movement brings his knife up into the other man's leg. It happens so fast the newcomer barely even moves. He looks down at his leg, where dark blood is suddenly pulsing across his thigh. Melantho screams and puts her arms around him, trying to hold him up, but he's already sagging to the ground. Agelaus yawns, wipes his knife, and crawls back into his tent. The other men in the courtyard watch until the youth on the ground stops moving, then go back to their tasks. One picks up an axe to hack firewood from a stack of furniture. Another, his face tattooed with the pattern of a wolf's head, wets his razor in a barrel of water and begins to shave.

I grip the balcony rail and look down at the scene below me. At the washing lines festooned with young men's clothes, at the tents made of carpets draped over furniture dragged from the great hall, at the targets daubed on the walls, the piles of smashed jars, broken sticks and abandoned wineskins. I breathe in the stench rising from the pit they use as a toilet, and the fire of sawn-up furniture whose smoke is already dirtying the clean morning air. I watch a crow drop to the ground, hop forward on strong legs, and tear at some abandoned food on a tray under the colonnade. I don't want to think about what I've just seen: a man killed casually in a knife fight over a girl, his body left lying in a pool of blood. I try to remember what the courtyard looked like when I was little. I used to run after the gardeners who tended it each morning, their rakes sweeping arcs in the gravel. The whitewash was so bright it hurt to look at. Servants dozed away afternoons in the long, cool colonnade. There was a great jar of water always kept full, with a bronze cup hanging on a hook for anyone who was thirsty. On feast days, we draped garlands around the gateposts of the great hall, whose pillars were carved in the shape of boars' heads, my father's symbol.

"Telemachus." Eurycleia bustled along the gallery toward me, her face shocked.

"What is it?"

"Antinous is in Penelope's room."

I can hear the creak of my mother's loom from along the gallery. I race to her door and stop. My mother is sitting at her loom just as I would expect, eyes squinting at her skeins of vividly colored thread, small fingers thrusting her needle in and out of the weave. But she isn't alone.

Sprawled in a chair close by her, one leg hooked over the arm, is a heavily built, handsome young man wearing a silk dressing gown and rows of beads that tangle in the thick fur on his chest. As he watches Penelope weave, he's eating handfuls of nuts and dropping their shells on the floor.

Another line crossed. None of the young men have ever gone into my mother's bedroom before. I ought to shout. I ought to run forward and hit him, or draw a knife on him. But I can't fight Antinous. I know. I tried once, last autumn. Something made me crack and I hurled myself at him, fists pummeling his body, fingers ripping away layers of silk to claw at his flesh. I still remember the moment I encountered hard muscle under Antinous's layers of fat, and the shock of helplessness as he chucked me aside. I don't need another lesson. I'm sixteen years old, not yet fully grown, and no one has ever taught me how to use a sword. The visitors who have taken over our house are grown men. They're fighters.

"One day you'll be a fighter." My nurse, Eurycleia, used to tell me that.

I hardly knew what fighters were, then. Men on Ithaca are fishermen and farmers. I didn't know about the weapons and tattoos, the peacock clothes and jewelry, the plaited hair, the scars exposed like badges of pride, the furious arguments, knife fights, killings. Fighters—I'm surrounded by them now. They stalk the corridors of the big house like dogs, their aggression filling every room with a raw animal stench. Every day ends in drunken arguments. Fights—like the one in the courtyard earlier—happen pretty much every week. I still remember the first corpse I ever saw: a young man barely older than me, sprawled in the courtyard with his teeth grinning at his own blood while two others rolled dice for his shirt.

I'm neither a coward nor a weakling—at least I hope I'm not. But I can't do anything against men such as these.

How do I cope? I've learned different survival strategies instead. I've learned how to defuse ugly situations, how to swallow the petty humiliations that would make a fighter reach for his sword. Sometimes I don't feel like a boy at all. At sixteen I'm like an old man, with the skills of a practiced diplomat.

So instead of hurling myself at him, I just say, "Good morning, Antinous." Keeping my voice calm.

Antinous nods, not even looking at me. His fat tongue appears, searching his lips for a shred of nut. Antinous's features seem too small for his face, as if his pointed nose, girlish mouth, and small, bright eyes were designed for someone more delicate. Seeing him watch Penelope, his expression reminds me of Eumaeus, the farmer, looking over a pig he's fed up for slaughter. The thought makes me feel sick, but I don't show it.

"I thought you were in the kitchen." I heard him there earlier, giving Melanthius orders for this evening's feast: lambs to be slaughtered and spitted, fish to be gutted and stewed in squid ink. Antinous loves his food.

"I was in the kitchen." Antinous twists his thick neck and gives me a contemptuous look. "I'm not anymore."

I glance out the window to calm myself. Outside, sun shines on the olive grove, and the sea is a majestic blue. No sail in sight. It's a habit I've had all my life: to check the window each morning, just in case this morning—*this* morning, of all the mornings—there'll be a speck of white out there on the endless blue. A ship bringing Odysseus home to Ithaca. This morning I see nothing but a familiar cluster of fishing boats hauling in nets by the little islet of Asteris.

I go up to my mother, ignoring Antinous, and kiss her on the forehead. "How did you sleep?" I ask gently.

Penelope stops weaving and frowns, as if she's thinking hard. "Well," she says at last. "*Very* well."

When Odysseus married her, Penelope was said to be the prettiest girl on the islands, and her looks have barely changed. Past thirty, her skin is still smooth, her hair black, her figure as light as ever. It's inside that the years of loneliness have eaten her away. Until recently, she could still dress for dinner, put on her jewels and play the part of a hostess—as if the young men downstairs really were just guests in a big house. Now she weaves all day, sitting next to a window overlooking the harbor where she last set eyes on Odysseus. She eats nothing. She hardly leaves her bedroom. There are good days, but they are becoming fewer and fewer.

"We slept *very* well," Antinous mocks, in a high-pitched imitation of Penelope.

I look down at my mother's loom. In the past I used to love the pictures my mother conjured from wool: birds and trees, fishing nets and waves. After the first visitors arrived, three years ago, she wove pictures of men fighting, men feasting, men lying drunk on the shore. Then came the episode of the shroud, just after my grandfather's death last year, and everything changed.

The visitors were pushing her to name one of them as her second husband. Other than servants, Penelope had no one but a boy to protect her—me. One day she gave in. She said she had to weave her father-in-law's shroud, but as soon as it was completed, she'd make a decision. The day she began, I watched her work. Even I could see that it was really Odysseus's shroud my mother was making. I watched the boar turning at bay as it was cornered by a young Odysseus; I watched the stones of the harbor take shape, a crowd of people on the shore, and the billowing sail of the ship that took him away. Penelope worked swiftly, her thin, strong fingers nimbly twisting wool and snapping threads. By nightfall the shroud seemed almost finished. But when I ran into her room the next morning, I found only a few lines of thread at the foot of the loom.

"What happened to the boar?" I asked. "What happened to the ship?"

My mother was already growing thinner, already developing that remote gaze that would eventually shut the rest of the world out. I remember her laughing and rubbing the hair back from my forehead. "You must have dreamed them," she said.

I soon worked out what she was doing. Each day she wove the story of her husband's life. Each night she pulled the threads from the loom and burned them.

It didn't take the young men long to work it out either. They weren't fools. They forced her to finish the shroud. We buried Laertes, my grandfather. But Penelope still refused to choose between them. She wouldn't admit Odysseus was dead.

And she never wove pictures again. She works at her loom hour after hour, its noise creaking along the corridors of the big house. But the cloth she makes is filled with meaningless shape, glaring color, empty black space.

Antinous yawns and spreads his fingers in front of his face, inspecting them. "In the kitchen," he says, "I was planning the feast for tonight. We will eat a slowly roast lamb—a *young* lamb—wrapped in bay leaves and cooked in a pit. Melanthius is digging the pit now. With it we will drink a jar of the ex*quisite* . . ." He pauses and frowns, like he's checking whether the word is appropriate. "The ex*quisite*," he repeats, nodding, "wine from the second row at the back of the cellar. I have told Melanthius not to bring it up until after noon and then to leave it outside the kitchen door so that it is raised to the exact temperature"—he closes his eyes dreamily—"of a peach warmed by the sun."

Antinous is a killer. I've seen him kill. The man-of-luxury talk is an act, as phony as everything else about him—or else one pole of a character so split it leaves Antinous barely sane. I watch his face go slack now. His mood is turning. Suddenly he stands up and goes over to my mother. Putting his hands on her shoulders, he leans over and pretends to lick her cheek.

"I could eat your mother," he says.

The loom creaks and stops. I can see Penelope tense, eyes scared, then closed. Antinous's fingers, white and fat as worms, creep up her neck. He touches one earring and flicks it with his nail to set it swinging.

"Don't touch her," I say.

"Why not?" His voice is cold.

"I don't want you to."

"I don't want you to," he imitates. "She's going to have to choose." Slowly, almost tenderly, he cups his fingers around my mother's cheek. He's looking at me, not down at her. "We're going to have to choose." His voice is a singsong. "Which is the best man? Who do we want for a husband?" He leans forward suddenly and breathes deeply the perfume from her hair. "Who do we want in our bed?"

"Stop it." My eyes are full of tears. I can't help it, though I know that crying is the most contemptible thing a man—a fighter—can do. "Please . . ."

Did my father ever plead? Of course not. I can see the contempt in Antinous's face—a worthless boy unable to protect his own mother. A man would die rather than swallow an insult like this. All I can think is *If only my father were here.*

There's a step in the doorway behind me. Antinous looks toward the door with an expression of annoyance. Eurymachus, another of our visitors, is standing there.

He looks from Antinous, to me, to Penelope, sitting there in dread with her eyes closed. He can see what's going on. Eurymachus is no fool. He may be one of the visitors who have taken over our house, but he's the best of them, in a way. Sometimes I think he's ashamed of what's going on.

Antinous lets go of my mother's hair and takes a step back.

"What are you doing in here? This is Penelope's room." Eurymachus's voice is guarded. I can sense the tension: two dogs circling before a fight.

Antinous moistens his lips. "I was leaving."

"Leave, then."

"Why are *you* here?"

"I came from the gate. A visitor has arrived." Eurymachus looks at me. His expression seems a little puzzled. "He says he's an old friend of your father's."

I find the visitor squatting in the shade of the prickly
pears outside the gate, next to a flea-bitten mule with a
wooden saddle. The guards are eyeing him nervously.
He's an old man, an African with a face so dark it seems
to suck light into it, and a shock of wiry white hair. He's
wearing a stained leather coat tied at the waist with rope,
and a scarf fringed with sharks' teeth. But it isn't his clothes
that surprise me, or his color—we're used to travelers on
Ithaca. It's his eyes.

They're white. Not cloudy white like a blind person's. White
like ivory or horn. So pale the irises fade into the whites,
leaving his pupils as piercing black points.

"My house is your house," I say formally. The standard greeting to a guest, the law of the islands and the whole of Greece. No one turns a stranger away. Visitors are honored as long as they choose to stay. That's why my father's house is full of strangers.

The visitor stands and bows. Around his neck is a goat's foot hanging on a silver chain.

"Who are you?"

"My name is Mentes." The visitor's voice is deep, his accent foreign. "I am a friend of Odysseus. He traveled with me in Africa."

"Do you know where he is? Do you have any news?" I can't keep the eagerness out of my voice, but Mentes shakes his head.

"I came here for news. I heard Odysseus was missing. I heard there was a war. Are you his son? You don't look like him."

It isn't the first time I've heard that. "Delicate, like his mother"—that's what people usually say. "Not made for fighting." "Small."

"Yes."

"Then it's you I came to see."

I lead him down a back corridor to the great hall, hoping he won't see the chaos of the courtyard. He's beached his ship on the west side of the island, he tells me—that's why we got no message from the port. He has to sail for Corinth in an hour. The great hall is empty except for a maid sweeping the floor from last night's feast. Two logs smolder on the hearth, their smoke rising to the square opening in the roof, which brings in just enough light to see the brilliant images painted on the walls, of bulls tossing their horns and dolphins diving through waves. I call for bread and wine and watch the stranger settle on a chair, his gaze flickering curiously around the pictures.

Then he turns his disconcerting white eyes on me. "I hear there's been a war."

I can hardly believe my ears. Is there a man on earth who doesn't know about the war? Who hasn't been talking about it for sixteen years? I've never met one before.

"Yes, there's been a war. A great war. That's where my father disappeared."

"He was killed?"

"He disappeared."

"Tell me about it." He closes his eyes. "Tell me everything."

Easier said than done. The Trojan War, which ended eight years ago, was a poisonous mixture of trade, diplomacy, and sex that drew in every city and island in Greece. Troy, on the straits leading to the Black Sea, charged tolls on the straits trade and became richer than any Greek city. A Trojan diplomatic mission ended in disaster when Paris—son of the Trojan king and a fast-moving boy with a lady-killer's smile—broke hearts around Greece and eloped with Helen, the fabulously beautiful wife of Menelaus. Menelaus's brother, Agamemnon, happened to be Greece's most powerful warlord. The elopement was the excuse for a massive Greek expedition to eliminate Troy. Odysseus, chief of Ithaca, sailed to join it on a hot June morning with six hundred companions, leaving his teenaged bride, Penelope, pregnant and weeping on the quayside.

My mother, with me inside her.

Like most invasions, the Trojan expedition was expected to be short and glorious. Instead it turned into an attritional nightmare played out in Troy's mosquito-infested marshes, where the Greek leaders squabbled and the soldiers died in pointless skirmishes, while the massive walls of Troy, impervious to any technology we Greeks possessed, remained unbreached.

I know it's wrong of me to talk of the war like this. Fighters are supposed to love battle—it's what they live for—and I'm a fighter's son. In the mouths of storytellers, the Trojan War turns into something different: a heroic tale of valor and single combat, of bloody skirmishes and stirring speeches that keep audiences rapt in every tavern in Greece. When a new storyteller comes to Ithaca, the tavern is packed to the rafters, fishermen, traveling peddlers, and servants all listening with breathless attention. Even I get drawn into it then. Sitting under those blackened beams hung with ancient harpoons, fishermen's charms, and the dried-out beak of a swordfish, breathing in that reek of aniseed and grilled fish, eyes smarting from the charcoal braziers, ears filled with the storyteller's nasal drone and the thrumming of the instrument he plucks to accompany his tale, I hear my father's name, and suddenly the tears are running down my cheeks. By the time the story ends I'm sitting there quite sure—quite, quite sure—that my father, the hero of the Trojan War, is the greatest man in Greece.

I don't think it was really like that, though, so I tell Mentes the story the way I imagine it might actually have happened: war, pure, simple, and without heroics.

The war ended after eight years—ten, say the storytellers, rounding up for poetic effect—with Troy a smoking ruin and the surviving Trojan aristocracy herded aboard Greek ships as slaves. After much feasting, the Greeks built a massive shrine, hoisted anchor, and sailed for home, Odysseus and his Ithacans among them. One by one each leader reached his destination— all except my father, who was never seen again.

"He left Troy eight years ago," I say.

Mentes dips a morsel of bread in his wine and swallows it. For a while he doesn't speak. Then he says, "You're an unusual boy."

"I don't think so." I can feel his white eyes boring into me. I can't meet them. I can feel myself blushing.

"You're more like Odysseus than I thought when I first saw you."

"What do you mean?"

"You're clever, you're good with words, and you think things out for yourself. Have you heard any news of Odysseus since?"

"Nothing. We ask every ship that arrives here. There've been rumors. We follow them all up, but they never lead anywhere."

Mentes touches his goblet to his mouth but barely tastes the wine. "Meanwhile, what of your mother?"

I don't want to talk about my mother—not even to this old friend of Odysseus. "She isn't very well," I say reluctantly. But Mentes's brilliant eyes are staring expectantly at me, so I draw a deep breath and go on.

At thirty-two, Penelope is still the most beautiful and prestigious match in the islands, the daughter of a great chief, the wife (widow, say the young men who started to turn up three years ago) of another. Ithaca, the best harbor in the Ionian, is an idyllic island kingdom. No young fighter will ignore a prize like that.

Eurymachus was the first to arrive. I was waiting at the gate, excited at the idea of a guest. Eurymachus was tall, slim, and charming, and he carried a bunch of flowers in one hand.

"To pay my respects," he said, and squeezed my shoulder. "I happened to be sailing past." He put down his bag. "Is your mother here?"

Penelope was different back then. She was still well, still young, still smiling. I remember her running in through the gate, sucking her thumb where it had been pricked by a thorn. Eurymachus bowed formally as he took her hand. Something shifted then. It was the first time I saw Penelope not as my mother but the way other men saw her: as a beautiful woman, a prize.

Another young man arrived only two days later. He too just happened to be sailing past Ithaca. He wanted to say how sorry he was about Odysseus.

"My father isn't dead," I told him.

"Of *course* not," said the young man, gripping my hand. "Is your mother here?"

By harvesttime the guest rooms were full. It wasn't polite to ask how long a visitor would stay. Penelope arranged walks and hunting. There were feasts every night—the custom for honored guests. New arrivals were crammed into servants' rooms; baskets of fish were brought to the kitchen door each morning; sheep were slaughtered. I remember Medon, our steward, gloomily counting jars of wine in the musty cellar. Each night Penelope dressed carefully in front of the polished mirror in her room. She hung gold chains around her neck, made up her eyes and mouth, and into her hair fixed the tiny enameled boar that her husband had given her on the day he sailed away.

For the first year they were in awe of her. She laughed politely at their jokes, froze them when their laughter became too coarse. My mother was a chief's wife, after all; poised, immaculate, perfectly bred. She was Odysseus's wife. More than once I saw those young men glance nervously at the door, as if my father was about to stride in, sea-stained and soiled, gaunt from war, with his sword dripping at his side.

One of them tried to string my father's bow. I found him in the hall, holding it—the hunting bow that hangs on the wall, a massive thing of yew and ivory with a quiver of arrows next to it. He was weighing it in his hands when I came in, then pretended he was just interested.

"You mustn't touch that," I said. "It's my father's."

"I know that!" he snapped. But he put the bow back on its peg, and I never saw anyone touch it again.

Penelope's defenses decayed as the house did. It didn't happen overnight. Gradually the guests took to sunbathing in the courtyard, then leaving furniture out there. They summoned Medon for wine instead of waiting to be offered. Someone told an improper joke in Penelope's presence. I remember the uneasy pause before the laughter, but once that barrier was crossed, their speech became less and less restrained. My mother took to leaving feasts early. The visitors didn't dare enter her room, but when she came out they crouched around her like vultures on a wounded bird. Weaving was a form of self-defense: it kept her hands busy and her eyes fixed on the wool. I never knew what they said when I wasn't there. Sometimes I found her walking down corridors with a young man muttering in her ear. Once she hurried in from the garden with tears staining her cheeks.

"They want to marry her," Eurycleia told me after my grandfather's death. Her stern, old face was grim. "It's time you knew."

I'd already guessed that. "What about my father?" I said. "My father will come back and kill them." It's easy to be brave at fifteen. At the time, saying the words made me feel better, but there was an ocean of emptiness behind them.

"Of course he will," said Eurycleia.

Penelope never did make her choice. Instead, she withdrew into her bedroom, and the young men destroyed our house. They emptied the cellars, built tents in the courtyard, hung targets on the walls. Their rough voices filled the colonnades, coiling up the stairwells like the eternal stink of cooking from the kitchen. On my sixteenth birthday they threw a party for me and made me drunk for the first time. I was alone. I had no father. There wasn't a thing I could do to stop them.

I don't tell Mentes everything. Not about the night I overheard a group of men talking so coarsely about Penelope that I had to stuff fingers in my ears to stifle their voices. Nor about what happened at the end of the birthday party, when they dressed me in one of my mother's robes, painted my face, and made me stand on a chair to sing to them. Some things hurt too much to share with anybody.

"And so," says Mentes in his strange, slow voice, "your father's house is full of men. They go into your mother's room. They touch her. You can't stop them."

I don't say anything. Suddenly his arm shoots out and grips my wrist. I'm surprised by how strong the old man is. I try to pull my hand away but can't.

"Only a boy," he says, releasing me, but he says it without contempt, simply as a fact. "You can't protect her."

"My father will come back."

"Will he?"

"He must."

"Where is he?"

"I don't know."

Mentes leans toward me. I can smell some odd perfume from him, some spice or oil mingled with his sweat and the sea-reek of his clothes. "You must go and find him."

It's the last thing I expect him to say. I don't know what to reply. I've never thought of going to look for my father. I've never left Ithaca. "Who would protect my mother?"

"You can't protect her yourself."

"I don't know where to look."

"Go to Pylos. Nestor, the chief there, hears many things. Ships put in. People pick up news." Everyone's heard of Nestor. He's said to be the oldest man alive.

"My father will come home." I can hear a hollow echo to my own voice, like I'm not convincing even myself. "Odysseus will come home and drive them all out. He'll kill his enemies. He'll save both of us."

Mentes just looks at me. "You sound like a child," he says.

He stands up. I follow him to the gate, where the midday heat burns down on beaten white soil. Two dogs lie panting across the threshold. His mule waits in the shade, flicking its long ears to keep off the flies. Suddenly I don't want Mentes to leave. Here's a man who actually knew my father. Knew Odysseus, traveled with him.

"What was he like?" I ask, wishing I didn't sound so young.

Mentes looks down at me. Suddenly I realize he hasn't smiled once since he arrived. Not smiled, not frowned, not shown the least sign of emotion. His face looks like it's carved from a slab of wood.

"He was like you," he says. "Good with words. *Too* good with words, some people say. He was clever, like you. *Too* clever, perhaps. A lot of people hated him for that. Perhaps they'll hate you too."

It isn't like a person talking to me, it's like an oracle, impersonal. "What do you mean?" I feel breathless. My head's spinning. This isn't the Odysseus of my mother's stories. "Everyone loves Odysseus. Everyone admires him. He's a fighter. Everyone knows that. He won the Trojan War."

"Perhaps."

"So why do you say people hated him? *Why* did they hate him?"

Mentes looks down at me from the saddle of his mule as he turns it away. "Because he was a liar," he says quietly.

When he's gone, I slip down the alleyway that runs along the side of the big house, following it to the strip of beach that fronts the town. Boatbuilders make and mend fishing boats here. I need to be alone.

A gang of boatbuilders is at work now, planing planks whose fresh, clean smell drifts across to where I'm standing. Two gaily painted hulls lie on trestles beyond them. Nearby, an old man is slapping varnish onto the upturned hull of his boat, a can of pitch bubbling on a small driftwood fire next to him. Familiar scents drift toward me—of fishing nets suspended on poles outside the doors of the low, white cottages, of drying seaweed, of the shining fish that two men on the beach, legs silver with scales, are gutting and tossing into a bucket between them. Beyond them, two boys are throwing pailfuls of charcoal into the furnace where they make bronze. The sky shimmers in the heat above it, as if the air itself is being smelted into hard metal.

I don't want the fishermen's company today. Instead, I turn away from the town and pick my way over the rocks to the headland that closes one side of the harbor. Clambering down to the water's edge, I settle myself on a round stone lapped by clear water. The sun is at its height, the horizon a brown smear of heat. Sometimes, after a winter storm, you can see mountains on the mainland and the silhouettes of the other islands. Today they're no more than ghostly shadows. Haze shrouds the horizon over which my father vanished on a hot day like this one, sixteen years ago.

What did Mentes mean when he called my father a liar?

I should have run after him and called him back. I was too shocked. It's only now I think of everything I should have said, everything I should have asked.

Waves wash the stones below my feet. I can see delicate black urchins clinging to the rocks below the surface and a seashell encrusted with barnacles. I'm thinking, *How can the world—this familiar world—be changed so much by one word?* My father not a hero but a liar. Is that possible? To the people of Ithaca, Odysseus was a man of action. A brilliant strategist and fearless fighter: that's what I've believed all through my childhood. Those are the stories I've been brought up with—about Odysseus's strength, his courage, his sharp wits. I'm thinking, *Does my mother know people call Odysseus a liar?* And *why* do they call him that? Perhaps Mentes was lying himself. But why would he lie if he was Odysseus's friend?

Three pelicans fly low over the sea's surface, their slow wings almost grazing the waves. I feel lonelier than ever before. My father might have been missing, but at least I was sure *what* he was—brave, admired, unbeatable. Now I don't even know that. I don't know who Odysseus is—even my missing father has gone missing. If he doesn't come back to Ithaca, I'll never know what he was like.

I try to imagine Odysseus clutching the steering oar as Ithaca disappeared behind him. Did he look back? Look back at the crowded quayside and the huddle of cottages, the plane tree whose branches shade the square, and the white house from whose window Penelope would never stop watching for him? Or did he just square his shoulders and keep his eyes on the horizon ahead? What did it feel like simply to sail away? Sometimes I've helped fishermen with their nets. That's the farthest I've ever been from the shore of Ithaca.

The pelicans are almost out of sight. I pick up a stone and flick it over the sea, watching it skip twice before disappearing beneath the wave's smooth surface.

By the time I get back to the big house, dusk is falling and torches have been lit at the main gate. A great fire is blazing in the middle of the courtyard, its flames crackling as high as the gallery above and painting the walls with savage shadows. Antinous is watching it with satisfaction, one hand raised to shield his sweating face from the heat. Tables have been dragged into the courtyard. Young men are drinking and rolling dice. A dog, tethered to one table leg by a leather leash, barks monotonously at the moon, which is just rising in a swollen, perfect orb above the roof.

I pause under the colonnade, watching the fire. Euryma-chus sees me and comes over. Tall and good-looking, Eury-machus is a favorite to everyone—even, perhaps, my mother. He's the only one of the young men who ever tried to befriend me. I remember talking about my mother for hours on end while Eurymachus nodded sympathetically. He really seemed to care how she felt. Sometimes he's tried to keep the others in check.

"I saw you out on the rocks," Eurymachus offers. "Needed some time alone? I don't blame you. Thinking about your father?"

"Yes."

"I know what it's like. I lost my own father, you know, at about your age. Did I ever tell you that?"

"Often," I snap, and turn away. I need time to think. I watch Antinous, over by the fire, wave his hands for silence.

"Our lamb," he announces in his most irritating manner, "will not be ready for another hour. I suggest we use the time to amuse ourselves. My friends, I propose a story."

There's a shout of approval. Some of the men start rhythmic clapping. Everyone in Greece loves a story, and a new storyteller arrived in the harbor only yesterday. A young man dressed in a threadbare robe is pushed through the crowd to the front. He's blind, like many of the storytellers, and carries his instrument in a travel-stained sack tied with rough cord. As he fumbles the sack open, he raises his head to the crowd. "Which story shall I tell?" His voice half-chants, half-drones his repertoire. "The story of Achilles's fury, or the gods' battle with horse-monsters? The golden apple, or the tale of Jason and his voyage to the east?"

I haven't planned what I'm going to do. It's as if the words come out all by themselves. Before anyone can speak, I step forward and say, "Tell them the story of Odysseus."

There's dead silence. I can hear the crackle of flames on the fire. I can even hear my own heart beat, but it's too late to go back. Suddenly I remember what Mentes said: that I have my father's gift for words. Maybe that gives me courage. "Tell my father's story," I repeat. "This is his house. Tell his story. Tell how he fought in the Trojan War and planned the fall of Troy. Tell how he slaughtered his enemies."

"Tell how he died," calls a voice from the back.

"Odysseus isn't dead," I say quietly. Somehow I know that so long as I keep my voice calm, the young men will go on listening. "He's alive," I repeat firmly. "And there's something you should know." I pause. My mouth is dry. Greece, which seemed so small when I was sitting on the rocks, suddenly seems to have expanded into a universe. "Tomorrow I'm going to leave Ithaca. I'm going to travel wherever I have to, go to every island in Greece if I must. I'm going to find my father and bring him home."

I've said it. I didn't mean to. I didn't think I'd reached any decision out there on the rocks. But as soon as the words are out I realize I never had any choice. There's no turning back, and I'm glad of it. In dead silence I walk out on them, walk out through the side door into the moonlit olive grove, and it's only there I stop, with cicadas shrilling about me, and my heart beating as if it's going to explode.

That's when the flaw in my plan hits me, and I wish I could stuff the words back into my mouth. I can talk all I like about searching every island in Greece. How am I going to leave Ithaca when I don't even have a ship?

As chief of Ithaca, Odysseus kept five warships beached permanently in the harbor. He could have them at sea an hour after ringing the bell that hung on the roof of the big house, men straining at the oars while Odysseus steered. That—so everyone says—was Odysseus at his happiest, legs planted on the deck, body swaying to meet the waves.

For the Trojan expedition, merchants queued in the town square to lease him the extra ships he needed. When he was still two short, he rejected all but three of the unseaworthy tubs, cranked lighters, and overblown fishing boats they offered him, then sent men to fell pine trees on the mountainside, shave sweet curls of wood from the planks, and boil pitch to caulk the new ships. All within a week. Odysseus was never without a ship to put to sea in.

It isn't quite like that for me.

There are fishermen's caïque drawn up on the beach in dozens, brilliantly painted, but they're too small for the deep-water journey to Pylos. There are usually three or four merchant ships in the harbor, round-bellied but sturdy, most of them with ten or twelve oars per side and a single square sail hoisted on a stumpy mast amidships. Any of those would do well enough—I don't exactly need a war galley. But none of the merchants would detour south to Pylos, and I don't have the money to charter a vessel like that.

Colonists stop at Pylos on their way west. Their ships are crammed with children and animals, bags of seed, bleating young goats. But they're heading away from Greece toward a new life—not back to Pylos.

The young men in the big house all arrived by ship. There are always half a dozen light racing galleys hauled up on the sand, with bored-looking sailors playing dice next to them or dozing under makeshift awnings. But they're the last people in the world who would want to lend me a ship to find my father—even if I could swallow my pride to ask.

The only ship I can call my own is a wreck.

It's an old war galley Odysseus rejected sixteen years ago, and its remains have lain on the sand at the far end of the beach ever since, timbers bleached the color of bone by sixteen summers, seams gaping, lizards scuttling through holes where planks have been pried off for firewood. I remember playing in the wreck as a child, pretending I was a fighter sailing off to war. I could never move the steering oar—it was always buried too deep in sand—but I gripped it anyway. I pretended to steer and stared up at the stump of mast as if a sail billowed from it, then jumped down onto the beach to look up at the carved beak, from which every shred of paint had been scoured by winter gales.

I can't imagine the work it would take to make that wreck float at all, let alone brave the Ionian Sea.

No ship, no crew. I go back to my bedroom but don't sleep much. I doze off just before dawn, then an owl wakes me, hooting softly as it returns from its night's hunt. It's as I blearily open my eyes that I see the answer. The town council.

Greek chiefs aren't like kings. They don't control things outright. People—towns, islands—accept their leadership . . . but only so long as they lead well. Big decisions get put to the vote at noisy meetings, where every detail is debated endlessly and furiously. That's how it is in Ithaca, anyway. My grandfather Laertes once told me it was Odysseus's skill at managing those meetings that gave him such power over the island.

"He always spoke last," Laertes said. "A good trick—remember it. Odysseus would see which way the meeting was going, then stand up and turn it, just like you'd steer a boat. You should have heard the speech he made the day they voted for war. I was there. People weren't sure before then—most of them had never heard of Troy or Agamemnon. It was going badly. Then Odysseus stood up, and by the time he finished, I swear that old men who could hardly walk would have strapped on their swords and hobbled down to the boats to fight if he'd only let them."

Since Odysseus's disappearance—and with Penelope refusing to declare him dead so that a new chief could take over—the town council, gathered under the huge old plane tree in the square, has made most of the decisions on Ithaca. I remember my mother taking me when I was a child. She was always treated with deference—everyone loves Penelope—but I never heard her speak. Me, I've always looked forward to meetings. I love the packed benches dragged from the tavern for the occasion, and the old men clicking their fingers to applaud speeches they like, or hooting if they disapprove. Decisions on even the simplest matters can take all day. Sometimes it's late into the night, with oil lamps winking on window ledges, their light glimmering on the animated faces of the fishermen, old women, and tired children in the square before a vote is taken and the tavern-keeper rolls a barrel of wine out into the square to seal the agreement.

The town council can vote me a ship and crew.

Any of the island's elders can call a meeting. Within an hour I'm up at the hut of Eumaeus, my father's old farmer. Hanging over a sagging log fence, I explain what I want while he swills pig feed into a trough between two black sows.

"Oh, they'll give yer a ship, all right."

"You're sure?"

"To find Odysseus?" The old man straightens up, grimacing as his back stiffens. "Do anything for Odysseus, this island would. They'll vote for yer. Vote for the chief's son. You just tells 'em what yer arter, they'll give yer a fleet."

The sows nose forward into the trough, grunting happily. I can remember when this pen was full of pigs, with dozens more snuffling for apples in the orchard behind. The young men's feasts have taken their toll. Now Eumaeus won't let Melanthius, the cook, anywhere near the pig farm. Our guests have to make do with lamb and kids.

There's something else I need to ask the old farmer. It seems odd, now, that I've never asked him before. I try not to sound too hesitant.

"Eumaeus, what was my father like?"

"What was 'e like? Odysseus? 'E's the chief, ain't 'e?"

It isn't quite what I was expecting. And suddenly the old man seems very busy with swill, sluicing his leather bucket in the water butt and shaking out every last drop.

"Was he a great fighter?"

"You know 'e was."

"Did he tell lies?"

The old man shakes the bucket mechanically. I'm willing him to say no. Instead he puts the bucket down.

"They was more like stories," he says. "Always had the gift o' the gab, Odysseus did."

"What do you mean?" My mouth is dry.

"I don't mean nothin'. 'E was a good talker, is all."

"Was he a liar?"

Eumaeus looks me in the eye then. His eyes are as clear, as weathered, as the Ithacan skies under which he's lived all his life. "Some trusted 'im, some didn't," he says. "Like anyone else. Far as I'm concerned, 'e's the chief, an' that's all."

It can't be all, though, can it? Walking down to the town, I can feel uncertainty humming inside me like a wire. I expected Eumaeus to scoff at the idea my father was a liar. Who was Mentes, after all? A stranger. A man who told lies himself, for all I know, a man with a grudge. But Eumaeus didn't scoff. Lying in bed, playing the scene out in my head beforehand, I imagined him blazing up in fury at the least slur on my father's truthfulness. Instead he plunged his bucket in water, avoiding my eye.

On the outskirts of town I pass one of Odysseus's old fishermen sitting on the porch outside his hut, stitching nets with a big wooden needle. Word of the town meeting, run ahead by one of Eumaeus's boys, is already spreading.

I stop. I wouldn't normally. "You're coming to the vote?"

He nods, pulls his thread to its full extent, and tugs. Some of the old islanders don't say much.

"How well do you remember Odysseus?"

"I remember 'im."

The knot of worry tightens inside me. It isn't the response I want. Why haven't I noticed it before? All my life I've been certain of Ithaca's love for Odysseus. But why have I been so sure? My mother always said they loved him. So did Eumaeus, his favorite. But have I ever heard it from the other islanders?

"What do you remember best?"

The old man tugs at another knot, then tests the net by pulling at it with fingers like bronze claws.

"'E talked too much," he says.

Sitting in the square later, as villagers slowly flock out of their houses, worry pulses inside me like a stubborn headache. I know my father is a hero. I've heard the storytellers' tales. I've seen his hunting bow on the wall at home—I've even lifted his sword in the shrine. But now, unexpectedly, there's another Odysseus taking shape behind that armored fighter. A shadow, a man with the same outline but a different core. Too clever, too good with words. A liar.

The meeting starts at midday, with the sun at its zenith, driving the square under the plane tree into deep black shade, people packing the benches around it. I sit with my back to the tree. Its roots coil and plait around me like serpents burrowing their way into the ground. There are no rules about who can attend a town meeting. Children scramble on and off the benches. Visitors are welcome—people even give them a respectful hearing if they choose to speak. Women heckle from the upstairs windows of the tavern. I've seen meetings turn in seconds from orderly debates into screaming matches, even fistfights. Speakers get booed off. Arguments cause family feuds that run for years. But this should be over quickly. All I'm asking for is a ship.

I watch Mentor, one of Odysseus's old friends, take his place in the front row, accompanied by his wife and four sons. I wish my mother were here, but she stopped attending meetings a year ago, and I couldn't bear to add my troubles to her sorrows. I watch widows dressed in black clamber up onto the tables at the back of the square. The sight of them makes me confident. These are the women whose husbands and sons sailed for Troy and never came back. Surely they'll support a mission to find them? Then I see some of the young men from the big house, Antinous and Eurymachus among them, swagger into the square and take their places around the gathering. Not together—at strategic points, which means they're planning something—and that makes something lurch inside me. Antinous gives me an airy little wave as he sits down. He's wearing a bright red cape, and carrying—his latest affectation—a little tabby kitten he found in the storeroom and tamed. His plump, bejeweled fingers are scratching the creature's ears as the gathering falls silent.

I stand up. A novice. I've never addressed a meeting before. Every eye on Ithaca is staring at me, and my legs are trembling—I can't stop them. I notice little things—a woman in a window at the back of the square, whispering something to her friend. Then I see all the other eyes again, waiting for me to start.

"Sixteen years ago . . ." A bad start. Voice croaky, and too quiet. "Sixteen years ago . . ." Bellowing it—too loud, sounding like a child.

And suddenly it's going wrong. I know it from the first word. People aren't listening. Mentor looks nervous, which makes me feel worse, and I hear my voice wobble. There's no clicking of fingers, no rumble of approval as I list everything Odysseus did for the island. Maybe I do have a gift for words, but not today, not here. When I rehearsed the speech in the orchard, I imagined people stamping their feet as I reminded them how Odysseus rebuilt the harbor; they growled assent when I talked about the decision to go to war, wiped tears from their eyes when I mentioned Penelope. They even laughed at my only joke.

It isn't like that. I outline my plan for the journey, but by now the young fishermen at the back have lost interest and are whispering and giggling among themselves. My joke dies in silence.

I planned to wind up with an appeal to the islanders' sense of duty. Something tells me that's wrong. I always believed the Ithacans worshipped my father, but looking around the benches, I see that those familiar faces hold expressions I've never noticed before: bitterness, anger, resentment. It's as if I've never looked at them properly, as if they've suddenly turned into strangers; or as if they always were strangers and have suddenly turned into what they are—people.

"So what I really wanted to say," I end up, "is I need to go and find my father. My mother needs it. And I need you to help me. Please."

It sounds flat and I know it. Mentor claps twice. No one else does. I lean back against the tree, shirt soaked in sweat, exhausted. For a moment there's silence, then suddenly everyone's shouting at once.

It's an old woman who wins the floor. She lives in a hut at the end of the beach. I don't know her that well, but she's stabbing her shriveled finger at me and screaming, "Three sons . . . he took all my sons." Another woman follows, her voice rising to become the lament of the old beggars you see clustering the market gates—"No husband to care for me, no sons to look after me in my old age . . ." And sitting under the plane tree in the middle of a town meeting, I suddenly understand: Odysseus was the chief who took their men to war and never brought them back.

It's as if the floodgates have opened. A young fisherman stutters about the four brothers who never came back from the war, and he has everyone in tears. Eumaeus is sitting there in blank shock. Mentor, my father's old friend, does his best to change the mood. Face flushed with anger, he makes a long speech about the duty the islanders owe their chief. There are a few abashed faces around the square, but people keep interrupting. Eumaeus speaks gruffly and inaudibly. To my surprise, Eurymachus lifts his hand and makes a short, polished speech urging the islanders to give me their support. As he sits down, he catches my eye and gives a sympathetic shrug.

I'll still get my ship—surely I will. Eumaeus didn't doubt the vote for a second. But suddenly another voice rises above the hubbub, smooth, unctuous. Antinous is on his feet.

"My friends, *please* . . ."

In Greece, we show deference to guests, and that even extends to town meetings. Voices hush. People go back to their benches. Antinous is left standing, red cape flung over his shoulder, the kitten clutching his sleeve.

"Here's my reason," he says, "why we should discourage Telemachus from this journey. Because we love him. Telemachus, we want you here, close to us. We don't want to lose yet another of our sons. Telemachus . . ." His jeweled finger points straight at me. "Don't go!"

He's got their attention now. He makes a joke; they laugh. His fingers pluck points out of the air. People in the back rows are nodding. Was this how my father used to do it? Steer a meeting as you'd steer a boat.

"And there's one more thing," Antinous finishes, "for which we should thank Telemachus. Thank him, I mean, for calling this meeting." His face becomes suddenly solemn. "He's reminding us Ithaca's been sixteen years without a chief. A *long* time. This town has managed its affairs well . . . but for sixteen years Ithaca has been lucky. No enemies, no invaders—that won't last forever. And when trouble comes, this island will need a strong leader. Strong and experienced, a man who's seen the world, who's traveled, who knows how things work. I think what our boy is saying to us, what he's *really* saying to us, isn't about Odysseus. It's this . . ." And Antinous's voice drops to a whisper. "I need a father. Ithaca needs a chief."

I never saw this happening. How has Antinous twisted it around? I'm paralyzed. It's Mentor who rescues the situation.

"Vote!" he booms, standing up so abruptly that his stool clatters over behind him. "Vote!"

Eumaeus takes up the chant. It's a custom of town meetings that anyone with any kind of authority, or even just a strong murmur of encouragement behind them, can demand a vote at any time. So numbers are called, for and against. Hands are raised in the shade of the plane tree. There's no longer any doubt about the result. A dozen votes, no more, for offering me a ship, and the rest of the meeting solidly against me. The tavern-keeper's boys begin rolling wine barrels out into the square.

I stay seated against the trunk of the tree. I can't move. This time yesterday I was scared to leave Ithaca. Now, suddenly, it's become my prison. I *can't* leave. The sea is like a fortress wall—uncrossable, with my father beyond it.

Mentor comes over to me with his sons behind him, and Eumaeus as well. We stand in silence, shocked, beaten.

"Yer don't need to leave," Eumaeus says. "Yer dad'll come anyway."

"No!" I'm startled by Mentor's tone. To be honest, I've never much liked Mentor. He's stiff, full of his own importance, and doesn't have much sense of humor. But he crouches down next to me, and he's literally trembling with emotion. "He *must* go." He sounds passionate. I didn't think he could be passionate about anything. "You *must*. You *will*. I'm not a rich man, but I have some money set aside. Enough for a ship." His mouth twitches. "A small ship."

"But what about your sons? It's their money."

"No! We'll go to Pylos together . . ." He raises one hand, seeing I'm about to object again. "Odysseus was my friend, the best chief this island ever had. If he's still alive . . ." And suddenly there are tears in his eyes. ". . . if he's still alive, I want his son to bring him home."

So here I am, two days later, clutching the gunwale of Mentor's ship, staring across fretful waves at the rocks of Pylos, Nestor's territory, and wishing I were dead.

You'd think Odysseus's son would be a sailor. Perhaps I'm not his son. I used to think that: that it was all a mistake and there was some other kid somewhere—taller, braver, tougher—who was actually Odysseus's boy. Anyway, Odysseus was famed for his travels across the seas, while I'm hanging over the rail, vomiting like a sick dog.

The wind rose just a few hours ago—rose from nothing to a vicious storm that turned the Ionian Sea into our enemy. Waves batter the boat's hull. On the farm, back home, I've seen cattle stampede through a gate, their black, humped backs jostling together in a frightening torrent. The waves remind me of those stampedes, only vaster. Their expanse seems incomprehensibly huge—a broken landscape stretching all the way to the horizon. The sailors are cursing at their oars—they dropped the sail when the wind rose. Mentor's grimly clutching the steering oar. And I just want to die. My stomach's heaving with each lurch of the boat. The wind's shrieking in my ears, echoed by the gulls who glide past the mast, shrieking like demons. I'm soaked to the skin, and my bare feet are slipping in the mass of seawater and tangled rope that fills the bilges.

To take my mind off it, I think of the frantic twelve hours before we left Ithaca. I did get some consolation from the townspeople as they left the meeting. Quite a few came up to wish me well.

"If you'd asked five years ago, we'd all have joined, but we won't find the men now." That was typical. "Time to move on."

All of that made me feel a little better. But there was one encounter I still don't know what to make of. The square was almost empty. Mentor was bargaining with sailors to make up a scratch crew, while the innkeeper dragged benches back indoors. I was just going to return to the big house when a girl came up to me.

I knew who she was. She lives with her mother in a tiny cottage hidden behind a wall at the top of the town. There's always been something strange about those two. No husband and father to bring back food, yet the cottage is freshly white-washed and they both dress well—better than most of the townspeople, actually. They've always kept to themselves. The girl's a bit older than me, but I've never seen her mix with the town children. As she came up to me, I was wondering if I'd ever actually spoken to her. All the same, there was something familiar about her face.

"You'll find him, won't you?" She spoke before I could, and suddenly I saw she was crying. No sound, just noiseless tears pouring down her cheeks. She didn't bother to wipe them away.

"I'll do my best."

"You *must*."

Suddenly the girl reached into a fold of her dress, pulled something out, and pressed it into my hand. Before I could say anything, she was gone, walking across the square and disappearing into the alley that led to her home. When I opened my hand, I found a little carved wooden owl. A carved owl exactly like the offering Odysseus left on the altar the day he sailed for Troy.

I still don't understand. The girl, or the owl. Or maybe I don't want to understand. I can feel the owl now, squeezed inside my belt.

In any case, we were all too busy after the meeting to think of anything beyond barrels of water and wine, food for the sailors, gifts for Nestor. Mentor wasn't much of an organizer, it turned out. We had a few surprises. Men who voted against me came forward anyway to offer themselves as crew. Eurymachus tracked me down to the storeroom, where Medon and I were pulling out jars of wine, and pressed a small leather bag into my hand. Only gold weighs that much.

"For emergencies," he said with a rueful smile and a clap on the shoulders. "Listen—I'll do everything I can to protect your mother. I promise."

My mother was the last person I saw before leaving. I was dreading it—but when I went to her room, she was sitting at her loom, working as serenely as ever.

"I've come to say good-bye."

A little frown creased Penelope's brow, but she kept weaving.

"I'm going away. I'm going to find out what happened to Odysseus. I'll bring him home if I can."

She didn't say anything. For a moment I hesitated. I could still see Antinous's fat white fingers on her neck. How could I leave her? I shook her shoulders gently. "Do you understand?"

"Good," Penelope said. "*Very* good."

It was only when I hugged her, clutching her tight, feeling how thin and frail my mother had become, that she began crying too. Her last words made sense. "Be careful."

We didn't need to be careful for the first part of the journey. Mentor's ship, the smallest and cheapest merchant vessel Ithaca owns, slipped out of the harbor with twelve oars caressing the sea. It was only just past dawn, and the rising sun colored the water as if it was pouring oil from a jar. All day the crew rowed. Not a breath of wind; the sail stayed furled on the yard. I took my turn on the oars and tried my hand at steering. Dolphins rose from the depths, sleek, muscled bodies breaking surface in a thrilling burst of speed, then diving again to swoop and turn beneath our bow. That night we slept on the beach—ships never sail in darkness if they can help it. We rowed on before day broke. It was only late this afternoon, with the mountains around Pylos already in sight, that the sea shivered, suddenly, turned black, and began to heave and roll as if swarming with serpents.

I hear shouts and look up. There's a bustle of panic around me, and when I gaze blearily toward land, I can see why. The cliffs are shockingly close. The waves must have been driving us toward the shore. A plume of spray bursts from a rock, and I can hear its detonation and the hissing sigh as water sluices down the rock's glistening sides. I was scared before, and cold. Now I realize abruptly how close we are to death. Sudden death, unexpected and pointless. How could it find us so quickly, from a calm blue sea? I can feel the hull shuddering as each wave hits. It's no longer rising bravely to the swell. When the sailor beside me slips and falls sideways, the ship lurches, and green water swills over the gunwales. I watch the peak of the mountain sway into sight above the masthead. There's a goat watching from a ledge near the summit, watching us dispassionately: creatures about to die. It looks so easy to get to dry land, but between us and the land are jagged teeth of rocks. Water seethes past them, as if the cliff face is wetting its lips in anticipation. For some reason I think, *Perhaps this is how my father died*. I have a sudden vision of my own body lolling in waves, as his might have done. But Odysseus sailed the oceans, conquered Troy. His place in the stories was secure. What about me? Is this really all I can show for sixteen years? It mustn't be. It *mustn't*.

I do my best to think. Mentor said Pylos is in a bay—he came here once before—but there's no sign of a break in the hurling surf. We have to get away from the cliff face. The sailor next to me curses, struggling for a foothold as he heaves at his oar. Mentor is wrestling with the steering oar, desperately trying to turn the ship's bow from the rocks. I'm scared. I'm sick. But my mind's still working. I think, *Why doesn't the crew use the sail?* The sailors are never going to be able to row against that current. The sail's the only force strong enough to pull us clear, and the wind is backing off the rocks; it could drag us back out to sea.

I shout and point, but the sailor next to me is too exhausted to understand. They're too busy heaving blindly at the oars, too tired, too scared to think clearly. No one else is going to do anything about it, so I crawl to the foot of the mast. Ropes are knotted around the bench under it. I pull at the knots with frozen fingers, but the wet rope is jammed solid. One of the sailors watches, puzzled, then his face clears as he sees what I have in mind. He pulls a knife from his belt, saws through the rope, then turns and yells through the howl of the wind. Sailors drop their oars, struggling with ropes. There's a clap of wet cloth above us; then it feels as if some massive hand has grabbed us underwater. We lurch; the mast swings; and suddenly we're veering sideways with water sluicing over the gunwale. Someone screams. Mentor's feet lift off the deck as he clings to the steering oar, which seems to be snared deep in some furrow in the sea. The sail's dragging us away, though, the boat's careering away from the rocks, barely under control. I grip the mast and retch, but when I look up, the mountain is gone. Mentor is pointing ahead to a gap at the base of the cliffs—the entrance to the inlet at last. As I watch, it opens to become a narrow passage. The sail claps, then billows out again as we turn. One last time a wave lifts us; then we're gliding across the smooth waters of a long bay fringed by hills.

The silence feels solid after the roar of the open sea. To my right, I can see the lights of a little fishing village. It's nearly dark. The first stars are showing above the skyline, and a bright, low planet, maybe Aphrodite, is too. My lips are caked with salt. Suddenly I realize I'm trembling.

Mentor comes toward me. One of the sailors has taken the steering oar. He grips my shoulder, squeezing so hard it hurts.

I say, "I'm sorry."

He looks puzzled. "Sorry?"

"I was sick."

To my surprise, Mentor reaches forward and hugs me. "You did well," he says quietly.

I'm not sure what he means. I was scared. I did the obvious thing—what was so good about that? Suddenly I'm blinking back tears of nervous exhaustion. I don't want Mentor to see I'm crying like a child, so I stare out across the bow.

That's when I realize we aren't heading for the town. Instead, the helmsman has turned us left, into the shadow of the mountain. Screened from the wind, the sail hangs slack. One by one the men pull out oars and begin to row the boat forward along the length of the bay. Ahead, low down on the waterline, I can see a point of orange light. It's only when we get closer that I can make out what it is. A huge fire of driftwood is burning on the beach. There are people around it, black figures dancing across the flames. Closer in, I can hear chanting and the lowing of cattle. It seems to be some kind of festival. A branch on the fire flares up, suddenly, each leaf blazing distinctly. Then points of light appear at the water's edge. The men stop rowing. We rock slowly forward as the lights drift away from the beach. When they come closer, I see that each is a little floating raft with a candle surrounded by a wreath of flowers. The rafts rock as they drift past and float silently on into the bay's darkness. Looking behind, I can see candles spread across the water, as if it were a night sky garlanded with stars.

"Look," someone says.

There's a larger raft floating toward us, piled high with petals and tiers of lights. Their flames light up a wooden carving of a god, the height of a man.

"Poseidon," says a voice.

We watch as the raft floats past with the god's blank eyes staring out into the bay, drifting smoke and the smell of scorched flowers.

"It was Poseidon who saved us from the storm," someone says, and there's a rumble of agreement from the crew.

I don't say anything. I watch the flaming statue of Poseidon disappear into the darkness behind us, then Mentor gives an order and oars dip into the water. Their festival over, the crowd on the beach is waiting for us, with the fire's flames mirrored in the black water. As we draw closer, I can see the carcasses of slaughtered bulls lying next to a small altar. The sand is soaked dark with their blood. Priests stand to either side of an old man sitting on a litter. There are fighters there too, in polished armor, and musicians with curled brass horns I haven't seen before.

Mentor points at the old man and whispers, "Nestor."

Everyone has heard of Nestor, the oldest man on earth. He fought alongside Hercules and Jason—fighters from so long ago that these days they're talked about like gods. The chief of Pylos is small and bald, with a large head surrounded by wisps of snow-white hair.

Our ship crunches sand, but when I jump down onto the beach, my knees give way. The motion of the sea, fear, exhaustion—suddenly I don't have any strength left. All I can do is cling to the ship's prow with the warm, salty water tugging at my calves. I can feel the heat from the fire.

All I can think is *I'm alive.*

One of the priests calls out, "Who are you? Where are you from?"

The old chief lifts one hand to silence him. When he speaks, his voice sounds too loud for his frail body.

"Welcome to Pylos," he says.

I 'm Telemachus of Ithaca."

I can see the effect it has. Eyes widening, groups drawing together, and a whisper running all along the beach: "Odysseus's son . . . *Odysseus's* son . . ."

I hear Mentor clamber down onto the sand beside me.

"Odysseus's son?" I step forward, and Nestor grips my hand with fingers as dry and light as twigs. Up close, his eyes are covered by a milky film. People say Nestor is a hundred years old, maybe even more. I feel a papery hand pass over my face as if a moth is brushing it in the night. "And is this my old friend Mentor? I see him now. Polycaste, bring a cup of wine for our guests from Ithaca."

A sulky-looking girl is standing behind him. She's about my age, and looks bored. She takes cups of wine from a servant and passes them to us without a word or smile. She's taller than me, with curling, golden hair, a round face, and strongly marked black brows.

"My daughter," Nestor explains. "My *youngest* daughter. I have many children, you know. All now scattered except for Polycaste, the comfort of my old age." He turns back to me. "Odysseus's son. *Odysseus's* son. Do you bring news of your father?"

It takes a moment for me to realize what the question means. "I came here for news." I can't keep the disappointment out of my voice.

"For news of Odysseus? We have no news here. I am sorry—sorry, indeed. But still, if you are searching for him, then perhaps we can help. Odysseus's son, here in Pylos! A great day, to be sure. We will talk of Odysseus later. Tomorrow. Perhaps. Tonight we must celebrate your arrival." It feels like he's getting into his stride. I can't get a word in edgewise. "And Mentor, a pleasure to see you again! But look at you both, half dead with exhaustion. No easy journey today, I imagine. We have been celebrating the festival of Poseidon, an old tradition at Pylos begun by my father more than a hundred years ago. We like to keep up the old traditions, whatever the young think of them . . ." He glances at his daughter, who rolls her eyes. "But here you are, standing on the sand while the night grows cold. We must go back to my house and take care of you!"

No news of Odysseus. The disappointment leaves me numb. I'm tired. We've just escaped drowning. Ithaca feels a long way away. For a moment I wish I'd never left home. Even the olive groves smell strange in this new land. The priests' robes are different from the robes on Ithaca. There's an odd perfume coming from the fire, some kind of incense, and the line of

48

mountains above us is nothing like Mount Nirito at home. Everyone looks threatening. One of the fighters is missing an arm. Another has a scar where his left eye should have been. Feeling lost and scared, I watch the group by the fire break up as mules are led forward. The altar is packed into a wooden crate. Four soldiers lift Nestor's litter on poles. Polycaste mounts her mule, waving aside the soldier who steps forward to help. I find myself heaved onto a saddle and clutch the wooden pommel.

Servants raise torches of flaming pinewood to light the way, and slowly the procession moves off into the olive groves behind the beach. My mule rocks from side to side, brushing trees as it climbs the narrow path. Ahead of us, chains of torches lead up the hillside. I'm so tired I can hardly keep my eyes open. Two or three times I doze off and wake clutching at the saddle. Branches loom out of the darkness, framing a star-studded sky that might have been cut from purple velvet. Bats flicker across it. I hear the gentle hoot of an owl out in the olive groves. Cicadas shrill around us. In front, Nestor's litter sways on brightly painted poles. I drift in and out of sleep. Sometimes I think I'm still on the swooping deck of Mentor's ship, then wake to the mule beneath me.

The last time I wake, it's to the bustle of orders being shouted. We're outside a large house—bigger than our house in Ithaca—with whitewashed walls and soldiers on guard at the gate. Torches hang in brackets on the walls, casting a flickering glow across a forecourt of beaten earth, where Nestor is being helped down from his litter. People are dismounting their mules. Yawning, I follow my host into a wide courtyard of raked gravel, where Nestor stops me.

"You need to rest," he says kindly. "We won't eat straightaway. Come to the hall when the bell rings."

All great houses are supposed to be laid out the same way, but I've only ever seen the house at Ithaca. Everything here seems unfamiliar: the color of the walls, the height of the corridors, the carvings on the gateposts. I follow a servant down a corridor to a small room with a ceiling of wooden beams, its walls decorated a warm earth-red. A delicious smell fills the air. Under the window there's a hip bath half-full of water—Nestor must have sent servants ahead to prepare it. A slim servant girl comes in through a door carrying a steaming pitcher, which she empties into the bath. Opening a wooden chest, she throws handfuls of rose petals, sprigs of rosemary, and crushed bay leaves into the bath. After the terror of the storm, it feels as if I've been transported to heaven.

"Clothes." Her accent is foreign. She has a dark, delicate face, and her black hair, tightly curled, is braided on her head with a ribbon. She tugs at her light green dress to show she means clothes and opens a painted wooden chest to point out stacks of neatly folded gowns. Suddenly I'm aware of my own filthy clothes, still damp from the sea, of my hair caked with salt, my skin itching from two days' journey. When she's gone I peel everything off, step into the bath, and sink down into warm, perfumed water. It comes up to my chin, rose petals and sweet herbs revolving on the surface. I breathe in the deep, warm fragrance and close my eyes, feeling days of anxiety, of anger, of fear all soaking off me along with the salt that crusts my skin.

The girl comes back in, carrying another steaming pitcher. I do what I can to cover myself, but she just laughs.

"Close your eyes."

I close my eyes, bow my head, and feel a delicious stream of hot water cascade over me.

"Sit up."

I smell sweet soap and feel her strong fingers massaging it into my scalp, combing through the tangle of hair.

"What's your name?" I ask.

No reply. The soothing touch of her fingers is almost sending me to sleep, so I sink back and close my eyes. Drowsily I ask, "Where are you from?"

She doesn't answer immediately, so I repeat the question. When I open my eyes, she's over by the door, holding the empty pitcher, but there's something in her face, something wrong. She looks desolate.

"Troy," she says. Then she's gone, door closed.

And suddenly I'm wide awake.

Troy. How often have I heard that name? The Trojan War is part of my life—it's part of all our lives. How often, crammed into a corner of the tavern, have I heard storytellers describe the city the Greeks hurled themselves against year after year? How often have I closed my eyes as the thrum of their instruments quickened pace and their voices tumbled over the words, picturing hordes of Trojan soldiers bursting from its gates? Troy, the city that emptied Ithaca of men and filled it with widows' black. Troy, from which my father was meant to return.

But in all this time I've never seen a Trojan.

She isn't a servant girl, I realize suddenly. She's a slave. We don't have slaves on Ithaca, but they exist all over Greece. Prizes of war—high-born women, some of them, laboring in their conquerors' houses, and sometimes in their beds. There aren't many male slaves. When a town is sacked, the men are slaughtered. It's the women who become possessions, machines, trophies.

That explains the look of desolation. Who has she lost? A father, brothers. She was there—that's the thought I can't get over. I don't know how many times I've heard the story of Troy's last night, imagined the shrieks and the crackle of fire, seen flames leaping from houses and burning temples, pictured oil blazing in the streets from smashed shops, piles of bodies, soldiers breaking down doors and dragging Trojans out into the streets. She was there. A child, maybe, but that last night is still in her mind, seared there forever. She was there, dragged out into the street with her mother sobbing and the body of her father, slashed by Greek swords, slumped on the floor of a home she'll never see again.

She was there. And so was my father.

In the great hall of Nestor's house, two massive pine logs smolder on the hearth. Beyond it a table is spread with dishes of meat and baskets of bread. Servants—slaves—are pouring wine from pitchers. Cooks turn fat little sausages on a griddle.

A young man, a fighter with hair oiled and his arms covered in tattoos, greets me and pours me wine. "Are you really Odysseus's son?" He sounds eager, almost shy. "What was he like?"

"I never met him. He left Ithaca before I was born."

"What do you think happened to him?"

Bewildered, I stare at him. "That's what I came to find out."

"Are you Odysseus's son?" A girl in a long robe. And there are others behind her, a whole crowd pressing around me. "Do you know what happened to Odysseus? Where is Odysseus?"

Nestor rescues me. The crowd parts for him, and I find myself clasped in a weak embrace that leaves behind it an old man's smell and the feathery brush of Nestor's parchment lips.

"Telemachus. And Mentor. So great a pleasure. I am only sorry I can give you no news of Odysseus. No *fresh* news. Let me tell you about the last time I saw him . . ." Nestor leads me to the high table and settles himself comfortably against a pile of cushions, waving to a servant for wine. "On the beach at Troy, in fine spirits . . . as we all were, you can imagine. He had a bandage on one arm, his left, a wound from the night Troy fell. His men were stacking treasure in the ships. There is nothing left of Troy, you know, not even a village. No one to live there. It is gone as if it never existed, a graveyard, even the temples of the gods destroyed . . ." He frowns suddenly. "I fear that is the source of Odysseus's trouble. A vengeful god punishing the man who planned Troy's fall, for it was Odysseus's stratagem, you know, his *plan*, explained to us in council two nights before, that caused Troy's downfall. I can't say no one added to it. I myself made some helpful *modifications*, which, I flatter myself, contributed to its success . . . perhaps even *ensured* its success. Odysseus, though, was the guiding spirit. A *clever* man, which is why hope must still remain. If anyone could get himself out of some scrape or danger, it would be your father . . .

"Where was I? Standing on the beach, then. We embraced. 'Nestor,' he said, 'I will visit you in Pylos on my way home.' That may be significant—do you see? He had no plans for a detour. Home to his wife and his baby son . . . Oh, yes, he knew all about you. Messages traveled between Greece and the camp at Troy. 'Telemachus!' I remember the night he got the news. A great feast on the beach, sheep slaughtered, jars of wine looted from one of the little villages around Troy. We all toasted you, my dear boy, and here you are in the flesh, as it were, a young *man*. You don't, if I may say it, *look* like your father. Yes?"

The sulky-looking girl is tugging at her father's arm. "The food's ready." She doesn't pay any attention to me.

"And I have been talking . . . but we won't talk any more tonight." Nestor lays a light hand on my sleeve. "As I say, I have no hard news, but there are *rumors*. I know where you can find news. All that must wait for tomorrow, though, when heads are clear and we are both rested from our exertions. For now, we will celebrate your arrival in Pylos. We will *feast*."

It's quite a feast, I have to say that. I'm used to the chaos of our house at Ithaca, where rooms stay unswept for days, guests drift in and out of the kitchen, and servants come and go without warning. At Nestor's home, dishes are served and then whisked efficiently away. When I drop a cushion, unseen hands seize it from the floor and stuff it behind my shoulder. The slave girl who bathed me keeps stepping forward to fill my cup with wine.

I'm sitting next to Nestor, with Polycaste, his daughter, beyond him. Most of the talk is a monologue by Nestor that rambles wherever his mind wanders: his sons, now scattered across Greece . . . the old days . . . feasts of Poseidon . . . the harvest . . . the pictures on the walls of the great hall, copied from some he saw on a voyage to Egypt years ago. Most of the stories are about himself. I soon realize that Nestor's fusty charm hides a strong streak of vanity. And I notice something else. The doddery impression he gives—a pleasant but scatterbrained old man living happily in the past—isn't the whole story. He's cleverer than that. His rambling, impossible to interrupt, has a purpose: so long as he's talking, no one else can. Once, I ask a direct question about Odysseus, and he brushes me off. I ask something about the war—same reaction. Each time, he waves his hand and we're back on stag hunts in the hills of Thessaly or craftsmen who make rings of solid silver in Athens. It doesn't take a genius to get the message. Nestor will talk about my father when he's ready. For the moment, Odysseus is off-limits.

Polycaste, his daughter, looks bored and doesn't say much. Sometimes she tightens her lips at some story of her father's she's obviously heard a thousand times. The other guests get slowly drunk, which is what always happens at feasts. Eventually Nestor raises his hand, and the hall falls silent.

"We will have a story," he announces. "Tonight, in honor of our guest, we will have the story of the fall of Troy."

It's hardly new to me. Or anyone else—everyone in Greece can tell you about the fall of Troy. After eight years of slaughter under Troy's impregnable walls, with the Greek leaders squabbling, soldiers dying of disease, and the great Trojan adventure starting to look like a fiasco, Odysseus—my father—came up with the trick that finally pried open Troy's bronze gates.

The Greek armies retreated to the beach. With Trojan soldiers watching from the ramparts, the Greeks struck tents, sacrificed to the gods, then clambered back onto their ships and rowed away over the horizon. Several hours went by. At last a wary Trojan reconnaissance band, heavily armed, came out from a side gate to see what was going on. They found all the mess of an army that had been encamped for eight years: abandoned tents, piles of rotting food, stinking latrines . . . and the Greeks' final offering to the gods, the gigantic wooden statue of a horse.

They found something else as well: a half-crazed soldier hiding in a trench. When they dragged him out, beat him, and hauled him before Priam, Troy's king, the soldier babbled out the whole sorry tale—of aristocratic infighting, illness and indiscipline, mutinous, half-starved troops and adverse omens—that led to the Greek capitulation. That was when it came home to the Trojans that their nightmare was finally over. Heaving open the gates for the first time in eight years, they all flooded out onto the plain of Troy—soldiers, old men in litters, women and children, priests and slaves. They picked through the abandoned camp, traced the furrows of Greek ships that still marked the beach, kicked out the ashes of their enemies' campfires. The horse, chocked up on tree trunks, they hauled back across the plain to the great temple of Troy, where garlands of victory were already being hung and fires were lit as the town gave itself over to celebration.

Odysseus was inside the horse.

He and twenty companions, sweating, teeth clenched, gripping breastplates and shields so no clink of metal would give away their presence. They crouched in darkness for twelve hours, unable even to relieve themselves in case the stink gave them away. They felt the jolt as the horse eased over the threshold of Troy's main gate. They heard the Trojans singing and rejoicing, and smelled incense and roasting meat through the horse's timbers. Only when the last noises of celebration had died away did they let themselves down from the belly of the horse and open the gates of Troy to the Greek army. Because the Greeks hadn't really sailed away. They'd hove to beyond the horizon, and the moment night fell, they returned to the beach.

No storyteller on earth could describe the slaughter that followed. The Trojans were bemused, befuddled, unprepared—they had no chance of organizing any resistance. And after eight years' fighting, the Greeks showed no mercy. Women and children were killed, old men cut down in the streets. The Greeks hunted Priam and his children to the steps of the temple. Shops were set on fire, and fire spread across the doomed town, choking streets in oily black smoke, drowning children's screams with the crackle of flames. By the time dawn broke, Troy no longer existed.

I can still remember the first time I heard the story of Troy. It reached Ithaca via a storyteller on a merchant ship. The versions I've heard since have added detail—increasingly colorful—but to me, there's one image that always sticks in my mind. My father—my *father*—crouching in the horse's belly, doomed to almost certain death but feeling no fear. I remember what I felt the first time I heard it, and I've felt the same thing ever since: I couldn't do that. The story doesn't bring my father closer. It drives him further away. Odysseus the fighter, Odysseus the hero. Each time I picture my father's jaw set, his hand sweating on his sword hilt, and I know—I *know*—that whatever blood runs in his veins doesn't run through mine.

The version told at Pylos makes a few changes. It turns out Odysseus originally suggested a dog, not a horse. The horse was Nestor's idea. It was Nestor who modified the design to include a trapdoor and rope ladder. Nestor checked each man's equipment, ran through the final orders with Odysseus, and rehearsed the actor the Greeks left behind to sell the story to the Trojans. Plus, at the last minute he ordered the horse's head to be lowered slightly, otherwise it wouldn't have fit through the gate.

Apart from that, the storyteller at Pylos tells it well. Most of the changes are wasted anyway, because Nestor sleeps through it, waking only just in time to join the applause at the end. After that he rises unsteadily to his feet and says good night, ordering me not to get up too early in the morning.

I do wake up early, though. I wake with the feeling I've let something slip through my fingers. There's a conversation we've barely even started. About my father: about who he is, and where he might be now.

In the great hall a table is laid with baskets of bread and dishes of yogurt and honey. Polycaste is already there, shredding a roll.

"Apparently I've got to show you around."

"Show me what?"

"The house. The farm. Anything you want to see. Come on, you can eat while we go. That way we won't have to talk."

I try to anyway. "I enjoyed the story last night."

"Did you? It makes a change. Normally we have Jason and the Argonauts. My father was one of the Argonauts. This is the storeroom. Wine. Oil."

"Did your father really meet Hercules?"

"Yes. Amazing. Kitchen."

"You think people like that only exist in stories, and then you meet one of them." It sounds pretty weak, even to me.

"Maybe one day you'll be a story yourself. Probably a really boring one. This is the office where my father does his accounts, meaning sleeps. This is the courtyard, which you've seen. Upstairs is like any other big house. Let's go outside."

As we walk out into the sun-baked earth of the vegetable garden, I say, "Don't you like your father?"

Polycaste stops and turns on me, eyes blazing. "Of course I do! I love him! What's that got to do with it? I suppose you wouldn't understand if you don't have a father yourself." She pauses, anger ebbing away as fast as it came, and looks at me as if she hasn't really noticed me before. "What's your mother like?"

"She's not well."

"Ill?"

"She's very quiet."

"Everyone says how beautiful she is. Was. I suppose no one's seen her for years, except you. This is the orchard."

I say, "Why are so many of the men injured?"

It's something I noticed last night and again as we passed through the house. One of the men stacking tables in the hall had a scar under his eye. Others were missing hands. One man, who pushed open a door for us, had lost both legs and pushed himself around on a little trolley, his hands wrapped in bloodied linen rags.

Polycaste gives me a pitying look. "Why do you think? The war. They came back like this. Everyone was scarred by the war. What's wrong with you? Isn't Ithaca full of veterans too?"

I say, "No one came back to Ithaca. They all disappeared."

"Oh." Polycaste looks away. "I hadn't thought." After a moment she goes on, "There are loads of them 'round here, veterans. All the villages are full of them, the farms. Lots of men took to the hills. Eight years fighting in Troy, they couldn't get used to ordinary life again. Seeing women, living with children. Some became bandits. Some just scratch a living out of the forest. You'll see them if we go to Sparta together."

"Sparta?"

"That's my father's plan. Hasn't he told you yet? He will. There was a story last winter, of a war veteran living in a little village up there, a shepherd. They were snowed in for a month. When the snow melted they found he'd killed his whole family. Wife, three children, just killed them. I suppose it's still in their heads, killing people."

Suddenly I realize how remote Ithaca is. I always thought it was the center of the world. It isn't. It's a backwater dozing in the far west, cut off from everything on the mainland. All over Greece people are living through the aftermath of the endless, bloody war. For us on Ithaca the war is just an absence—the absence of the men who never came back. Everywhere else, it's real and you can see its marks—in wounded limbs and scarred memories, in slave girls, in veterans pushing them-selves around on trolleys, hands wrapped in bloodied cloth.

In things people don't know how to talk about.

We get back to the great hall about noon, as bells ring in the villages around the house and cicadas shrill in the olive trees. The sun has turned the courtyard into a furnace, but it's still cool in the hall. The fire has dwindled to a single sputtering log, kept aflame only for ritual's sake. A slave comes forward with a cool jar of water and a linen cloth to wash the dust from our hands and faces.

Nestor seems refreshed by his night's sleep. He lifts his cheek so Polycaste can kiss it, then gestures to a door in the side of the hall and leads me into a small office with a single window too high to see out of. Unlike the great hall, it contains no luxury. It's plain and simple, with no furniture but a couple of chairs and a wooden table.

"My thinking-room." Nestor eases himself painfully into one of the chairs and gestures the servant to leave. "No clutter. We must talk." But he doesn't. For a moment he just looks up

at the deep blue outside the window. Following his gaze, I can
see swallows darting across the sky.

"You know how this will probably end?" he says at last. He
looks at me, and there's something piercing in his filmy eye,
a flash of the wisdom he's famous for. "It's more than likely
your father is dead. You must know that. If you have a fraction
of Odysseus's brains, you'll know that."

He falls silent again, for a long time, then sighs. "We've heard
rumors, of course. I'm sure you've heard rumors in Ithaca.
Odysseus was seen in Africa. He drowned in a storm off Cape
Tenaros . . . There are any number of fates one can imagine. A
storm? A mutiny? A quarrel with people ashore? You would
think, wouldn't you, that after eight years of fighting together,
the Greeks would be united. Nothing could be further from
the truth. There were jealousies and resentments in the Greek
camp that will endure for generations. Leaders who felt they
weren't shown enough respect, contingents who didn't get the
booty they thought they deserved. In some ways, you know,
winning is far harder than losing."

Easy to say. I think of the desolate slave girl from the night
before.

"So maybe Odysseus went ashore on some island for water
and food, and ran into a fight," Nestor goes on. "Or he was
blown off course. Or he lost his way. There are as many possibili-
ties as there are rumors: the sea holds many perils. But nothing
worth acting on. You could spend a lifetime chasing rumors."

"I know he might be dead," I say.

"Good." Nestor rubs his chin thoughtfully. "You're right to
search, though. It's better to be sure. Nothing saps courage like
uncertainty, and from what I hear of affairs in Ithaca, you will
need all your courage. Who is looking after Penelope while
you are gone?"

"The servants."

His mouth tightens only slightly, but it's enough to make me wince. My mother, alone in her room. Antinous.

"Can you fight?"

"No." I can't see any point in lying.

"A pity. Somehow you must learn. If any of my sons were here, they would teach you."

I say, "Tell me about my father."

"Are you sure you want to know?" I'm almost certain he expected the question. Again I sense that piercing gleam in the old man's dull eye. "I wonder if any of us can really know our fathers—really *know* them. We see them through veils of . . ." He lifts one withered hand. "Awe. Resentment. Love. We spend so much of our time trying to be different from them—"

"I don't know what he's like," I interrupt. "I don't know how to be different."

"A fair point." Nestor's chin sinks to his chest. He seems weary, suddenly. "What have you been told about Odysseus?"

"What the storytellers say."

"There's truth of a kind in stories. Our greatest hero. A fighter. A strategist. All true." He pauses, his voice fading. "But not the whole truth, of course."

"Someone told me he was a liar."

For a moment I can hear the swallows shrieking outside the window. The old man slowly shifts himself on his seat, like he's looking for a comfortable position and not finding it.

"Who?"

"Mentes, a friend of his from Africa."

"Mentes? The African? I heard he died. But listen . . ." Nestor looks closely at me with a pained expression on his withered face. "There is no whole truth about a person. People are too complicated, they have too many sides . . . I will tell you the trouble with Odysseus. Your father was eloquent—a talker— and people distrust talkers. They distrust words, and Odysseus was a master of words. A liar? Yes, some people called him that. I prefer to call him a storyteller, a spinner of yarns. That was how we survived eight years of hell . . . yes, *hell*. Can you imagine what the war was really like? Forget the storytellers. Agamemnon was no leader. Our best soldier, Achilles, refused to fight, and the rest of our men were no match for the Trojans. Odysseus kept us going, because he always had another idea, another tale that would save us all, a god who would come to our rescue, a spy who promised to open the gates for us. Scheme after scheme . . . Lies? Most of them, yes, but he believed them before we did.

"That mad scheme of the horse . . . there was only one chance in a thousand it would succeed . . . It was Odysseus's plan, of course—who else could have come up with it? We went along with it because to hear Odysseus speak, to see him in the assembly, you would feel all objections fall away. That was Odysseus's genius: people *believed* him." Nestor shakes his head. "While they were with him. Afterward, of course, the doubts crept in . . . 'Was that *really* true?' Your father was a complex man. Not everyone liked him. Not many trusted him. Brave? Yes, when he'd convinced himself of some hare-brained scheme. At other times a coward for whom the rest of us had to cover up." He sighs. "I'm assuming that, as his son, you're no fool yourself, which is why I am talking to you as if you were a grown man, not a boy of sixteen who has never learned to fight."

Nestor falls silent. Questions crowd into my mind—a lifetime of questions. But one look at the old man's face stops me from asking them. Nestor is too exhausted to trouble with more questions.

"Why do you want to find him?" he asks after a pause.

"For my mother's sake."

"Now I think *you* are lying."

"For mine, then."

"And what will you do if you learn nothing?"

"Declare him dead, raise a funeral pyre, and let my mother marry again."

"The best thing, perhaps. But whatever happens, it won't be easy. Listen to me, Telemachus. Don't judge your father too harshly. Odysseus was just a man. Better than some, no worse than others." He lifts one finger. It has a chief's ruby ring on it. "And here is another piece of advice. Don't set too much store by finding Odysseus. You think that finding your father will explain everything about you. It won't. I barely knew my own father. Hercules killed him . . . and later, Hercules became my friend. It's a strange world. I'm one hundred and ten years old—imagine that. For decades I enjoyed how people honored me for my age and wisdom . . . now I sometimes think I understand nothing at all. They still flatter me. I pretend to enjoy it. I'm too tired to explain it means nothing to me. But enough." He lifts one weary hand. "Now I must tell you what to do next. Listen." He reaches to a tray, pours a little water into a cup, and sips it.

"When Odysseus left Troy he was healthy and had good ships. He was planning to return straight to Ithaca, via Pylos. He would have had to sail around the south of Greece, where two capes jut into the sea, Malea and Tenaros. More ships are wrecked on Malea and Tenaros than anywhere else in the seas. I have sailed around them myself and always been fortunate . . . but if your father was wrecked, it was probably on one of those points. Both lie near Sparta, Menelaus's kingdom. You must go to Menelaus in Sparta."

"Menelaus!" Menelaus is the brother of Agamemnon, leader of the Greeks. Since Agamemnon died, Menelaus is the richest and most powerful king in Greece. It was Menelaus who began the war after his wife, Helen, ran off with a Trojan prince.

When the war ended, he took Helen back to his palace at Sparta. If I go to Sparta, I'll meet Helen herself.

"Think," Nestor goes on. "Menelaus and his family, the Atreids, control the whole east coast of Greece. If anything happens in the east of Greece, they know of it. Besides, Menelaus has traveled since he left Troy—to Crete and beyond, to Egypt. He has agents everywhere. News reaches Sparta. If anyone on earth knows Odysseus's fate, it's Menelaus."

Nestor stops and clears his throat. "My daughter Polycaste will accompany you. I won't deny I have my own reasons for sending a mission to Sparta." He smiles wearily. "If you are truly as astute as your father, you'll guess them soon enough. Pylos is small and peaceful. Sparta is large and hungry for war. Friendship alone prevents the Atreids from gobbling us up. I have not visited Menelaus since the war, and I should have done. I am too old to travel now, but Polycaste can go in my place. She cannot cross the mountains without a companion. There—you will be doing your father's old friend a favor by going."

He blinks like a little white owl. I've tired him—it's time I went. But before I can leave, Nestor lays a soft white hand on my wrist. It seems to weigh nothing. It's almost a bond to my missing father—these feathery fingers that once clasped Odysseus's hand.

"Odysseus was my friend, Telemachus." He sounds oddly husky. "So many battles together. So many arguments in the Greek council. I can hear his voice now . . ." His eyes half close as he remembers the voice I've never heard. For a moment I think he's fallen into a reverie. When Nestor speaks again, his voice is so low I have to lean closer to hear him. "I can't offer you anything more than advice, Telemachus. But my prayers will be with you. Good luck."

6

Polycaste and I set off the next day on two mules, with a third to carry our baggage. The plan is to travel to the edge of Nestor's realm and pick up a guide to lead us across the mountains to Sparta. Mentor will stay in Pylos with Nestor. All this is decreed by the old chief, who allows no alternatives. I wonder why he is so insistent that we travel alone. Maybe it is a test of some sort—for Polycaste, or me, or both of us.

On the first day we travel through gentle hills covered with olive groves and little farms. This is Nestor's country, and everyone knows Polycaste. Children run after us when we ride through villages. A farmer draws us water from his well in an ancient leather bucket. When the sun is at its hottest, we shelter for an hour or two in the shadow of an outcrop of rock, but we don't talk much. To be honest, I'm scared of Polycaste—scared of her caustic tongue and quick boredom. In the evening we drop down to the shore of a bay with some fishermen's cottages and a little tavern clustered around a beach lined with fishing boats. We kick off our shoes and paddle in the soft, silky water while the mules are led away to a shed at the back of the village. On the far side of the bay are mountains, the highest I've ever seen, way higher than Mount Nirito at home. When we look to the right, past a headland, we can make out open sea; to the left, where the bay ends, is the smoke of a little town.

"That town's where we're going," Polycaste says. "Over there"—she points out to sea—"is Tenaros. The mountains run all the way back along the peninsula and inland. We have to cross them to get to Sparta."

"Have you ever been to the town?"

She shakes her head. "It's outside my father's territory."

We eat fish grilled over olive branches on the beach and sleep on piles of nets in a low shed that reeks of fish oil. Its rafters are hung with spare oars, masts, and rolled-up sails. Another day of travel brings us to the outskirts of the town.

A rough ditch signals the boundary. Beyond it, the track runs across beaten earth marked with the outlines of houses. It feels like the town used to be bigger. Starved-looking children stare at us from shelters made of bent branches, but they seem too apathetic to chase after us or even beg for food. Our mules pick their way cautiously through heaps of debris and the ashes of old fires. The track dips down, then climbs over leveled banks of flattened earth.

"There used to be walls," Polycaste says. "Ages ago. My father told me."

"What happened?"

"It was sacked."

"Who by?"

"People in boats. A long time ago. Trojans, maybe." She shrugs. "Enemies."

From outside a low, unpainted cottage, an old man watches us approach. Scrawny chickens peck at the dust under his bench. A dog lies at his feet, its head on one side. It bares its teeth as we halt but seems too exhausted even to get up and bark.

"We're looking for Nauteus," Polycaste says.

The old man carefully looks us over, like he's trying to memorize our appearance, then says, "He's sick."

"Where will we find him?"

"Up by the stronghold, next to the cistern, but I told you, he's sick. Everyone's sick."

As we ride away, he shouts something after us. It sounds like "Watch out for . . ."

"What did he say?"

Polycaste shrugs. She leads the way along narrow streets, past houses that mostly look abandoned. There's an open space that might once have been a market square, and a taller building, its roof recently patched, that could have been a temple. Apart from two mules tied up outside a house, there's no sign of life. The town is nothing like the bustling little villages in Nestor's world.

Polycaste pauses in the square. To the right, a track leads down to the beach. To the left, another climbs upward toward a ruined tower. She guides her mule toward the tower, and almost immediately the road widens around a circular stone structure whose walls are choked with weeds. There's a cottage next to it with fishing nets hanging from the eaves. A bench stands outside the door, but the shutters are closed. Polycaste frowns, then clambers down from her mule to knock at the shutters.

A woman's voice answers. "Who is it?"

"I'm looking for Nauteus. Nestor sent me."

"He's sick."

"Is this his house?"

The door opens and the woman appears. She's gaunt and stooped, not old, but so bowed by work that she looks much older.

"I'm Polycaste, Nestor's daughter. My father told me to find Nauteus. He said he would guide us through the mountains to Sparta."

"Nauteus is sick," the woman says. Her eyes flicker suspiciously over us from a face burned almost black by wind and sun. "He was vomiting all night. I offered a jar of oil at the temple, but he's no better."

There's something imperious in Polycaste's expression. "He *has* to get better," she says. "He has to take us to Sparta."

"He isn't taking anyone anywhere. The way he is now, he won't see another night. Then where will I be? No man to look after me, no one to feed my children, no one to bring us food . . ." Her voice is starting to take on the whining, chanting tone of professional beggars.

I swing myself off my mule and pull a loaf from the sack on my saddlebag. "Here's some bread for him." The woman's lament stops abruptly. She eyes the bread greedily, but I don't let her take it—not yet. "Is there anyone else who can guide us?"

The woman shakes her head. "Everyone's sick. There's no luck in this town. The fish went away, the trees died, the animals died . . ." She's starting the beggar's drone again. Her black eyes don't leave the little loaf of bread. "People say some god hates us, maybe Poseidon. We gave him too poor a sacrifice one year and he's hated us ever since . . ."

"Do you know the road to Sparta?"

The woman falls silent, still staring at the bread. "There's only one road," she says at last. "Over the mountains. There are tracks in the forest, but only one road."

"Where can we stay the night?"

"Not here. If you have any sense, you'll go back to Pylos. Take the young lady home to her father."

"I can look after myself," Polycaste says.

The woman gives a short laugh. "I wouldn't spend the night here. It's dangerous. You'll get the sickness."

"Is there a tavern?"

"The people in the tavern are bad."

"An empty house?"

"Not here."

Polycaste says, "My father will be angry when he hears you turned us away."

The woman looks at her with a sour expression and clicks her tongue. I let her take the loaf of bread, climb back onto my mule, and turn its head away. I can hear the hooves of Polycaste's mule behind me. It's a moment before she catches up.

"Why did you give her the bread?"

"She needed it."

"She should have helped us."

I don't want to argue about that. "Do you know the way to Sparta?"

"She said there's only one road."

"Is it dangerous?"

"I'm not afraid if that's what you mean," Polycaste snaps.

"I meant, is it sensible for us to go without a guide?"

"Of course we'll go!" She stops her mule, so I have to stop as well. "My father sent us to Sparta, so that's what we'll do! I'm not going home because we're scared!"

I force myself to stay calm, to sound reasonable. I know how to deal with angry people. "All I meant is, your father wouldn't want us to go without a guide and no one to guard us. If it's too dangerous . . ."

"Who cares what my father thinks? We set out for Sparta, so that's where we'll go. What's wrong with you? You can't fight, you turn back at the first sign of trouble . . . anyone would think you're a coward."

I don't answer. Maybe I am. I look at her angry, flushed face and feel tears prick the backs of my eyes.

"Don't you want to find your father?" she says.

"Of course I do."

"Then we go to Sparta." And she turns her mule away from the town, toward Sparta.

We spend the night in a ruined farmhouse just outside the town, surrounded by vineyards that are already being reclaimed by the forest. The mountain looms above us. It seems like the farmers left in a hurry. A child's robe, bleached white by the sun, still flutters on a washing line. The track runs past the front door, plunging beyond it into a gorge from which we can hear the sound of running water. I gather sticks and make a fire. We eat staling bread and strips of dried fish, but don't talk much. In the morning we wash in the stream, then ride on up the track, which climbs a narrow ledge along one side of the gorge, with pine trees falling steeply away to our left. When we look back, we can see, framed by the hills' cleft, the sapphire blue of the sea and beyond it, blurred by morning haze, the shore of Nestor's territory. I can even make out the little fishing village where we spent the first night.

"Come on."

Reddish cliffs rise above us on either side. The track's too narrow to ride side by side. It widens only when it leaves the gorge and turns into thick forests of oak and chestnut. From there we can see ridge after ridge of trees ahead of us, cut by gorges and rising to peaks of bare rock that gleam white in the morning sunshine. The track's easy enough to follow, marked by deep wheel ruts through the undergrowth. Riding behind, I watch Polycaste sway easily to the motion of her mule. Her hair is tied up in a black ribbon, and her quiver of arrows hides a darkening patch of sweat on her back. I'm scared of her, I realize. Scared of her composure, her beauty and her anger. Scared that she seems to know so much more than I do, to feel so much surer of herself.

I'm watching her so intently I don't even see the men coming.

They surge up from behind rocks above the path, eight or nine of them—it all happens so quickly I don't have time to count. They're wearing the remnants of armor and clutching short swords and spears. One grabs the bridle of my mule, another tears the sword off my saddlebag. I feel my leg pulled, and suddenly I'm pitching sideways off my mule. A knee lands heavily on my chest. A short, dark man with desperate black eyes is pinning me down, while hands grab at the locket around my throat.

"Stop!"

It's Polycaste. She's moved faster than me, and her commanding, flat voice freezes the little clearing where the ambush has taken place.

Somehow Polycaste has dismounted and unslung her bow. Somehow she's twisted an arrow out of the quiver at her back. And the arrow is pointing right at the throat of the outlaws' leader.

I know he's the leader because everyone else is looking at him for orders. He's taller than the others, with a brown, unkempt beard and a scrap of red cloth tied jauntily around his neck. His hands are half raised—he's dropped his sword.

"A girl," he says. His expression is half-wary, half-amused, like part of him wants to laugh at her and the other part is thinking, *That's a real arrow.*

The tip of the arrow doesn't waver. It's no more than an arm's length from his throat. One move and he's dead before he can reach her.

Polycaste says, "Let him go."

The man kneeling on my chest looks to the leader, who nods, then he slowly stands up. I get to my feet. The bandits are scattered about the clearing. One holds the mules. Two others must have been ripping open the contents of the saddlebags when Polycaste's order rang out.

"If anyone moves, he's dead." Polycaste sounds calm. Her eyes are narrowed, like she's aiming at a target, not a man's throat.

Without taking his eyes off the arrowhead, the leader says, "Shoot the arrow, they'll have you."

"You'll be dead."

"So will you."

I can almost smell the tension in the air. The men are starving—I can see that now. They seemed terrifying enough in the first moment of attack, but now that I have time to look at them properly, I'm seeing ragged clothes and dirty bandages. They've only got three swords between them—the rest of the men are armed with sticks. One man is leaning heavily on a staff, his knee twisted awkwardly to one side.

"Who are you?" I ask. Get them talking.

The leader frowns. He's concentrating on Polycaste's arrow, the little bronze tip that could end his life.

"Who are you?" I repeat.

I know about angry men. I know about violence. I've seen it at home on Ithaca, felt the surge of it in the hall as wine is drunk and tempers flare, felt the moment when raised voices turn suddenly to weapons and blood. But I've also sensed that moment of sudden flatness when voices are still raised but the impulse of violence has passed. It's like a wave flowing on up the beach—when men don't want to back down but have lost their urge to kill.

I can sense that now. The men in the clearing are scared.

"My name is Telemachus," I say, like I'm chatting to strangers in a tavern. "I come from Ithaca. My father is Odysseus. This is Polycaste, the daughter of Nestor, chief of Pylos. We're traveling to Sparta to visit Menelaus." Clear and steady. Sound weak and men become cruel; aggressive, and they'll bristle at the challenge. The tone that works is calm. Talk steadily and confidently, and you can lead them to a quiet place just like you lead a bull back to its field.

"Menelaus's men are meeting us at the frontier. They're expecting us. They're waiting for us . . . actually we're late. We ought to be there already. They may be coming along the path to find us. What's your name?" I aim that directly at the leader. People can't ignore a direct question, clearly put.

Without taking his eyes off Polycaste's arrow, the leader says, "Thoon."

We're at a turning point. I can't say how I know. I just sense it, like I can tell when two of the young men at Ithaca are going to fight and one's going to back down. It's like a waver in the air—an opportunity. Right now the leader is uncertain. He doesn't know how to deal with the situation. He doesn't know whether he can trust the others. Will they let Polycaste kill him? Maybe the men will think it worth sacrificing their leader to win these two prizes. I can almost see Thoon calculating, but I get to the answer first. The only way Thoon can retain control is by backing down but keeping his pride intact. So I have to make that happen. I have to give him a small victory but set limits too—that way I keep control.

"You look hungry," I say. "There's bread in the saddlebags. We'll share it with you. There's gold too, but you can't have that. It's for Menelaus. Would you like bread?" I don't let the question lie—it's important I'm the one doing the talking, setting the pace. "I'll get it."

I walk across the clearing, not hurrying, to where the mules are cropping grass as if nothing is going on. The man by the saddlebags stands back to make space. I pull out a bag of rolls and give one to the nearest outlaw, who drops his weapon and starts tearing at it with his teeth, stuffing it into his mouth so fast he can hardly chew.

As I walk around the clearing handing out bread, I keep talking in the same quiet voice. "You were fighters in the war, weren't you? Perhaps one of you saw my father, Odysseus of Ithaca. Or maybe you fought alongside Polycaste's father . . ." I'm giving the leader time to reach the same conclusion I did: that he has no choice but to back down.

"We'll take the bread," the leader says, getting there at last. "All of it."

That's what I was waiting for. Thoon needs to keep status in the eyes of his men. Otherwise they'll kill him.

"We need enough to get us to the border," I say. "You can take the rest."

From the way the men are eating, that'll be enough of a victory for Thoon to keep control of them—at least for the moment.

"You need to go now, though. Before Menelaus's soldiers arrive."

Thoon looks at Polycaste and takes a step backward. She doesn't fire. He takes another step back. The arrow is still aimed at his throat.

"Take the bread," the leader orders the others, his voice false-jaunty. "We'll let these two go for now. I knew Odysseus."

One by one the men pick up their weapons and back away, toward the town. The tip of Polycaste's arrow tracks them out of the clearing. She only lowers her bow when they're out of sight.

For a while neither of us says anything. Two eagles are wheeling across the sky overhead. Their distant mewing is the only sound in the clearing.

"I'm sorry," Polycaste says.

"Sorry?"

There's an odd, troubled expression on her face. "Sorry I called you a coward."

That night we camp against a rock face by a stream. Branches close above the cold, brown water that tumbles over stones, tugging at stray branches caught on the current. In a clearing beyond the stream there's a little half-ruined shrine with a wooden statue of the goddess, its walls hung with dusty offerings from travelers. The floor is covered in owl droppings, but there's an oil lamp burning on the altar. Some passing traveler must have lit it for protection against the dangers of the journey.

Polycaste watches me break sticks for our fire and heap them up on a flat patch of earth next to the stream.

"How did you know what to do?"

"I'm used to men fighting."

"Why?"

I look down at the half-laid fire, not at her. "What do you know about Ithaca?"

"What people say."

"Which is?"

"There are a lot of men there." I can hear awkwardness in her voice. "Who want to marry . . . Penelope." She was about to say *"your mother."*

"They live in my father's house." Mechanically I straighten the sticks on the fire. "They drink a lot. They fight. There are no other men to help. I'm the only one. I have to keep them under control."

"How long's it been like that?"

"Years. When my grandfather was alive things were easier. Then he died, and my mother became ill. Then it was just me." I ball a handful of dry grass and thrust it into the fire.

"What do they do?" Polycaste's voice is quiet.

"Whatever they want. They're guests. We can't turn them away. They eat. They drink and argue. They pester my mother, and I do what I can to protect her. It isn't much. I can't fight them. I don't know how to fight."

"But you have protected her, haven't you?"

"So far. Maybe we've just been lucky."

"I don't think so. You know what to say. You knew what to say to those men back there."

"I said the first thing that came into my head. You were the one who fought back."

"I didn't think. I just wanted to kill them." Polycaste drops her chin onto her knees, hugging herself. I spark flame from tinder until the dry ball of grass smolders and a thread of smoke rises up into the evening air.

"Tell me what it's like in Ithaca."

The fire crackles. I stay on my knees in front of it, watching the first flames catch at the grass, then at the smaller sticks and kindling. The smell of burning wood spreads through the clearing.

Almost without thinking, I start to talk. I tell Polycaste about the courtyard, about my father's wrecked storerooms, the feasts, the young men sprawled across landings and corridors each morning. I tell her about my mother. I tell her about the humiliations: Antinous's contempt, Eurymachus's phony friendship. Maybe I sound bitter, or angry, but I don't care. Suddenly I'm telling her things I've always kept to myself, things I never imagined being able to share: the way they forced me to drink, until my words slurred and they roared with laughter. The way they dressed me up. The time one of the young men tried to get into my room and I had to push a cupboard against the door and spend the whole night awake, begging the goddess for help.

"Did anything happen?"

"No. He was drunk. He went away."

"I can't imagine what you've been through."

It's starting to get dark now. Firelight winks on the stream as it bubbles over the rocks next to us. Fireflies glow on the bank opposite.

"We ought to eat."

"There isn't much left."

We share two rolls and some dried meat the outlaws didn't find, and drink from the stream, the water so cold it numbs our lips.

"What about you?" I ask.

"What about me?"

"What's it like being at home with your father, when he's so . . ."

"Old?" Polycaste laughs softly. "You might as well say it. He was already old when he left for the war. I was like you. He left before I was born. I grew up without any father at all. People talked about him. My brothers and sisters joked. To me he was just a name. Then they all came home, and there he was, this old man. They made me kiss him. He smelled old and dirty, but I made myself do it. He gave me a present, a piece of silk. He said, 'This is from the greatest of their temples.' It still had blood on it. I was eight." Polycaste pauses, her mouth twisted.

"Then I watched the slaves landing. All women. Their hands still tied, some of them. Dresses torn. You can imagine what it was like on the boats. Crying. And filthy, with bare feet and breasts. Some of them were children, girls my age. No men. That's what happens when they sack a town. The men killed, the women . . ." She falls silent, her face dark, then says very quickly, "That was when I knew what I had to do. I said to myself, 'That's never going to happen to me. If they come to Pylos, I'll fight too. I'll be killed rather than carried off as someone's slave.' I got one of my father's men to teach me. Aiming a bow, fighting with a sword. My brothers laughed, but I didn't care." She tosses her hair back. "All we hear about is the war. *Their* war. The fights, the glory . . . To hear the storytellers, you'd think it was . . . *fun*. I don't think it was fun. I think they were all destroyed by it. Look at them . . . the men who attacked us today. The women who were left behind . . . your mother. Your father never coming back . . . it's us who pay for it, isn't it? And keep on paying . . . it doesn't *end*. It's what happens afterward . . . like what happened to Agamemnon, the biggest chief of all."

"What did happen?"

"You don't know?"

"Some of it. I don't know everything."

Polycaste takes a deep breath. "It started while he was away. His wife, Clytemnestra, was left behind. Agamemnon told his cousin, Aegisthus, to mind the kingdom. Eight years he was away. Aegisthus and Clytemnestra started an affair. Then the war ended and Agamemnon came home. You can imagine . . . the great warlord, leader of the Greeks in the great victory. He comes back to his palace . . . ships full of treasure, rows of slaves . . . And Aegisthus and Clytemnestra murdered him. Killed him in his bath. The leader of the Greeks killed naked without even a sword in his hand." She pauses.

"Agamemnon and Clytemnestra had two children. I played with Orestes when he came to Pylos once. He was a bit older. The daughter, Electra, was our age. What could Orestes do? Code of honor."

The code of honor. Iron law across the mountains of Greece, among shepherds and farmers as much as chiefs and warlords. A death can only be wiped out by another—or by blood money, calculated by priests and paid, sometimes, over many generations. A stain on a man's honor is visible to all, as vivid and disfiguring as a scar on his face—until he kills in his turn and wipes his honor clean. On sleepy Ithaca, where most men work the sea, you don't much come across it. But we all know how powerful a grip it holds.

"So Orestes killed Aegisthus and Clytemnestra . . . slaughtered them both. And now he's on the run, with Aegisthus's people searching for him. A death for a death . . . He was a sweet boy, I liked him, but they'll kill him sooner or later, it's the only way it can end. So you see? We, their children, are still paying for what happened in the war."

There's a silence. The fire crackles. Somewhere, away in the woods, an owl softly hoots. We can see the dark mass of the shrine in the trees across the stream.

"It's not as if we'll be any different," Polycaste says.

"What do you mean?"

"You'll be a fighter, like your father. You'll find some war to go to, some town to burn. You'll fight duels. You'll get your hair plaited and have a tattoo."

"No."

She's laughing, but her voice is serious. "What else is there?"

"I don't know."

"What, then?"

"I don't know. It's just . . ." I think of the young men sprawled around tables in our great hall. Speech slurred, knives sharp, fingers drumming on the tables as they wait for the insult that will bring someone to his feet. Bored, vicious, carrying their honor inside them as if it were a precious glass they mustn't allow to break. "I know what they're like," I go on quietly. "I don't want to be like them."

"What else is there for a man to do?" I hear the crackle of leaves as Polycaste rolls over to look at me. "I'd give anything to be a fighter. It's the only way to be safe. Be stronger than anyone else."

After a moment I go on, "Just before I came to Pylos, I met a girl in the town. I mean, I knew her before, but I'd never talked to her. She came up to me. She was holding a charm, exactly like the one my father left at the goddess's shrine before he sailed to Troy. She said, 'Bring him back.'" I pause, seeing the girl's pleading face all over again. "I still don't know what it means."

Polycaste snorts. "It's obvious, isn't it?"

"Is it?" I know what she's going to say, but I don't want to hear it. I suppose I've been refusing to admit it ever since the girl walked away, leaving the little owl in my hand.

"Your father kept a woman in the town." Polycaste shrugs. "She's his daughter. He wouldn't be the only one. My father was the same." She laughs with something almost like affection. "Not anymore, obviously. He's too old."

"Don't you mind?"

"You can't mind about everything." She reaches out, suddenly, and squeezes my hand. "Can you?"

Next morning we start at dawn, aiming to travel as far as we can before the day becomes too hot. In the higher mountains the trees are short and stunted. We don't see anyone except two copper miners, father and son, who are making charcoal next to a hollow in the rock. Smoke seeps from a mound of black earth, which they douse with water whenever a flame breaks through it. One of the men thrusts a wooden dipper into his bucket for us to drink from. From the top of the pass we can see the sea as a distant line of blue both ahead and behind. There's a little temple to Apollo, the sun god, and we stop to light candles in the dusty, dark interior. Someone, perhaps the miners, is looking after it. The floor is swept, and two twig brooms stand neatly in one corner.

"Do you believe in this?" Polycaste asks without looking at me.

"In the gods? Of course."

"*Really* believe." She glances quickly at me. "Between you and me."

I look at the statue of Apollo on the altar. It's wooden, worm-eaten, with one glass eye missing. Someone has hung mountain flowers around its neck. A tiny silver chain, a bracelet, has been crumpled up and thrust between its wooden feet as an offering.

"My grandfather told me Odysseus speaks to the goddess. She meets him and they talk, just like you and me talking now." I pause, remembering what Nestor said about my father, the teller of tales. "I don't believe that."

"If you'd spoken to her, maybe the goddess could have told you where your father is."

I shrug. "Perhaps Menelaus will."

"He will." Polycaste sounds certain.

"How do you know?"

"Menelaus is the most powerful king there is. He knows everything. Servants everywhere. Messengers coming and going. It's not like Pylos. He'll know."

"Do you remember Sparta?"

"I only went there once, six years ago. I remember the palace, most of all. It's huge, bigger than anything you've ever seen. It's what everyone must dream of, to be a king like that, in a palace like that. My bed was so big I cried, because I thought I'd get lost. Then my father was angry that I might wake up Helen."

"What's Helen like?"

"Beautiful." She shrugs. "That's all I remember. Just beautiful. You look at her and you can't imagine taking your eyes away. You don't think . . . I don't know . . ."

"What?"

"That this was the woman who started the war. About all the men who died because of her. At least I didn't, then."

There's a moment's silence, then Polycaste reaches forward, suddenly, and touches my arm. "Menelaus will help you. You've got to believe that."

Beyond the pass, the trees change to pine, filling the overheating air with the smell of resin and dust. Cicadas shriek in the trees around us. When it's time to rest, Polycaste pulls her scarf over her head and shakes out hair dark with sweat. The mules switch their tails angrily at flies. We hear falling water ahead of us. Dismounting, we lead our mules through an overgrown track that leads off the path. It twists around a rock and suddenly we're standing by a wide, black pool with a little waterfall tumbling over rocks at one end.

Polycaste drops her mule's reins, and it wades eagerly forward to drink. She follows it. "It's cold. Freezing. Meltwater. We can camp under the cliff."

We eat the last of our bread and some figs we find growing wild among the rocks, and we drink the frigid water from the pool. Close to the shore, stones shine under the surface; beyond them the water plunges into icy blackness.

"What are you worrying about?" We've eaten and are lying in the shade of the trees that fringe the pool.

"I'm not," I lie.

"Yes, you are. You haven't said a word."

I guess I'm finding it hard to break a lifetime's habit of secrecy. I haven't gotten used to the idea there's someone I can tell things to. Other people have friends. I never did.

"Fighting, I suppose."

"*Fighting?*" Polycaste sounds amused.

"Because I'm going to have to. Sometime. And I don't know how."

"Come on, then." Polycaste scrambles to her feet and holds out her hands. "I'll teach you."

"You?"

"Why not? You've got to learn from somebody. We'll start with wrestling. That's how Elatreus started with me." She drops to a crouch. "It's all about balance. Once you've learned balance, you can fight with anything. Sword, spear, whatever. Look, stand like this."

She tenses on the balls of her feet, arms out and ready. I do my best to copy her, and she doubles over laughing. "You don't have to look so fierce. I mean, not with me. Try again. Grab me by the arms and throw me."

She drops to a crouch again, and we circle. Each time I move forward, Polycaste sways back out of my reach. I make a sudden lunge, then feel my leg slip from under me, and suddenly I'm lying on my back looking up at branches.

Polycaste's face appears. She's trying not to laugh. "You lost your balance when you reached too far. Stand up." When I'm standing, she takes me by the waist and pulls me forward abruptly. "See? When you're off balance, it's easy for me to throw you. I can use your own weight. One leg to kick your foot away . . ." Her bare foot kicks me expertly on the ankle. "And you're over. Now try again."

We try again. And again. Each time I lunge forward, she dances away from me. Once, Polycaste feints, and when I stumble back she uses my own weight to trip me. I'm a bit stronger than her, I soon figure. Using that, I grip her around the waist and feel her rib cage crush against me, then I'm suddenly rolling backward, feet off the ground, to land, stunned, against a tree.

She laughs. "You're not bad, actually. At least you might be all right one day. Come on."

She reaches out a hand and pulls me up. We circle again. I feel sweat in my eyes and wipe it away. Polycaste uses the distraction to spring forward, but this time I'm quick enough to seize her waist as she closes in and roll backward, just like she showed me. It nearly works. Polycaste jams her foot between my legs as we turn, and we land heavily on the ground together, with her on top, weight crushing me, laughing.

"Nearly. Well done."

Her hair tickles my face. She's lying on me, panting, and suddenly I feel embarrassed. I'm aware of her closeness, of the smell of figs on her breath, of the broad pressure of her chest. Polycaste looks down at me. She knows what I'm thinking; suddenly her expression's sardonic. I stare past her small ear, fixing my eyes on the leaves, dreading what she's going to say. But to my surprise, she gives a short laugh.

"You're sweet," she says softly.

She leans down and kisses me gently on the cheek, then rolls off, walking down toward the stream. As she walks, she pulls her gown over her head and strides into the stream with her back to me.

"It's freezing," she says in a normal voice. "Icy." Then she's gone, splashing out into the deeper water.

She turns, swimming back toward the bank with her chin high out of the water.

"Aren't you coming in?"

"I'm all right here."

"Coward. It is cold, though. I'm getting out. Don't look."

I don't look, but sit with my head turned away, listening to Polycaste cough out water and dry herself.

"You can turn around now."

She's sitting wrapped in a white sheet, hugging her knees. "Look at you," she says.

"What?"

"Solemn." She pulls a long face. "You ought to swim, you know. It makes you feel alive." She gives a short laugh. "Don't worry. I won't look either."

The next morning, an hour or so after leaving, the path breaks through trees to a hillside, where we look out over a flat plain divided into neat, square fields. A stone blockhouse bars the road. We can see a haze of smoke above a town in the distance.

Polycaste turns in her saddle and grins at me.

"Sparta," she says.

T he soldiers from the blockhouse spend more than an hour searching our saddlebags. Neither of us is quite sure what they're looking for. The men are polite but thorough. They nod respectfully when we tell them our names, but they go on searching anyway.

More soldiers throng the villages we pass as we ride down to the plain, led by a mounted escort commanded by a young officer with a sandy beard. To me, it feels quite different from the gentle hills of Nestor's territory. Faces watch us curiously from the cottages we pass, but no children run out into the streets to greet us. At each village our escort stops to exchange passwords with the garrisons who man the village gatehouses. A soldier keeps a firm grip on the bridle of my mule.

When it reaches the plain, the road runs straight and dull, chalk white, through fields of wheat. There are men and women harvesting the crops. They move in straight lines through the fields, backs bare and shining with sweat, slashing at the wheat stems while overseers watch from high stools. Sparta itself is a main street of taverns and workshops, prosperous but dull, with six dusty plane trees shading the square. Everything is dominated by the palace that rises beyond it in tiers of columns and terraces.

A broad flight of marble steps leads up from the square. Menelaus is waiting for us on the first landing.

I recognize him from his red hair. He's famous for it— "redhead Menelaus," the storytellers call him. It falls over his shoulders in luxuriant waves, while his beard, flowing softly over his chest, is streaked with silver hairs that somehow make him look even more distinguished. A gold medallion hangs in the red curls that show thickly through his silk robe. Soldiers line the step behind him.

"Friends." His voice is a low purr. Menelaus comes down the steps and puts an arm around each of our shoulders. He smells of some expensive perfume. "My friends' *children*—that makes you *my* friends." He squeezes us both tighter. "Look— my palace." He spins us around suddenly to look up at the steps, the soldiers, and the columns that flank the entrance beyond. Statues line the terrace, beyond which we can see the leaves of a garden. "You like it?" Menelaus says. "Yes? Later, I'll show you around. You had a good journey? Yes? Were the soldiers rude to you? They'll be punished. Look . . ." Gripping our shoulders before we can answer, he turns us to look across the dusty square. A man is leading a cart piled with wheat. Menelaus watches it approvingly. "My town. Let me tell you something—you know why my town means so much to me?" His voice drops a note. "It's because of the people in it. *My* people. Come. You're tired. You need to wash. Come into my palace."

Still grasping our shoulders, he leads us up the steps to a broad, paved forecourt. Soldiers guard the gate that leads into the palace. The two columns that flank the gate are carved with the faces of lions, symbol of the Atreids.

But Menelaus stops us again.

"I want you to be my guests," he says, and smiles, perfect white teeth showing through his beard. "I want you to be happy here. I want this to be your *home*. Telemachus." He says my name clumsily, like he hasn't learned it properly, and kisses me formally on each cheek. "Polycaste." He kisses Polycaste the same way. I can feel her wince. "My guests *matter* to me. Welcome."

There isn't a moment to ask about my father. Menelaus sweeps us with him up the massive flight of steps. The palace is spectacular. The corridor beyond the gate is lined with servants holding torches, and decorated with statues in niches. At the far end it opens onto a courtyard twice the size of the ones at Ithaca or Pylos. There's a pool of water reflecting rows of columns, and an upper story painted red and black. At one end stands an overblown marble altar, and at the other, a life-size statue of Menelaus.

"This is my courtyard," Menelaus tells us. "My altar to Hera, my favorite goddess."

He turns us toward the other end, where the statue of him stands on a fat block of granite.

"Me," he says, as if we hadn't noticed. "I had marble for the statue brought from Attica. Fifteen shiploads. Any flaw in the stone, we threw it overboard. I said, 'I only want the best for my statue.' Helen, my wife, agreed. The sculptor? I only wanted the best in Greece. He was working in a town in Thrace, so I went to the town. I sacked it. I said, 'You only work for me.' He made the statue, he died. A tragedy. He was my friend. I said to him, 'At least now you're dying, you can say you've made a masterpiece.' I'll never forget the tears in his eyes. Gratitude. That's the staircase leading to my guest rooms. This is my great hall."

Like the courtyard, the great hall of Sparta dwarfs the halls at Ithaca or Pylos. Columns support thick wooden beams that are carved and painted in the shapes of wild beasts. The walls are decorated with frescoes. Four soldiers stand on guard around the hearth, whose smoldering logs fill the room with a sickly reek of incense. On each of the columns hang huge bronze shields, and more war trophies decorate the walls above the frescoes: a breastplate molded in the form of writhing snakes, helmets, a war chariot's gilded yoke.

"My trophies," Menelaus says, pointing. "From Troy. Later, when you've rested, I'll describe them to you. You can't wait? You want to hear about them now?" He gives a low, indulgent laugh. "Then I'll tell you. This is the armor of Hector, greatest of the Trojan fighters. His helmet. Two wheels from his chariot. This is Paris's armor. The shield of Priam . . . Priam, king of Troy—greatest city in the world—his shield on my wall. The breastplate of Deiphobus, solid gold, I cut it from his body myself. He was still alive. I said, 'You anger the Atreids, you pay the price.' His shoes. The shield of Hippodamus, son of Priam, the spear of Chersidamas . . ."

The recitation seems to go on forever, shield by shield, spear by spear. Just when we're hoping it's over, Menelaus claps his hands for a servant, who brings in trays of jewelry, copper bars, temple offerings, each one in a case lined with red silk. Each has a story that Menelaus tells us in detail. Sometimes he pretends to forget a name and claps his hand for the servant, who steps forward and mutters in his ear.

"Doryclus," Menelaus says. "Inside the citadel. Third door on the right. His wife is my slave. Do you know, I can see the citadel of Troy today as clearly as if I was still walking through it. And both of your fathers . . ." He comes forward and engulfs us in another hug. "Both of your fathers were right behind me. The loyalest friends I knew. 'Odysseus,' I said, 'You take the streets on the right. Nestor, the left.' They obeyed my orders." He clicks his fingers. "Like that."

"My father . . ." I say, thinking I'll be able to get in a question, but Menelaus is on to the next shield, the next glittering dagger. It's over at last. A maidservant comes forward at Menelaus's command and shows us the way upstairs—with a strict order to return when the bell rings—to two luxurious guest rooms whose windows overlook a garden of gravel paths and orange trees. We collapse on chairs in Polycaste's room.

"He's a fool," she says scornfully.

"He can't be that much of a fool."

"He behaves like one. 'My dining table. My chair.'" She stabs a finger at her chair, which is upholstered in crocodile skin dyed a vivid purple. "I can't believe it. He's supposed to be the greatest king of all.

"'My palace . . . My guests . . . I want this to be your home.'" Polycaste shakes her head. We're laughing now.

"I want to meet Helen."

"We will."

When the bell rings, drinks—delicately spiced wine in silver cups—are served on a garden terrace lined with orange trees. You can smell their sweet fragrance drifting across beds of well-tended plants. We're so high up we can't even see the town. A servant stands behind each chair to refill our cups. Both of us are washed and dressed. In each of our rooms we found a deep marble tub filled with water that actually spouted from pipes in the shape of dolphins' beaks. Next to each stood cedar chests filled with soft silken robes, Polycaste's blue and mine white, which we're wearing as we recline on wooden benches, listening to Menelaus talk.

"So you've come to bring respects. I'm glad you've come. Polycaste . . . Telemachus . . . I'm glad you're my friends."

But I can't wait any longer now. "I came for news of my father," I say.

There's a moment's silence. Menelaus makes a funny, troubled frown, like I haven't understood the rules. He brushes the frown away as if it were an annoying insect. "Your father," he says. "Odysseus. Odysseus—my friend."

Polycaste says, "Nestor, my father, sends his respects. His *deep* respects. He thought you might have news of Odysseus."

"News. Do you know, I have messengers who can reach the coast in two days . . . the coast anywhere in southern Greece. Horses . . . I have horses that can gallop all day, horses never seen in Greece before, I brought them back from Troy. Tomorrow, I'll show you my stables."

"Have your messengers ever brought news of my father?"

Menelaus looks away across the terrace, where we can see distant peaks of mountains inland. His face is serious, suddenly, and so, when he speaks, is his voice.

"Yes, I have news of Odysseus," he says quietly.

Suddenly my hands are shaking. My throat feels so full I can hardly speak. "Tell me."

"Not now."

"Please."

He shakes his silky red hair. "Tomorrow you'll hear for yourself."

"Is my father still alive?"

Menelaus looks at me then. "Yes. Odysseus is still alive."

"Where is he?"

Menelaus raises his hand warningly. "No more for now."

There's a long silence. I don't know what to say, what to ask. "Tell me about him," I say at last, in a weak voice.

"About Odysseus?" Menelaus juts out his lower lip, brooding. "He was a hero."

"Some people call him a liar."

"Ignore them." He speaks without a moment's hesitation. "People are jealous. They try to tear great men down. Your father was a hero. That's all you need to know."

"Tell me . . ."

"Enough." Menelaus lifts his hand imperiously. He's looking across the terrace toward the house. "Here she is at last," he purrs in a different voice. "My wife."

I turn. Helen of Troy is walking toward us across the gravel. My mind is still full of what I've just heard, but even so, Helen is overwhelming. She's more beautiful than any woman I've ever seen, more beautiful than any person ought to be. Her cheekbones are high, like a cat's, her eyes green, wide and somehow caressing, as if they bless everything they touch. She has golden hair tied carelessly up in a simple ribbon. There's no point decorating it—any ornament would look drab on that face. Her nose is straight, her lips parted in an expression of slight amusement, like someone's just told her a joke and she wants to please them by smiling. She's wearing a simple gown of green silk, caught in gold clasps that show off her long, shapely arms. A simple bracelet encircles her right wrist. I can see soft shadows under her collarbones.

I stand up.

"Telemachus." Helen's voice is low and thrilling. "Odysseus's son. Polycaste . . . you've grown so *beautiful*."

Helen's lips brush my cheek, leaving behind a faint cloud of rose petals and lavender. I stand there gawping as she moves on to embrace Polycaste. It isn't just her beauty. It's what that name means—Helen of Troy. I'm thinking, *This is the woman they fought the war for.* How many people died because of her? Thousands? And what did it feel like, to have caused all that? Death, destruction, the end of a city. Bloody slaughter on the battlefield, a town in flames.

Helen sits down on one of the wooden couches. "It's cold," she says, yawning. "Too cold to be sitting out. The sunset is lovely, though." Her green eyes turn toward me. "So you're Odysseus's son. Odysseus was my friend." Her voice grows even more thrilling as she leans toward me. "I hope you will be too." I don't know how she does it. There's something in her voice that seems to plead for protection—and suddenly I realize I'm ready to do just that. I'd do anything she asked.

Helen glances at her husband before going on—a flickering glance with something of a challenge in it. "I remember Odysseus coming to Troy," she says in the same caressing voice. "He broke in through a side door by himself . . . can you imagine the courage? Disguised as a Trojan, wearing clothes like theirs. *Reconnoitering.*" Her voice mocks the military word. "And he bumps into me, poor man, out walking with my women. Our eyes meet. Well, we knew each other before, of course, before the war. I knew him straightaway. And do you know what I *felt*? Do you know what I felt?" She presses one hand to her chest and leans forward, her wide, beautiful eyes full of tears. "Just seeing him, I wanted to cry. His face said, *Greece.* It said, *Home.* My women thought I was ill. I didn't give him away. I told my women, 'Just leave me a moment, I'll come back alone.' I wanted to talk to Odysseus. To your dear, dear father. The moment we were alone, I embraced him. I couldn't help myself. Dear Odysseus from dear Greece. Troy, you know, by then . . ." She looks up at the darkening sky, fanning tears from her eyes. "It was a prison." She looks beseechingly at us. Polycaste's face is set. Menelaus isn't saying anything, but he's glowering at his wife as she talks. There's trouble coming. "It was *hell,* sheer hell. I used to go up to the walls every night. I'd stare out across the plain, and in the distance . . ." She lifts one hand, pointing. "I'd see the Greek campfires burning, and I'd think, *There are my friends. Odysseus, dear Nestor . . . and there . . .*" Her voice catches. ". . . *there's my darling husband, Menelaus . . .*" She swallows and stops, eyes glistening.

Menelaus clears his throat deliberately.

Helen puts her fingers to her temples. Her voice is almost inaudible. "It takes time, you know, to recover . . . Some things you can't forget, you're too young to understand that. Every night I'd go back to that man . . . that *awful* man Paris, the one who abducted me. I'd lie next to him in the dark and think, *How many more days?* I knew we'd win in the end, you see. I knew Menelaus would come for me . . ." She gives her husband an adoring smile, leans forward, and reaches out a hand to clasp his.

Menelaus doesn't take it. He's scowling now, his big-man, goodwill expression turned into vicious anger. When he ignores her hand, Helen stoops and fiddles with her sandal, like that was why she reached out in the first place.

"Your father," she goes on with a bright smile, "was the first Greek I'd spoken to in eight years. Eight *wasted* years. I couldn't stop crying. He drew me into a doorway so we could talk. That's when we came up with it. The wooden horse. I said, 'You'll never break the walls. They're too strong. This is how to get in.' Odysseus was *so* clever. I showed him the temple where the horse would be brought. I said, 'This is the message to give my husband . . . "Then . . . this was the worst, the *worst* bit . . . I had to go back to the palace and pretend to all the Trojans I was still on their side. Even pretend with that man, that *dreadful* man . . ."

She stops. Menelaus has leaned forward. Slowly, deliberately, he knocks three times on the table in front of him. His eyes are on his wife, his face full of contempt. He knocks again, three times. Helen is staring at him. Now she looks scared.

"When you get older," Menelaus says quietly as he sits back, "you'll learn memory plays tricks. Isn't that right, *darling?*" Helen winces at the sudden viciousness in his voice. Menelaus leans forward again, muscles bunching under his soft silk gown. "I was in the horse that night. With your father . . ." He's talking to us but looking at his wife. "Twenty men. Twenty brave men crouched in the darkness, not making a sound. We felt the horse move. We heard them celebrating outside. I was *there.*" He seems a different man from the host who showed off his palace and treasures this afternoon. Smaller, nastier, but more real. "We waited until the celebrations were over. They'd lit fires. We saw them glow through chinks in the wood. We thought they were going to burn the horse and us in it. But the fires burned down. It was dark. Still we waited. Then what did we hear?" He stares at his wife. "Voices. Two voices. One of them I knew." By now he looks as if he's about to pounce on Helen. She's twisted away from him. Frozen. Contemptuous. "My wife. The woman I hadn't seen for eight years—the one so many good men had died for. The man with her? Paris." He sits slowly back again. "Drunk. But I heard her . . . we all heard her . . . 'Don't trust them. Don't trust them. I know Odysseus. It's a trick.' Nothing from Paris. Then what?" He leans forward and raps slowly three times on the table. "She's knocking on the horse. She knows it's hollow. 'Is there anyone in there? Hello?' My *darling* wife. Who missed Greece *so* much, and couldn't *wait* to be back with her friends . . ." Menelaus picks up his silver cup and throws his head back, draining it in one draft. "Paris was drunk, thank the gods. He didn't listen. Two hours later, I killed him myself."

Helen laughs suddenly. A low, thrilling laugh. "I wish he wouldn't," she says. "Joker. He knows it drives me wild." She stands up. "We should dine. In honor of our *guests.*" She stresses the word, but Menelaus doesn't stand with her. Watching her, he holds his cup out to a servant, waits for it to fill, then drains it again.

"She has a chest in her room," he says. "Treasures from Troy. Everything she misses."

His voice is thickening. He's drunk. I'm wondering if this bitter little scene is played out every night, in the luxurious palace that's turned into their private hell.

"I don't know about anyone else," Helen says, ignoring her husband. "I'm starving." She goes over to Polycaste and takes her by both hands. "I *so* hope we're going to be friends. I *love* your dress, by the way."

"It isn't mine," Polycaste says coldly. "I found it in my room."

"You wear it so well. Come on, *do* let's eat."

She leads Polycaste through to the great hall. After a moment's hesitation I follow them. Menelaus stays out on the terrace. A table's been laid, groaning with luxuries, and to add to them, servants bring gold dishes of food I've only ever heard about in stories: stuffed snails in their shells, piles of tiny roast birds, a whole suckling pig surrounded by mushrooms. Music plays from a gallery overhead: a flute, harp, and tambourine.

"My husband's been through a lot," Helen says, looking at each of us in turn and talking in a hushed, confidential voice. "You have to understand, it was hard for him . . . *so* hard." Suddenly she grips both of our wrists. Her fingers are warm and surprisingly strong. "You *do* understand, don't you? And for me. Paris was violent . . ." Still holding our wrists, she looks down at her plate laden with delicacies. "Horribly violent . . . He forced me to go up to the horse. Thank the gods I'd worked it out with Odysseus beforehand." She squeezes my hand. "Your dear father. I said, 'They'll make me say things. Don't answer.' Thank the gods, not one of them spoke . . ."

"Has she told you her version?" Menelaus is standing in the doorway, holding his empty cup. He comes over and sits down heavily at the end of the table. "She always has a version. So. Memory plays tricks. She hated Paris. She hated Troy. She longed to come home again. Eight years."

"Perhaps he could have stopped me leaving in the first place."

"Perhaps she could have restrained herself."

"Perhaps there was nothing to stay for!"

They pretend they're talking to us, but they might as well have been alone together. For a long moment silence hangs in the great hall, the music playing behind it as if nothing's wrong. Slowly we feel the violence wash away through the echoing room. No one speaks. Then Helen turns her beautiful head to look at Polycaste.

"What lovely earrings," she says.

The rest of the evening goes the same way. Menelaus drinks, occasionally rousing himself to boast about the treasures on the walls around us. Helen talks like we're young children. After a time she gets bored and goes to bed early. Polycaste takes that as an excuse to follow her. For a while I sit on with Menelaus. It's the wrong time to ask questions about my father, though. At last, when he seems to have fallen asleep, I leave.

I can't sleep. Maybe it's the heavy scent of flowers hanging in the room, or the heat of the plains that stifles the whole palace. When I do fall asleep at last, I wake up sweating, my mouth dry. I need water. There isn't any in the room, so I make my way out into the corridor, hoping to find the kitchen, or a cool jar of water in the courtyard downstairs. There's silver moonlight on the floor. Suddenly I hear voices coming from the corridor to my right. Moving as quietly as I can, I make my way toward them, keeping one hand on the wall. There's a crack of light under a door at the end of the corridor. From behind it comes the rumble of a man's voice, then Helen's, shouting something in reply. I'm sure it's Helen, but she doesn't sound anything like the languid hostess who greeted us this afternoon. Her voice breaks off in a wail—"I'd rather one night with Paris than a lifetime with you . . ."

The words are shrieked rather than spoken, like the howl of an animal in pain, or the moaning laments you hear from women at funerals—a sound that comes not from the mind but from a deeper instinct of hatred or fear. There's nothing I can do. I feel my way back to my room, and at last I fall asleep.

I wake up early. The palace is silent, but I find Polycaste, already dressed, leaning over the balustrade of the courtyard.

"Come on."

"Where are we going?"

"Anywhere but here. I can't stand another moment."

We make our way to a balcony with steps leading down into a garden. In it we find a doorway, unlocked, with a stair that looks like it will lead to the town but ends in a walled courtyard. We've been wondering about a rhythmic sound, a sucking sound like an octopus being slapped against the harbor wall to soften it. When we reach the courtyard, we find out what it is.

They're flogging a man. His tunic's been stripped from his back and he's tied to a post, with a leather strap between his teeth to stop him from screaming. A soldier, sweating in the early-morning heat, is whipping him with a flail. Blood showers the sand around our feet.

"It's him!" Polycaste runs forward just as I recognize the sandy beard of the officer who escorted us to Sparta the day before. "Stop! What are you doing?"

The man with the whip pauses only for a moment. Still tensed for the blow, he eyes Polycaste's furious face, then swings his arm forward, lashing it across his victim's back.

The officer whimpers through his leather gag. Blood spatters sickeningly over the sand and on the hem of Polycaste's dress.

"Stop!"

"Orders." The man's voice is flat. His eyes are weird. Glazed. Unfocused. Clumsily he pushes Polycaste aside to take another blow.

"We didn't say he'd been rude. We didn't ask for him to be punished. It's a mistake!"

"Orders." The man lashes again, and again the officer moans, his body convulsing against the post.

I tug Polycaste by the arm. "Come on."

"I won't. He's got to stop."

"He won't stop. He's been ordered. We'll only make things worse."

Polycaste gives a strangled sob but lets me pull her back across the deserted courtyard. We go to the garden and find a bench under a eucalyptus tree. Neither of us speaks until the slapping noise has stopped.

Then Polycaste draws a deep breath. "I can't stand this. This place is awful. What's wrong with him?" We both know she means Menelaus.

"He's angry."

"With that soldier? He didn't do anything."

"Not just with him. With everybody." For some reason I'm picturing not Menelaus but Antinous's small, mean eyes, shining with malice when he's invented some torment for a new arrival—or for me. "He's angry about Helen . . . about everything. And he has the power to make everyone else suffer."

"They're all mad." She says it in a near whisper. "*All* of them who went to the war. It hasn't made them happy, has it? Fighters . . . they're all *damaged*. Odysseus missing, Agamemnon dead. Menelaus trapped with a woman who hates him. What did they do it for? You hear the storytellers: 'Glorious Menelaus won the war . . .' It isn't like that, it's a nightmare. And it's *us*, isn't it, who have to pick up the pieces, get on with life, while they live in this hell." She breathes more slowly, eyes closed, one hand on her chest. "And it was all for her. That's the worst thing of all. She's so empty, so *false*. Why would anyone fight a war over *her*?"

"Menelaus loves her."

"*Love?*" Polycaste stares at me. "What are you talking about? She's a trophy. 'The most beautiful woman on earth.' What man wouldn't love her?" She shrugs. "Isn't that what men are like?"

"And she loved Paris. I think she really did."

"You think she's capable of *love*? *Her*? Look at her. The war was vanity, too. 'Thousands died for me.' Do you think she cares about any of them? She's proud of it. She's *empty*."

"No. Even if she's hard, and vain, she's still . . . a *person* . . ." I know I'm not finding the right words, but somewhere in my mind I've got an image of a younger Helen who might not have been thinking about war or consequences. Who was just swept away by a feeling she hadn't known before. I don't like her. But for that younger, foolish Helen I can only feel pity.

Polycaste says, "You're nicer than me." She's looking at me with an odd expression, half affectionate, half angry. "You think more."

"No."

"If I hate someone, I just hate them. I'm simple. And I hate her. She's false."

"You're not simple."

"You don't think so?" She stands up, shaking back her hair.

"Nobody is."

At the doorway to the palace a servant is waiting for us. He leads us to the town square, where a chariot with gilt wheels is standing under the shade of the plane trees, harnessed to two lively black horses with their manes braided in gold thread. One servant holds their bridles while another stands by with a tray of steaming silver cups and fresh rolls.

Menelaus, dressed in a leather coat and carrying a whip, drains his cup and puts it back on the tray. He looks as if he hasn't slept.

"Breakfast," he says, gesturing to the tray. He sounds grim. There's no sign of the expansive host of the day before. "Then we leave."

We take cups and sip at a warm infusion of herbs. The rolls are flavored with honey and sweet spices. Menelaus, tapping the handle of his whip against the rail of the chariot, waits impatiently while we eat and drink. There's no sign of bodyguards. As soon as we climb up next to him, he flicks the servant away and we set off with a lurch, the horses pawing at the square's baked earth. As soon as we're clear of the town, he lashes the horses with his whip and they break into a wild gallop, dragging the chariot along at a pace I've never experienced before. The chariot's platform bucks and rears. I look down and see the ground whipping past just a hand's breadth below. Gripping the rail, hands and legs shaking, I'm thinking, *Surely it can't take the strain.* The dust blinds me. A hot reek of horse fills my nostrils. Beside me, Menelaus is cracking the whip over the horses' heads, urging them to a still-crazier pace.

Only when the road begins to travel upward, passing olive groves, then pine trees, does he haul on the reins, slowing the chariot, then bringing it to a halt at the side of the road.

He looks at me. "You were scared," he says. His face is masked with dust. He draws a sweaty hand through it, leaving it streaked like war paint.

I step down onto the warm grass. My legs feel so weak from the pounding of the road that I can barely stand. I have to keep clinging to the rail of the chariot, but I manage to shake my head.

Menelaus gives a snort of disbelief. "Now we walk."

"Where are we going?"

"Follow me."

"Are we going to see my father?"

He doesn't answer. He leads us up a mountain path. We have to scramble over rocks and press through thick, clinging thorns, but eventually the way grows clearer, winding in loops up the side of a bare mountain. Halfway up, we can see far across the dusty plain of Sparta, past the roofs of the palace and town, past square, flat fields to the distant sea. The sun, burning through a cloudless sky, grows hotter. Lizards flick their way into crevices. I can feel sweat pooling in the small of my back.

"Stop." Menelaus pulls a leather water bottle from his belt and passes it to each of us in turn. Polycaste throws back her head and sprinkles water over her face and neck.

"I brought the horses from Troy," Menelaus says. "The fastest in the world." But his heart doesn't seem to be in boasting today. He looks up at the mountain. Two eagles are wheeling above its summit. "Do you know where we are?"

"Of course not." Polycaste looks mutinous. "How could we?"

Menelaus only glances at her. "Mount Aroania. Up there." Menelaus points to a cleft between two peaks. "The source of the river Styx." He looks down at us. "That's where we're going."

He won't say any more. We reach it two hours later, sweating and exhausted from a climb over bare, unshaded rock and burning stones that skitter away underfoot. A last twist of the path brings us to the lip of a crater. Below is a round, black pool of water.

A wooden shack stands to one side. A tall, elderly man dressed in black appears, stooping, at the doorway. His robe is embroidered with rich gold thread, but the sleeves are stained with oil. Gold thread braids his dirty white hair. He bows to Menelaus, who begins to scramble down the side of the crater. From above we watch him draw something from the chest of his leather coat, kiss it in his balled fist, then hurl it high above the pool. It flashes once as it's caught by the sun then falls into the water without a splash. We watch the ripples widen outward and die against the pool's rocky banks.

Menelaus clambers back up the crater and stops just below its rim, looking up at us.

"When we left Troy," he says, "the gods were against us. They hated us for destroying the city. They hated us for burning their temples. You know how they punished my brother. I too have suffered . . ." He pauses, wiping one hand across his mouth and red beard. "At Cape Malea the gods sent a storm. It drove us far south, to Egypt. I met a man there, a priest who could see things . . . he read them in the smoke of incense. I asked him which of us had perished since leaving Troy, and who was still alive. He told me the names of the dead. Agamemnon, my brother, was among them. I didn't know my brother was dead. They killed him, Aegisthus and that whore, his wife. I didn't know that, then, but the priest told the truth. I brought him back here to Sparta."

"Have you seen my father?" I try to keep my voice steady. "Do you know where he is?"

Menelaus shakes his head. "The word of the gods is good enough for me. Lector!" He turns to the old priest, who nods, disappears into the hut, and returns carrying a brazier, his hands wrapped in cloths to protect them from the heat. He sets it on a level piece of ground outside the hut and disappears inside for a round metal dish, which he sets on the brazier. Into the brazier he throws a handful of brown powder that he scoops from a small, enameled box.

"From this place." The priest's voice is deep and sonorous, strongly accented. "The waters flow deep underground through caverns where no living man can follow them. This is the river Styx, the river of the dead." He pauses and throws another handful of the powder onto the fire. Brown smoke coils up from the dish as it heats.

"All those who die come to the river's shores. Charon the ferryman awaits them. In his boat they cross to the underworld, the realm of Dis, never to see light again. They walk the shades forever as ghosts." The priest bows suddenly, plunging his face into the reeking smoke and breathing deeply. When he straightens up, his eyes are closed and he sways, gripping the handles of the brazier so hard his knuckles whiten.

"Charon!" he moans. "Of those who left Troy's shore, who has crossed your stream into the realm of the dead?" He plunges down again, burying his face in the smoke. Polycaste has come forward to stand beside me. Menelaus is watching with narrowed eyes. I notice a little bird, a sparrow, bobbing and dipping on a rock at the black water's edge. A gust of wind blows the smoke toward us. It has a faintly acrid, sweet tang.

"Agamemnon!" The old man's face is running with sweat. His eyes have rolled upward until only the whites show. "Ajax!" He plunges his face back toward the dish. For a long time he breathes its vapors, but when he stands up again, he's silent.

"Odysseus?" Menelaus says. "Ask about Odysseus."

The priest breathes slowly in through his nose. When he opens his eyes again, they're back to normal. "He said nothing of Odysseus." He steps away from the brazier and drops to a crouch, hanging his head between his knees to recover. Gradually the smoke from the dish thins, replaced by the reek of scorched metal.

"Enough!" The priest stands, sweeps the dish from the fire, and drops it on the ground with a clang. Then he turns and disappears back into the hut.

"Now you've heard it for yourself." Menelaus nods at me. "Your father is alive. Yes?" He glances down at the black, unrippled surface of the pool. "Now we go back to Sparta."

❧

"What are you going to do?" Polycaste says.

We found mules waiting for us at the foot of the track. Menelaus climbed into his chariot and rode ahead. Polycaste and I went back to the palace at a slower pace and washed away the dust of the journey. There was no sign of Helen. A servant brought us a message that Menelaus had been called away on business, and showed us a tray of bread and cheese set out on the table in the great hall. When we'd eaten, we retreated to the garden just as the evening began to cool. Over thickly flowering plants I can see the bare tops of the mountains we climbed earlier.

"Nothing."

"Why?"

"I'll go home to Ithaca." I don't look at her. "I'll build a tomb and say prayers for my father."

"But the priest said Odysseus was alive!"

That makes me angry. "Has anyone seen him? Does anyone have any news of him? He's gone. A priest from Egypt . . . a fortune-teller . . . that isn't proof. If he's alive, why haven't we heard from him? Why hasn't he come home to Ithaca? Surely *someone* would have met him . . . a sailor in a port . . . Five hundred men don't just disappear. Even in a storm, wreckage is washed ashore . . . oars, timbers. If he was in Egypt, Menelaus would have heard. If he was in Africa, I'd have heard from Mentes. If he's dead . . ." I shake my head wearily. "*Since* he's dead, it's better to move on. For me, for my mother, for everyone. I'll build a tomb for him in Ithaca."

I can remember the funeral of Laertes, my grandfather. We built a pyre for the old man's body on the mountainside where he lived out his last years. Cedar logs, stripped of their branches and cut to equal length, were stacked first one way, then the other, with pine twigs crammed into every joint. We laid Laertes's body on top of it, washed, perfumed, and dressed in rich white robes. His old bronze sword, the blade nicked from many fights, was placed on his chest, and his spear, with its insignia of a boar, hung on the pyre beside him. We left the gold rings on his fingers. His women servants twined ivy in his scanty white hair.

I remember the way his hair—all I could see of him from the ground—was feathered by the mountain wind as we waited for the ceremony to start. Only when the sun touched the horizon did the priest step forward and thrust a torch into the pyre. It took a moment for the pine twigs to catch, then a roaring came from the base of the mound, a sudden crackling and a waft of heat that washed across the little knot of spectators: me, my mother, a dozen servants. Laertes's old friends were all dead. The young men in the big house stayed away.

It didn't take long for the flames to take hold. A tongue of fire split a cedar log. Black smoke curled up into the sky. As we watched, more flames appeared, licking around the ends of logs, exploring each crevice of the pyre until, as the sun finally disappeared behind the mountain's edge, the fire roared and crackled, bright orange flames and clouds of sparks rising up into the sky and thickening the night around us. The priest and his assistants stepped forward, shielding their faces from the heat, to throw incense onto the flames. Its sickly, rich perfume masked the stench when the fire reached Laertes's body.

Gradually we shuffled backward, driven by the heat. From the edge of the forest we watched until the flames slowly began to subside, charred logs gave way, and Laertes's pyre collapsed into embers.

The next morning I climbed the mountain again and found nothing but a mound of grey ash.

My father, Ithaca's chief, deserves something more permanent. "I'll build a tomb by the harbor," I tell Polycaste, "near where he sailed away. A domed tomb of cut stones. I'll hang his bow in it, and his weapons, and burn a ship on the beach outside. I'll make a pyre of cedar logs and resin, and sacrifice to the goddess to protect Odysseus's soul." I look down at my feet, scuffing the dust with my toes. "I've got to go home to Ithaca."

"Stay with us at Pylos first."

"I can't. My mother has no one to protect her. I've got to go home."

Home. I think of Ithaca. But home doesn't mean comfort and safety. It means Antinous sneering at me and Eurymachus pretending to be friendly. It means young men washing in the courtyard, brawling voices and violence always waiting to break out. It means the clack of my mother's loom, her empty smile, her fingers plucking listlessly at the chain around her neck. And once I announce Odysseus's death—once the flames of his pyre have died to ash and the smoke has faded from the sky—it's going to mean something worse. I know that. I'm not under any illusions. Those young men want Penelope. They want Ithaca. They want me dead.

"What will happen there?"

"My mother will marry again. Someone will have to rule Ithaca. I suppose there'll be a fight."

"We'll help!" Polycaste squeezes my arm. "My father will send men. I'll fight with you."

I lay my hand over hers, where she's holding my arm.

"Are you all right?" she says.

"Yes."

"I'll teach you how to fight on the way."

I make myself grin. A sixteen-year-old fighting Antinous. Fighting Eurymachus and Agelaus, challenging the tattooed young men in the courtyard with their spears whose shafts are scored with notches—one notch for each life they've taken. And I have no choice, because I'm a fighter's son and must be a fighter myself, even if my only fight ends at the gateposts of my home.

"We'll leave tomorrow," Polycaste says.

I nod. As I stand there with Polycaste, I know how my story is going to end. It can only have one ending. In a week's time, little more, women will shriek my name across the harbor at Ithaca, and my mother will kneel on the sand with her dress torn and ashes in her hair. The pyre by the harbor won't only be for Odysseus. It will be my tomb as well.

PART TWO

8

Nausicaa loved stories.

Stories of fighters were the best of all. She loved the story of the Trojan fighter Hector and his wife, Andromache, when Hector was going off to the war to fight. Andromache came to say good-bye to him, and they were both in tears, and Hector played with his baby son, Astyanax, dandling him on his knee and putting his great war helmet on the baby's head.

It was just a shame Hector was horribly slaughtered a couple of hours later.

She loved—maybe best of all—the story of Helen and Paris, because Helen was so beautiful and they were so in love. Even after the storyteller would finish his tale, at the end of a feast in the great hall of her father, Alcinous, chief of the Phaeacians, Nausicaa would go on imagining their lives—how Paris would come back from a day on the battlefield, grimy, sweating, and covered in blood, and Helen would wash him and bind up his wounds, then maybe cradle his head in her lap and sing to him.

Nausicaa would love to marry a fighter. Unfortunately most of the Phaeacians were sailors and merchants, most of them only interested in profit from the seashells they turned into purple dye in the stinking vats at the top of the town or in abstruse points of navigation, which they could discuss for hours on end, and frequently did at the feasts. Living at the farthest edges of the civilized world, the chances of her meeting a genuine fighter were practically zero.

Even though her father was chief, Nausicaa's life was dull, with nothing she actually had to do except lead the girls down to the river where they did the washing. Her mother was always busy weaving cloth for clothes, all of it dyed purple. Everyone in Phaeacia wore purple, thanks to the seashells, the source of their wealth. Phaeacian merchants kept the best cloth for export, though, so they all wore the cloth that had come out a bit wrong, ranging in shade from crimson to lavender. When the streets were thronged with people hurrying about their business, this variation in color gave the town a vivid appearance that visitors always remarked on, but Nausicaa was fed up to the back teeth with it.

She hated purple. She would have given almost anything for a glimpse—just one glimpse—of a man in white, wearing bronze armor and carrying a sword instead of a counting-frame.

Nausicaa sighed and rolled over in bed. It was washing day today—as it seemed to be pretty much every day. But today she resented the work slightly less than usual. Her favorite dress—green, with an embroidered pattern—had been out of action for a month, awaiting mending, but was now ready to wash. She would slip it in among the interminable purple gowns of her brothers, the crimson tablecloths and lavender sheets, and win at least something back from the morning. She would wear it at tonight's feast, and the young merchants from the town would all fall in love with her.

For what that was worth.

Nausicaa got out of bed, shaking out her long golden hair. She brushed it, listening to the sounds from the courtyard: someone drawing water from the well; a creak of baskets as her women brought the washing downstairs. When she went out onto the gallery, she saw there was a mountain of it: four baskets, each piled high. She stood for a moment, thinking, her pretty mouth twisted, then ran down to the great hall, where her mother was spinning purple yarn and her father was flicking beads on a counting-frame of time-blackened oak.

Nausicaa kissed her mother, then went behind her father and wound her arms around his neck. He kissed her absentmindedly.

"Father?"

"Mm?"

"I was wondering . . ."

"Mm?" Her father flicked two beads across the counting-frame, frowning.

"Could I possibly . . ."

He said, "No."

Nausicaa stood up, pouting, and dancing her fingers on his shoulders. "There's four baskets of it."

Her father frowned and looked up, attending for the first time. "What is it you want?"

"The covered wagon. To carry the washing."

"Oh, yes . . . if you must. Get Halius to put the mules to it."

"Thank you!" She kissed him lightly on the head and ran out into the courtyard, snatching up an apple for her breakfast as she went.

The girls were already outside. It only took a moment to bring the wagon around and talk two of her brothers into loading it up. Then they were spinning out through the gate and past the dye vats, taking the beaten chalk road over the fields.

Nausicaa drove. She liked driving and was good at it, even though the girls screamed when she went too fast and her brothers scolded her for wearing out the mules. There must have been a storm the night before. From the cliff at the edge of town she could see that the waves were still high, crashing viciously onto the rocks and scratching the blue sea's surface with white breakers. The olive trees in her father's grove were still tossing in a high wind, their leaves flashing green and then silver, and the beach, which the road skirted, was strewn with foam and driftwood. She hoped all the Phaeacian ships were safe in harbor, their long black hulls, distinctively curved, sheltered by the breakwater or drawn up safely on the sand.

The girls chattered in the wagon behind her. Nausicaa swung the mules inland, following the track through olive trees and wheat fields to the washing place, where the island's river, bearing cold, fresh water from the mountain, formed a little bay with its own sandy beach, a short walk in from the sea. There were stony shallows in which they could trample the dirty clothes, and stunted little bushes on which they could hang them to dry while they picnicked afterward.

"Picnic?" Nausicaa called, suddenly worried.

"I've got the basket!" shouted a voice from the back.

Nausicaa flicked the whip expertly over the leading mule's ear and took the turn down to the river slightly too fast, lifting one wheel off the ground and evoking screams of outrage and excitement from the back. In one of her dreams—one of the stories she told herself—she rode in a fighter's war chariot, gripping his muscled arm as they hurtled across the plain of Troy past heaped bodies and fallen ramparts, with the wind blowing her long hair out behind.

It didn't take long to do the washing. Each basket was emptied out into the rapidly flowing stream, then, hitching their skirts up to their thighs, the girls waded, screaming, into the icy water to tread the heavy cloth with their feet, kicking up spray and screaming again as it splashed them. Streamers of purple dye trailed away downstream.

Like blood, Nausicaa thought. For a moment she looked left, toward the river's mouth. It must have been some storm last night. The thick bulrushes that fringed the river were blown flat, and driftwood had been washed all the way up from the beach.

When the washing was trampled enough, they hauled each piece out, heavy with water, wrung it out, and hung it on the bushes to dry.

"We'll swim!" Nausicaa ordered.

They all swam. The girls copied everything she did. Glancing around to make sure no male eyes were watching, they pulled their light dresses over their heads and waded out into the deeper water, splashing each other and shrieking. Nausicaa swam the farthest. Afterward they dried themselves in the sun on the bank, then dressed again, unpacked the picnic, and ate bread, fish, and apples from Alcinous's orchard. The washing still wasn't dry.

"We'll play ball!" Nausicaa commanded. She was annoyed with the washing. She needed to be back home in time to dress for the feast, which always took hours, but the heavy cloth remained stubbornly damp. One of the girls got a ball from the back of the wagon, and they picked their way along the bank to a meadow nearer the bulrushes. They formed a ring and threw the ball to each other, sometimes bouncing it, sometimes full toss. Nausicaa lobbed it, and the ball sailed over the girls' heads to disappear in the rushes beyond.

"I'll get it!" Nausicaa shouted.

She ran across the grass to the rushes and began to pick her way through them. The stems pricked her bare feet. The ball must have gone farther than she thought. There was no sign of it, so she kept on, steadying herself on the branch of a little bog oak. The ground was marshy and uneven. Nausicaa stumbled once, slipped on the edge of a hollow, and then stopped.

There was a man lying in the hollow beyond the tree.

He was sunburned and caked with brine, his beard tangled, the hair on his chest and shoulders all white with salt. His legs were drawn up under him.

He was naked.

Nausicaa clung to the tree branch. The sound of the girls' voices seemed very far away. Was he alive or dead? He wasn't moving. The wind fluffed his curling brown hair. Maybe he was dead.

She reached down and touched him, then almost screamed as the man moved.

He sat up with a start, eyes staring, fingers clutching for something he couldn't find—a ship's oar or a sword. They found Nausicaa's wrist instead and gripped it. She found herself staring closely into two blue, bewildered eyes. His breath came in hoarse pants.

Actually, his breath stank a bit.

She said, "It's all right. You're safe. I'll look after you." She swallowed. His grip hurt. "We'll look after you."

"Nausicaa?" The girls were shouting her name.

"Just coming," she called.

Frightened, the man looked past her shoulder. "It's all right," she said. "They're my friends. Everything's all right." It was so like her dream. He was even handsome, like the men in her dreams. "We'll take care of you. Are you hurt?"

The man thought for a moment, then shook his head, bewildered. He tried to say something, but his lips were too dry.

In fact, he was a bit older than Nausicaa had first thought—perhaps even as old as her father, although it was hard to tell. Suddenly the man seemed to become aware of his nakedness, and he squirmed away from her, trying to roll over and cover himself.

"It's all right," she said. "I'll bring you some clothes. Wait here."

Her own mouth was dry as she clambered back through the rushes. The girls stood in an expectant circle on the edge of the meadow.

"You haven't got the ball," Nereis said.

Thegea said, "What's happened?"

Nausicaa drew herself up. It was her role, as the chief's daughter, to be in charge of everything. "There's a man," she said as offhandedly as she could. "He's hurt. We need to help him. He needs clothes."

"Isn't he wearing *anything*?" Nereis squeaked.

"Just get some clothes," Nausicaa snapped.

They brought a purple shirt back from the bushes, still slightly damp. Ordering the girls to wait, Nausicaa carried it through the rushes to where the man still lay. She handed it to him, then turned her back as he pulled it over his head.

"What's your name?" she asked.

He didn't answer. He still hadn't spoken.

"Come with me."

She took him by the hand. The girls screamed when he rose up out of the rushes, but Nausicaa ignored them. He was limping, she noticed. There was a gash on his leg, caked with dried blood. His torso, under the curling hair, was knotted and crisscrossed by scars.

She had noticed that before he pulled the shirt on.

At the meadow, Nausicaa gave orders. "Thegea, get a jar of water. Nereis, get food."

The stranger ate as if he hadn't seen food for a month, squatting on the grass and tearing at the bread with his teeth. Nausicaa could see his shoulder muscles moving under the shirt as he raised the jug to drink.

Then he looked up at her. His eyes were the bluest she had ever seen, the color of the sea in the harbor's shallows, or the sky on a gentle morning.

He said, "Thank you." His voice was still hoarse. He wiped the back of his hand across his mouth. "Thank you." He looked around him, at the meadow, the stream, and the purple washing hanging on the bushes. "Where am I?"

"You're in Phaeacia. My father, Alcinous, is chief of the Phaeacians. I am Nausicaa, his daughter."

The stranger nodded, still squatting on his haunches. He said, "I need to wash."

"Are you hurt?"

He examined his thigh, running calloused brown fingers over his scar, as one might test the strength of a piece of wood.

"I can bind it up for you," Nausicaa said. "I know how."

"I need to wash first." The man looked confused. "But not while . . ."

Nausicaa blushed. "We won't look."

The girls stood on the bank in a prim line, facing the meadow, while the stranger washed himself in the stream behind them. Nausicaa could hear the water splashing over his body and his grunt as he dipped his head in the icy stream. She had already picked him something to wear from her father's clothes, a dark shirt, almost blue—like his eyes—and a purple kilt. But even she was surprised at the transformation when she turned around. His hair and beard were paler than brown, almost golden, and with his face clean of salt, the eyes stood out even more startlingly, if anything, against his deep tan. He didn't look quite so old.

Or perhaps, to be honest, still a bit old. His face was lined, and his hair was streaked with grey. Quite a lot of grey. But definitely better-looking.

"Shall I bind up your wound?"

"I've done it."

"Oh. Can you walk?"

He nodded. "Is there a town? A chief's house? Are we on the mainland or an island?"

Nereis said, "Don't you even know where Phaeacia is?"

Thegea said, "So were you shipwrecked or what?"

"Don't pester him," Nausicaa said.

The stranger looked over his shoulder, out toward the sea, where waves were still breaking in the brisk onshore wind.

"I was at sea for sixteen days," he said in a dazed voice.

"Did your ship sink?"

Thegea said, "Are you a fisherman?"

"Obviously he isn't a fisherman," Nausicaa snapped.

"I had a raft," the man said. "I made a raft." Suddenly his knees sagged, and he pitched forward. Nausicaa sprang toward him and gripped his arm as he fell. She found herself cradling his head. His hair and beard were soft. It was a moment before his eyes opened again, blue and unfocused.

"You're weak," she said. "We must get you to my father's house."

"I can walk."

"We've got a wagon."

It took two of them to help him into the wagon. Driving back to town, Nausicaa grew thoughtful. It was all very well to turn up in Phaeacia with a handsome stranger. That had happened really quite often in her dreams. But in real life it was a bit awkward. She knew how people talked. Girls weren't supposed to be on their own with men other than their brothers and close relatives. She was confident she wouldn't get in any trouble, but she didn't want to be teased afterward. She hated being teased.

She turned the wagon in by the back way, the track leading to the side of the courtyard. There she helped the stranger down from the wagon. His wounded leg almost gave under him.

"This way," Nausicaa said. "I'll take you to my father and mother. Lean on me."

lcinous, chief of Phaeacia, disliked interruptions. When he was working a problem through—his accounts, for instance—he needed to work them through to the end, balance weight of cloth against number of ships, length of journey, size of crew, and know that it all made sense. Interruptions caused mistakes. Mistakes caused loss.

His wife, Arete, knew that. She knew to keep spinning, for hours on end if need be, without talking, and the patient clack of the spinning wheel was oddly soothing to Alcinous's thoughts, suggesting that they too had the regularity and precision of a machine. Only when he sat back from the counting-frame with a particular sigh and pressed his two palms together did she smile and say something—usually a quiet question about the nature of his calculations, which allowed him to explain it all to her, doubling his satisfaction. She was, in every way, the perfect wife.

His daughter, Nausicaa, didn't understand about interruptions. She was forever breaking in on him with dramatic problems that required instant attention—usually a torn dress or lost hairpin, sometimes a hurt bird she had found in the orchard. And she always brought with her a crowd of girls, chattering, gasping and shrieking, who didn't understand about interruptions either.

Even for Nausicaa, though, this latest interruption went too far. When Alcinous looked up, the din of voices having penetrated a complex calculation involving seashells and Egypt, he found her standing in the middle of the hall, clutching a man.

The spinning wheel slowed and stopped. Alcinous stared at the man.

He didn't like him. The man was a fighter—he could see that straightaway. There was something in the set of his jaw and the bunched muscles of his shoulders; something about the scars on his bare arms and the way he stood like a dancer on the balls of his feet. His face was tanned to the color of walnut, and his beard was tangled. His eyes were a startling blue, and he was wearing Alcinous's shirt.

The Phaeacians were merchants and traders. They didn't fight. A generation before, they had departed their old home and settled here, at the end of the world, as colonists, precisely to avoid the aggression of warlike neighbors, horse-riders who preferred sacking cities and plundering to buying purple fabric, the Phaeacians' specialty. With relocation had come peace and abundant seashells, but also a need to develop the navigational skills necessary to access the markets they had left behind. Phaeacian sailors were the best in the world. Their ships, long and sleek, rode out storms. Their captains read stars and currents the way shepherds knew their pastures. Phaeacian ships could be seen in any port in the world. Some had even dared to voyage beyond the known world, out into the green oceans whose waves touched the clouds and whose mists shrouded islands of unknown men, demons, and monsters. The Phaeacians had traveled farther than any people before them.

But they didn't fight.

Alcinous knew about fighters, though. Violent, rapacious, and cruel, and—the thing that infuriated Alcinous and all trading men the most—so arrogant as to claim that their unabashed viciousness, their rape and murder, their burning of cities and desecration of temples, their plundering of warehouses and ransacking of treasuries, was not criminal but heroic—*heroic*, by all the gods—and worthy of being celebrated in poetry while sensible men who actually accomplished things were dismissed as dull.

Dull victims for fighters to kill and pillage, whose poverty and deaths were put in poems to entertain people. Storytellers were forever arriving at Phaeacia on returning merchant ships. They wasted evening after evening singing stories of war and love to a rapt audience. Nausicaa adored them.

Nausicaa opened her mouth to say something. Her eyes were shining. But before she could speak, the stranger limped forward, dropped to his knees in front of Arete, and clasped her ankles.

The traditional way of seeking help. It made him a supplicant, a guest. A duty.

"Our house is your house," said Alcinous, sighing.

"I found him in the reeds," Nausicaa said. "He was shipwrecked. He's got a cut all the way up his thigh."

Alcinous didn't want to know. The last thing he needed was a fighter sprawled all over his house, cut thigh or no cut thigh, with Nausicaa mooning over him. Half-healed, he would be picking quarrels with his sons, then leading his best sailors off on some voyage of rape and pillage. The man might be growing old—his hair was mostly grey. But he was still dangerous.

"What's your name?" Alcinous asked. "Where are you from?"

Still kneeling, the man looked up at him through his startling blue eyes. He didn't answer. He simply shook his head. That was a guest's right. You should be welcomed just as a guest, not for who you were. And since the tangled webs of kinship and old feuds, rivalries, oaths, blood brotherhoods, and ancient quarrels linked almost every family in Greece in ways so tortuous no one could begin to untangle them—even if they could remember them all—any traveler, arriving innocently in a town, might find himself hosted by a man whose cousin had killed the uncle whose blood brother had once saved his father's life, and would therefore be obliged to murder him. Many guests preferred to claim their hospitality anonymously.

"You're none the less welcome," Alcinous said drily.

This needed time to think through. Time to think through in private, not in a crowded hall with the young men casting admiring glances at the stranger's scarred arms, and the women hanging on his every word.

"You look tired," he said. "You must rest." He raised his voice, turning his next words into an announcement. "Tonight's feast will be postponed until tomorrow. Our guest needs time to recover."

Arete nodded. For a moment Nausicaa looked outraged, then gave a resigned shrug.

"He could never have danced on that leg anyway," she said.

Alcinous raised one hand, dismissing them all. He had bought himself some time. He knew what his strategy had to be. He must show the stranger every courtesy that the laws of hospitality demanded. And more. He would offer the stranger all possible assistance. Everything in his power—ships, men, gold—to help him travel wherever he was going when he was shipwrecked. To his home, to his friends, to whatever war he was planning to start. To the ends of the earth, if need be . . . just so long as it was far from Phaeacia.

Without, of course, being rude. He didn't want this man coming back with a shipload of vagabonds to sack the town, burn the house, and fill his ships with all the wealth he had glimpsed in Phaeacia's storerooms. Alcinous shuddered.

The stranger spent the rest of the day, and the morning following, lying in the courtyard on a low chair with his face up to the sun. His arms dangled on either side of the chair. On his left wrist was a thick leather bracelet stamped with the image of a boar.

Nausicaa and her friends clustered around him like hummingbirds around a flower, bringing him apples carefully peeled and cut into slices, cups of water, cushions. Once, when Alcinous crossed the courtyard, he found Nausicaa kneeling next to the chair, trimming the stranger's fingernails. Another time, to his extreme displeasure, she was combing his hair. The fighter seemed happy to let her do so. He whispered something to her as she combed, talking so low and fast no one else could hear.

Most of the time he slept, though. Or seemed to be asleep. Once Alcinous thought he saw a gleam between the man's closed eyelids. That was exactly what he would have expected from a fighter: guile, cunning, ruthlessness. Fighters were liars—he knew that well enough.

A couple of hours before the feast, Alcinous's sons and their friends arrived in the courtyard with a ball and began kicking it around. By then Nausicaa and her friends had disappeared upstairs to dress, otherwise they would have stopped them. From the office where he was checking accounts with his steward, Alcinous watched his son, Halius, go up to the stranger and shyly ask if he wanted to join in. The stranger simply shook his head and went on sleeping.

After a time, the boys tired of their ball game and, instead, started shooting arrows at a row of barrels at the far end of the courtyard. As always there was a lot of laughter, but most of the arrows missed. Archery was not a sport much practiced by the young men of Phaeacia. Again, Halius went up to the stranger, who this time seemed a bit impatient at being disturbed. Again he refused to join in the game.

When the boys were bored with archery, they started throwing spears instead. The courtyard of the big house at Phaeacia was rectangular, twenty paces wide and forty long. The boys had been shooting arrows the length of the courtyard, but none of them could throw a spear that far. Instead, they clustered in the corner where the stranger sat and threw their weapons at the wooden wall of the shed opposite. Not many of them managed even that. Most of the spears missed or, at best, hung for a second in the woodwork before sagging and drooping to the ground. Again, Halius eyed the stranger for a while, then went up to ask if he wanted to join in. The scarred, suntanned guest fascinated him. But again the stranger shook his head.

"Perhaps you're not much of a fighter, sir," said Halius. Alcinous could just make out the words from the window where he stood watching.

Halius didn't mean it rudely, but his words appeared to strike a raw nerve. Rage seemed to froth up inside the stranger like water spouting up through a geyser. One moment he was lying in the chair; the next he ripped the spear from Halius's hand, wound himself back, and hurled it. He threw it not at the wall but at the barrels at the farthest end of the courtyard. It hit the middle target dead center. The barrel exploded in a shower of splintered staves. Wine splattered the wall behind. In the bloodred stain that flowered across the whitewash, the spear stood quivering, not drooping but erect from the wall, haft buried deep in the plaster.

There was a moment of shocked silence. No one on Phaeacia threw a spear like that. Then the stranger clutched his thigh and sank to the ground, groaning. A shriek sounded from the gallery upstairs. Nausicaa came running into the courtyard.

"What have you done to him?" she shouted at Halius.

Together she and her brothers helped their guest back into the chair, his eyes closed and his face sheened with sweat. Alcinous turned away from the window, deeply troubled.

"Have we a ship ready?" he asked Prymneus, his steward.

"The vessel that came back from Tyre last week."

"To depart immediately?"

Prymneus pulled a face. "No food. No water. Repairs needed to the rigging and three oars missing."

"Get her ready," Alcinous ordered. "As soon as you can. Start now. Gather a crew. She'll be leaving within two days."

"Destination?"

Alcinous sighed. "I wish I could tell you," he said.

The guests arrived as soon as was decent for the feast in the great hall that evening. News of the stranger's presence had spread through town, along with the story that he had been seen riding back from the beach with Nausicaa and—a garbled account emanating from servants—that he had fought a duel with the chief's son, who was now lying at death's door. Halius's presence in the hall, pale but unharmed, was greeted by most of the arriving guests with evident disappointment.

As servants filled cups with wine and passed around trays of food, Alcinous sensed the excitement in the hall. The men kept turning to look at the stranger. The women shot covert glances to where he sat between Alcinous and Arete. The stranger ignored all of them. He ate greedily from the heaped trays the servants held out to him—lobsters and grilled fish, squid stuffed with bread and prawns in rich sauces of saffron and cream. But he barely spoke. When he wasn't eating, he sat with his head sunk between his shoulders, staring at the food in front of him. From the other side of the table, Nausicaa tried to engage him in conversation, without success. When Alcinous asked polite questions about the wreck that had landed him on Phaeacia, and how long he had been at sea, he answered as curtly as possible.

"Sixteen days."

"Where did you set out from?"

"An island."

"Its name?"

The stranger simply shrugged.

"Did you have a crew?"

"I was alone."

"Alone on a ship?"

"On a raft."

"A *raft*?"

The stranger looked down at his calloused, torn hands. "I built it," he said. "I made it from driftwood."

"Where?"

He shook his head again.

"Who was the chief there?"

"No chief." The stranger frowned, then looked at Alcinous through sea-blue eyes that suddenly seemed clouded. "A woman. It was *her* island."

At last the food was finished. Alcinous stood up and clapped his hands for silence.

"Tonight," he announced, "Demodocus will tell us a story from the great war." Demodocus was a new storyteller, recently arrived on Phaeacia. Alcinous reckoned that with a fighter present, and with so many rumors already swirling around town, he could hardly avoid one of the fighters' tales his daughter loved so much. He beckoned Demodocus forward. "We will have the tale of Odysseus and the wooden horse," he announced.

There were gasps of satisfaction. Everyone loved the story of Odysseus. Benches were pushed back and cups replenished. Servants crowded the doorway from the kitchen. Children were hushed. Demodocus was a good storyteller. Taking up his place on the step of the hearth, he began to thrum his instrument, a low, unearthly drone to accompany his words. He began the story when the horse had already been drawn inside the citadel at Troy, and he told it well. He described the joy of the Trojans as they hauled the clumsy wooden statue to the temple steps—a tribute, they thought, from a vanquished enemy. He described the throwing open of the temple doors and the crowds thronging the square, the priests' chanting and the lowing of cattle led forward for sacrifice, the gusts of perfumed smoke that rose from the altars on the steps. He described Helen and Paris leading the celebrations, women dancing, young men drinking themselves to a stupor. He described King Priam, in his palace, looking out over the roofs of the city he thought he had saved. And meanwhile Odysseus and his men crouched inside the horse's wooden belly, clutching their weapons. As moonlight kissed the waves, the Greek ships returned to the beach and the fighters jumped down onto the silvery sand: Agamemnon and Diomedes, Ajax, Neoptolemus. In silence they marched across the dark Trojan plain, over the sites of so many battles, over the graves where they had buried their friends. He described Odysseus, the author of the stratagem, unlocking the trapdoor and peering down into the empty square, still littered with barrels and smashed cups.

"For Odysseus," Demodocus said, "was the cleverest of the Greeks, brave in war, skilled in debate. Odysseus who had sailed from faraway Ithaca, leaving his wife and unborn child, to fight alongside the armies of Agamemnon."

Alcinous looked around the great hall as Demodocus performed. Young men were listening with their mouths open, women with their hands to their faces, as if struck with horror. But Nausicaa, instead of watching Demodocus, had her eyes fixed on the stranger. Her heartbroken expression startled Alcinous. He looked across at the stranger.

Tears were pouring down his cheeks. He made no sound, but his mouth was open, as if he'd been howling in pain. Shrunk in on himself, he no longer looked dangerous. He was more like a tired old man—tired and wounded.

Alcinous stood up, his chair clattering to the floor behind him. The thrum of Demodocus's instrument wavered and stopped. A kind of sigh ran through the hall as the story's spell broke.

"It seems," Alcinous said, "that this story gives our guest no pleasure." He looked down at the stranger's curly grey hair and sunken shoulders. "Sir," he said quietly. "I think you have your own story to tell. To start with, perhaps you should tell us who you are and where you come from."

There was silence in the hall. Everyone looked to the stranger, but for a moment he seemed unaware of it. Only slowly did he straighten himself and look up at the king with a dazed expression.

"I come from Ithaca," he said. "My name is Odysseus."

Alcinous cleared the hall before letting his guest continue. He looked too hurt, too ill to recount his story in public, and in no state to deal with the pandemonium that had broken out in the hall at his revelation. Odysseus, the conqueror of Troy, discovered right here on the island! The Phaeacians left in a hubbub of excited gossip, sweeping up children, scraping back benches until the hall was empty. The door to the kitchen closed. Nausicaa drew her chair next to Odysseus's.

Odysseus sagged sideways in his seat, as if he barely had the strength to hold himself upright. He had said nothing since revealing his name. Then he sighed, wiped the back of his hand across his tearstained face, and began again.

"Eight years ago," he said, "I left Troy." He paused and repeated more softly, "Eight years." Again there was a silence. Then he pulled himself upright in his seat and looked at Alcinous. "I thank you," he said in a more normal voice, "for your hospitality. All of you." He glanced at Nausicaa, whose hands flew to her cheeks. "Without you, I would have died. Sixteen days I clung to a raft. My water was washed overboard, my food. The raft broke upon the rocks. All I ask of you now . . ." Suddenly his voice broke, as if he was about to weep again. "All I need is your help in returning home to Ithaca." He stood up, suddenly, and dropped to his knees at Alcinous's feet, clasping his ankles in the suppliant position.

Alcinous stooped and placed one hand on Odysseus's head, then helped him to his feet.

"First," he said, "you must tell us how you arrived here. And where you have been traveling for eight years. Then we will help you return home." He glanced at his daughter. "It will be our pleasure."

A flood of tears silenced Odysseus. He fumbled his way back to his chair, reached for his cup of wine, and drained it. The wine seemed to give him strength. Alcinous motioned Halius to refill it. When Odysseus spoke again, his voice was louder.

"We left Troy on a morning in summer," he began. "Myself, ten ships, three hundred Ithacans—all who had survived the war. It was eight years since we had seen home . . . eight years of fighting. I had a son I had never seen, Telemachus. My wife, Penelope, was waiting for me. All I wanted was to be home." He paused and drained his cup again. Alcinous glanced at Nausicaa, who was frowning.

"Two days out we reached an island, Ismarus. My men landed there. We sacked it." He said it without emotion. "But they regrouped and attacked us as we were loading booty onto the ships. They fought us on the sand, killed sixty of us, the rest were lucky to get away. Six oars short in each ship, and the ships laden with water and food, laden deep, then the wind rose. We were heading southwest for Cape Malea but the storm caught us, three days. Have you ever seen lightning strike a ship at sea? The mast scorched, the sails flaming in rags? Three days . . ."

Odysseus paused. Despite himself, Alcinous found the words drawing him in. There was a kind of enchantment in Odysseus's voice as he spoke, the words low and murmuring, tumbling over one another like water over pebbles.

"When the storm ended, we didn't know where we were. The sun was high and hot. There was no wind. We rowed over water as thick and sluggish as mud. It was two days before we sighted land, a tall island with a mountain and an islet offshore. Our water was almost gone by then, so we put into the islet, found a stream and a herd of sheep grazing between the rocks. That was the first good luck that had come our way since leaving Troy. Big, fine sheep . . . we slaughtered three and spitted them over fires of driftwood. Then a dozen of us decided to row over to the bigger island to see what we could find. Why?" Odysseus shook his head. His eyes were clouded. "Because it was there. How do I know why? Because we were men . . ." He sobbed suddenly, unexpectedly, but mastered himself and went on. "People lived there . . . I say 'people.' There were signs of life. A stone quay. A track. We followed the track through bushes to a cave. Farther up the hill we could see stacks of firewood and dry stone walls, more sheep grazing. It was what we found in the cave, though, that made us glad we'd come. Someone lived there. The food! Hams hanging from hooks driven into the rock, big wheels of cheese, barrels of curds. The place stank of cheese, a shepherd's home. Piles of fleece as tall as I was, one of the men took a jump and landed on it. We were all laughing. I'd brought with me two skins of wine, the best we had on board, thinking we could exchange them for food, but there was no one there and the cave was full of all this wealth, so we stuffed our pockets with it, loaded up nets of cheese, sacks of bread we found in baskets.

"Me, I was calculating. How far could one storm have blown us off course? We couldn't be far from Cape Malea, with friends to help us on our way—Menelaus at Sparta, Nestor at Pylos. In a week, I thought, we could be home, and with all this food we need never stop on the way. *One good wind*, I thought, *that's all we need, one good wind*. Then I heard someone coming.

"The others heard it too and froze. I can still see them now, bread in their hands, sacks half full, no better than thieves. We just had time to dive to the back of the cave when he appeared in the door. A man." Odysseus swallowed and raised one trembling hand. "I say a man. A giant, the size of three men. One eye . . ." He placed a hand over one of his own eyes. "Filthy. He squints around. I think, *There's no hiding*, and we weren't going to fight the brute with nothing but short hunting spears. So I step out. 'Sir, I beg for hospitality. We're sailors. We're lost. We need food. Can you help us?' He just looks at me through his one eye. 'The gods love those who help strangers,' I say. He's looking at each of us in turn, counting. Then he moves—a big man, and he moves quick as a snake—grabs one of my men, and drags him away. The boy's screaming, 'Odysseus!' We're paralyzed . . . as if there was anything we could do against that brute. Drags him to a corner of the cave, sweeps up a stick on his way, and beats out my boy's brains against the cave wall. The screams stop suddenly. When he turns around . . ." Odysseus gave a sob. "When he turns around, there's blood on his mouth, he's been *eating* . . ."

Nausicaa gasped. The others listened in horror, without moving.

"'That's all the hospitality you'll get from me,' he says. We were wondering if he knew how to speak. He takes a huge stone, rolls it in place to stop the cave's mouth. 'Now you're my guests,' he says, and sets to milking the sheep he's herded in with him. Fine, fat sheep, glossy fleeces, a ram leading them—their bleating fills the cave.

"My men don't say a word, just stare at the corner where their friend's lying dead, then look at me to see what to do. I'd gotten them out of scrapes before. 'Don't make him angry,' that's all I can think to say. So we crawl to the back of the cave and lie there not sleeping while the giant goes to sleep, his snores shaking the rock. One of the men tugs my sleeve. 'We could kill him now,' he whispers. I just point to the stone at the cave's mouth. None of us could shift it. Kill the giant and that cave would have been our tomb.

"The next morning he goes out with the sheep. 'Be good,' he says. 'Don't touch anything. I'll know.' When he's gone, he rolls the stone back in front of the opening to trap us in. The men are at the stone at once, heaving together. Nothing. I had a plan, though. 'Get a stake,' I said, pointing. There was a stack of them piled against the cavern wall. Good olive stakes for fencing, as thick as your arm. I had them sharpen one end and heat it in the fire that was still smoldering. Heat it carefully, without burning, until the point was black and as hard as iron. Then we hid it behind some barrels.

"That was a long day. We ate. Covered our friend's body as best we could, with those teeth marks on his leg. Waited for the giant to come back. We heard him outside at last, then saw the stone move. In he comes, and his one eye's looking around the cave, checking. 'How are the thieves?' he asks. 'Travelers,' I say. 'Guests.' And his arm shoots out, seizes another of the men. This time he doesn't even drag him to a corner. Lifts him up in one hand and snaps his neck the way you'd wring the neck of a chicken—we hear the bones break. The giant laughs, lifts our friend's body to his mouth, and bites into his arm, blood running down his chin. I can hear the men whimpering behind me. One of them heaves over and vomits, but I know our only chance is if I play unconcerned. 'You'll want something to wash that down with,' I say. 'Did you ever drink wine?' He looks suspicious. 'What's that?' he asks. 'I've got some here,' I say, and I bring out the first skin. He snatches it, rips out the stopper, and drinks.

"That was strong wine," Odysseus said. "And he's never tasted wine before. Sucks out the first skin in one draft, and when he puts it down, his eye is already muddled. 'More,' he says, so I give him the other. He doesn't know what's happening. Sits down with a crash that shakes the cave, tries to steady himself with a hand on the wall. 'That wine's all right.' But his voice is gone and he starts laughing. Then he throws up. Everything he's eaten—wine, milk, human flesh . . . I nearly lost it myself. The giant's gone, though, flat out on the floor and snoring.

"We get the stake and heat it in the fire 'til the point's glowing. The giant's lying on his back, and we drive it right into his eye. Drive it in and twist, with the eye hissing, the flesh burning around it, and black blood pouring all over us . . ."

Nausicaa shrieked, but Odysseus ignored her. "The giant's screaming, tries to sit up, flails with one hand, rips the stake from his eye, while we run for cover. He's blundering about the cave, crashing into walls, howling. I would have felt sorry for him if it hadn't been for our friends' bodies still lying on the floor. He screams, 'Where are you?' but I gesture the men to stay quiet, and after a time the pain takes over and he forgets us. All night he's screaming and groaning. In the morning the sheep start bleating to be milked and let out. He milks them by feel, letting the milk spurt on the floor. Then he pushes the stone back. 'You'll not escape,' he says, looking 'round the cave with that awful, destroyed face, a bloody hole where the eye was. The sheep have to get out, though. He feels their backs, each one as it passes. But my men are clinging underneath, hanging on to the fleeces for dear life. They know what he'll do if he finds them. I'm the last, and I take the ram. Nose full of sheep stink, hands slipping on the greasy wool. He stops it, doesn't he? The ram, his favorite. 'Why did they do this to me?' he asks it. He's still a little drunk, and dazed with pain. 'I'll get them back, though. I'll do the same to them, one eye at a time.' I can feel his thick fingers grip the animal's fur. Then he slaps its rump and I'm outside.

"We should just have run and gone, but something made me stop. The thought of my dead men, the way he'd brained one and wrung the other's neck. So I turn and shout, 'You'll never catch us!' A stupid boast. He comes running out at once, hands flailing, and his face turning everywhere except where I'm standing. Then I really do start to run.

"I'd played a trick on him," Odysseus said. "When I was in the cave. On the first night he asked me, 'What's your name?' I thought fast and said, 'Nobody, my name's Nobody.' So now, when we're running, the giant howling outside his cave, his friends come out, each from a cave like ants from an anthill, a hundred of them. They're standing on the mountainside, men like you've never seen, thighs like tree trunks. There are dogs barking, an alarm sounding, one of them blowing a conch shell. Someone shouts, 'Who's attacking?' Our giant howls back, 'Nobody!' 'Who is it?' they say. 'Who's attacking?' 'Nobody!' he shrieks. 'So why are you bothering us?' they shout, and one of them heaves a rock at him. Rough men. It gives us just enough time to reach the ship, find our friends. They'd almost given up on us. 'Where are the others?' 'Dead . . . No time to explain.' He's coming after us by now, fumbling across the mountainside, hands in the gorse, blood on the rocks. He hears our oars, tears a rock from the ground. Not a loose stone, a *rock*. Hurls it wide. The giants still shouting, 'Who's hurt you?' 'Nobody!' he howls."

Nausicaa giggled. "He must have been stupid," she said.

Odysseus drew breath. "We made it. One rock he threw smashed oars on one side, but we made it. They had no boats. Shepherds, not fishermen. We tugged on the oars until our wrists cracked. I turn at the steering oar, he's standing on the beach, knee-deep in water with the blood dripping in the sea. 'I'm no *Nobody*,' I shout. 'My name's Odysseus, don't forget it.'"

He drew breath again. "So we rowed back into the cove, butchered two sheep and cooked them. Talked about our dead companions. We lit a fire and prayed before we sailed on. I still remember the moment that island dropped below the horizon . . ."

Odysseus paused and took a sip of wine. "After that we had three days at sea. Plenty of dolphin, a line over the stern, but we caught no fish. Then we see land to the east and make for it. A cove, one small village—colonists, I suppose. The man who ran it was called Aeolus. A magician, he could conjure winds. We found him on a rocky hill behind his house with a staff of olive wood as high as he was. He points it west and a west wind blows up, we can feel raindrops. Swings it to the south and the grass rustles, blows on my left ear. Suddenly I can smell hot desert, blown across the sea, palm trees, spices. All the way around he turns, points it to the north and we're shivering, smelling ice from the glaciers, pulling our cloaks around us to cut out the hail.

"He's heard of me. 'I'll help you,' he says. That night, dining in his hall, he brings in a leather bag. It looks like a sack you tie up cats to drown in, it's bulging all over. But when you touch it—nothing, it's empty. 'I've caught the winds in this bag,' says Aeolus, 'all except the southwest wind to blow you home to Ithaca.'"

Alcinous pursed his lips. It looked as though he was about to say something, but Odysseus went on.

"There's a twist of silver wire at the top, to hold it closed. 'Watch out for your crew, though,' Aeolus says. He was right. Six days on a warm sea, the southwester filling our sails, but I haven't slept a minute, steering the ship toward Ithaca. When we raise Kephalonia at dawn, the first familiar land since we left Troy, there are tears running down my cheeks, I can't help it. Then there it is—Nirito, the mountaintop of Ithaca, like a jewel on the horizon, the rock you'd put on a girl's finger, and suddenly I'm remembering the day I left—Penelope on the jetty, women hanging out of the windows around the harbor. Someone had hung a banner over the street. As I sailed through those waters then—the Ionian, deepest sea in the world, so blue it's almost black—as I sailed past Asteris then, I thought, *'When will I be back?'* And here I was.

"That was when I nodded off at the oar. Six nights without sleep! When I woke up, it was chaos. The winds roaring, waves rearing higher than our mast. There are men clinging to the gunwales, the oars gone, sheets gone, sail flapping in shreds from the masthead as if it had turned into a bird and wanted to fly away. I found out what happened afterward. They'd been gossiping since the day I brought that leather sack on board. 'What's in it?' 'The chief has some treasure he doesn't want to share with us.' The moment my eyes are closed they're at it, untwisting the silver wire. Every wind in the world, unleashed and furious, escaping from the bag at once. The sea whipped to frenzy, the sky gone mad . . ." He shook his head, dazed by the memory. "I don't know how we survived. The storm blew us back to Aeolus's island, but he wouldn't help us again. 'You had your chance,' he says, won't even let us land, he has the colonists drive us off with arrows. We could have fought them, but why? Who knows what other magic Aeolus had in that staff?"

Alcinous gave a little cough. He was still frowning.

"So we sailed on again. This time keeping the ships close. Water enough in our barrels, but our food's running low. When we see an island on the horizon, we make for it. Tall crags, big waves rising and crashing against them. When we sail around, though, there's an opening, and beyond it you can see a pool of black water. Not even a ripple to disturb the surface—a natural harbor. I watch the other ships run in one by one. I don't know what stopped me following them. Instinct? A god's voice whispering in my ear? 'There's no room for all of us,' I shout. 'I'll anchor outside!' And we tie my ship to the rocks outside the harbor mouth. Inside the harbor the ships lie as quiet as babies sleeping. Trees growing down the cliff face. Smoke from a farm somewhere inland. Colonists again, those islands are full of them. They sail west, find somewhere deserted and scratch out a farm. A peaceful life." Odysseus closed his eyes. "Peaceful, we thought. I sent a party off to find the farm whose smoke we can see. The rest of us lay down on the rocks to doze. Hot sun, it was noon. No danger. The first I know something's wrong, I hear a shout. Two of our men scrambling down the cliffs as if they had lions behind them. While we watch, men appear on the cliff edge, throwing spears, hurling rocks. One of our men, I see a rock crush his head, his face flowers blood, he's falling. They catch another as he tries to climb down. Cut his throat without even asking his name. All we're thinking now is *Get back to the ships*. The men start rowing out, swimming out. It's chaos. Some are dropping sails, others hoisting anchors before their friends are on board. Orders screamed and no one listening. Then the arrows start to fly. The pursuers have reached the shore, hundreds of them. Me, I've led my own crew out to the harbor mouth where our ship is moored. When I look back from there, I can see what happens." Odysseus gave a strangled sob. "A bloodbath. How could nine ships maneuver out of that harbor? It was a trap, like the hole you'd dig to catch a boar. One ship drifts ashore, they're on it like dogs, men butchered, the sea red. I watch them all slaughtered—my friends, nine ships, two hundred and more men who've been through everything with me. They survived the war at Troy . . ." He shook his head. "Survived that just to die in a bloody little bay on an island no one's heard of. And why?" Odysseus put both hands to his temples. "Gold. As the islanders take each ship, the bodies still on board, we can see them picking over it like flies on a carcass. Each man's treasure pulled from under his rowing bench. Treasures we won at Troy, you can see them glinting in the sun. Nothing but thieves.

"We only just made it to our own ship, moored off the mouth of the harbor. Dove off the cliffs and swam on board. I cut the anchor rope—no time to hoist it—and the wind took us away as the first arrows splashed the water behind us."

There was a pause. "Pirates," said Alcinous. "Our ships have orders only to land in ports with whom we have treaties."

Odysseus looked at him. "Very sensible," he said ironically, then shook his head and snorted. "But there was no such luxury for us. Sea beggars, that's what we were. I had one ship left, of all the ships and all the men who sailed from Ithaca. One ship left, my own.

"So by ourselves we plowed across the sea. It had never seemed so empty. No sailors shouting jokes from ship to ship. No friendly sails emerging from the darkness at dawn. Nothing but the sea and our one ship, alone in that vast plain of salt.

"God knows where we were. The stars were the only familiar sight. I sailed south 'til we saw a group of islands. We made for the biggest, saw a house on the hill, a beach with ships drawn up on it, but no one in sight. A bit odd, I thought." He looked at Alcinous. "Hardly a treaty port, but what else could we do? So we put in, ran our ship up the sand like the others, and sent a party up to the house to see. Ten of them. One came back running, Eurylochus. Arms flapping like wings, eyes staring, and his mouth wide open, screaming. We grab him, all he can say is, 'Pigs. Witch.' We throw him down on the sand, four men holding him, throw water in his face, he keeps moaning, 'Pigs. Witch.' At last I get the story, kneeling on the sand, my ear close to his mouth to hear." Odysseus drew a deep breath.

"They had followed the path up to the house, broad, well kept. There's a verandah around the house, no one in sight, but music from inside, or a wind chime. They're about to go in when four men run up. Men? They're frothing at the mouth, walking on all fours like dogs. One, when he sees them, puts his head back and howls. Wolf-men. My boys have their weapons out by this time, fight them off and the wolf-men run off into the trees. 'Into the house,' says one. 'I'm not going in there,' says Eurylochus. 'All right,' they say. 'You stay out here and keep watch.' 'I'm not staying out here either,' Eurylochus says, but they make him stay anyway, and go in. Nothing happens. Eurylochus waits, watches, keeps listening for the wolves. He's shaking already. 'Creepy,' he tells me, 'the place is creepy.' Then he hears this shriek inside the house, but not a human shriek. Squealing, grunts, cacophony, and then his friends are running out of the house, but not like people, they're down on all fours, squealing, biting the earth, they're pigs. 'This witch,' he says, 'she's turned them into pigs.' He took off and ran, I don't blame him, all the way down to the beach, mouth open and screaming. It took us an hour to quiet him down.

"I put on my armor, sword, breastplate, shield. I hadn't worn full armor since we sacked Ismarus. I had the men turn the ship around, stern to the beach and a gangplank, men at the oars. 'If I'm not back in an hour,' I said, 'just go.' 'Go where?' they said. 'Ithaca.' 'Which way?' they said, and I turned on them. 'How do I know?' I said, and walked off. Up the path, no one in sight. I saw the house ahead of me, no wolves. Then I hear a noise to the left, look around, and there's a farmyard, my men in it." Odysseus paused, recalling the sight. "It was as Eurylochus said. Like pigs, rutting and fighting. Faces smeared black where they'd been rooting in the ground, some had torn off their clothes." He shook his head. "I took out my sword and went into the house. A low place, built of wood, shutters all around. There's a smell of perfumed smoke, rugs on the floor, and a girl sitting on a low couch. I say girl . . ." Odysseus put his head on one side. "She was older than she looked. Gods, she was lovely, though. Wearing a white dress so thin you could see right through it. A child of nature, barefoot, hair wild. 'Drink this,' she said, and pushed a bowl toward me, cut from the bottom of a gourd. There's a gummy white liquid in it. I've seen that kind of thing before, traveling in Africa with Mentes. We came to a village, there was a witch doctor there made people drink this liquor he cut from a tree. They danced, screamed, howled. He could make them do what he wanted—the men laugh like women, the girls fight like men. I drank some and he had me on a branch, hooting like an owl. I pushed it back. 'You drink it,' I said. 'What have you done to my men? You've turned them into pigs.' 'Men *are* pigs,' she said. There's howling from the front. 'Or wolves,' she said. I put the tip of my sword between her breasts. She's interested now. She looks up at me. Her eyes . . . gods, how do I describe her eyes? 'Or lions,' she says, takes my hand, and leads me toward the couch . . ."

Nausicaa's cheeks were pink. Her father gave a meaningful cough.

"I stayed there a year," Odysseus went on. "My men, the drug soon wore off. The others, the wolves, she let them go. The ships on the beach were theirs. My crew rigged tents in the field behind the house. They were happy enough. There was good fishing in the sea, orchards, a farm. Circe, her name was. I don't know how a whole year passed. I told her about Troy and our travels. She told me about herself. Her husband had founded the colony, built the house, then died. There was a village the other side of the mountain, but we didn't go there much, she didn't want us to. A whole year . . ."

"Did you tell her about your wife and son?" Arete asked drily.

Odysseus looked at her. "I thought about them. More and more. Lay in a hammock on the verandah and thought about Ithaca. She knew something was wrong. The men were getting restless too. Nothing for them to do. They built her a new barn, did chores. One of my boys, Elpenor, broke his neck fixing the roof, drunk. She knew I wouldn't stay forever. Circe wasn't the type to cling, maybe she was bored of me too. 'Go, then,' she says. 'What are you waiting for?' I told her, 'I don't know where to go. I don't know if I'll ever see Ithaca again, hold my wife, see my boy. There was a man in Troy,' I said, 'Laocoon, he could see the future. I could have asked him, "Will I ever reach home?" He'd have told me. If I'd taken him captive, I'd have him here now to ask. Instead he was killed.' 'You want to talk to Laocoon?' she says. I just look at her. 'He's dead,' I say. 'Anyone wants to talk to Laocoon has to cross the river Styx and go to hell.' She looks straight back. 'I can do that,' she says. And she goes into her room, the room where she makes the incense sticks, pounds bark, fixes potions, all the things her husband taught her . . ."

Odysseus closed his eyes and rocked forward in his chair. When he looked up at them, he was hunched, as if in pain. He looked into each of their faces, very slowly, one by one. "What I'm going to tell you now," he said hoarsely, "you won't believe. No one could believe it. But I swear to you it's true. I swear on my boy's life."

No one said anything. After a moment Odysseus went on. "She came back with a bowl. I knew that bowl. 'Drink this,' she says. I'd never touched one of her potions before, but I look her in the eye, take the bowl, and drink." He touched his lips with his tongue and screwed up his face, as if he was tasting the bitter potion again. "It felt . . . I can't describe it. Like when you're sick and your head spins. Dizzy. I knew I was sweating, I could feel her hand behind my head. I thought, *'Gods, what has she done to me?'* I was lying down. My sight had gone. Then I was on the deck of my ship, standing. I don't know how it happened. My crew pulling at the oars. We were on a grey sea, no wind, the sail furled. Mist on the water, drifting in clumps past my steering oar. No birds. We rowed on like that for what seemed like hours, as if we could have rowed forever through the same mist. Then we see a rock and everyone stops rowing. Just a black rock, shining in the sea, a gull on top of it, but it's the first thing we've seen. Slowly we drift past. When it's almost out of sight, there's a hiss of water on shingle and suddenly we stop, we're aground. I go up to the bow, you can't see anything, there's mist all around, but I jump down anyway. I'm in water up to my thighs. One by one, the crew jumps down after me. We drag the ship onto a beach. It's shingle and mud, flat, bleak. No sign of a tide. We walk up the beach and there's some wiry grass, no color in it, and more mist.

"There's driftwood on the beach, so the crew gathers it and lights a fire." He shivered. "The first that was ever lit on that shore. It doesn't warm us. The mist gets in your clothes, freezes your bones. We're all shivering. We get a goat from the ship, from where we keep the livestock trussed in the bows. Slaughter it, catch the blood in a bowl as a sacrifice. Cook the meat, but no one wants to eat. Then someone says, 'There's a man.'

"There's more than one. Walking out of the mist, but not together. One by one, separated. We're all on our feet. I say, 'Draw swords, but wait 'til I speak.' Then I see it's Elpenor? The boy who fell off the roof? We all see it at once. Someone behind me gasps. His face white, black blood on his neck. 'Elpenor?' I say. He's holding out his hands. 'Bury me,' he says, his voice thin as the mist. 'If you love the gods, bury me, and tell my parents where I lie.'

"My mouth was so dry I could hardly speak. 'Where are we?' I ask. 'Where do you think?' he replies, 'on the shores of the underworld, where the dead go.' 'And all these people?' 'The dead.' That's enough for the men, I hear them scrambling back on the ship, but I just stand there. Somehow I'm remembering why I'm here. Laocoon, the prophet. I look around. Elpenor has slipped away into the mist. *Who else is here?* I'm thinking. Everyone who ever died, everyone who ever lived—how many is that? How far did that plain stretch? Mist and mud and dead souls, forever. But there's a stir in them now. The word has gotten around there are living people on the shores of hell. You can feel it like an eddy in the mist, a drift toward us, grey faces turning, one by one, people trudging toward us across the plain like starlings wheeling in the sky.

"Laocoon is with them. The last time I saw him was on Troy's last night. His eyes were locked on mine when I cut his throat, now he's looking at me again. 'I'm sorry,' I say. 'It was war.' He doesn't say a word, just gestures to the bowl of goat's blood by the fire. 'You want this?' He lifts it to his lips and drinks. Black goat's blood running down his white ghost's chin. It's as if his eyes focus then, and he sees me properly. 'Odysseus,' and he nods. I tell him what I want. Will I ever see Ithaca again? My wife, Penelope, the boy. I'm asking the questions and tears are running down my cheeks, hot and wet. 'You'll see Ithaca again,' he says, and then they're tears of joy. I drop down on my knees, squelching the mud, and try to grip his hand—except there's nothing there. I'm going to reach home!

"'I'll make an offering to the gods for you,' I say, 'the very day I land on Ithaca. I can picture it now. We'll sail into the harbor. The fishermen will have seen our sail, they'll be waiting for us. They'll line the streets with flags, like they did when we left. People will cheer. Penelope will be waiting on the quayside with the baby in her arms. I'll be holding her the moment my feet touch land. We'll walk up to the big house together . . . she'll line the servants up outside. We'll give thanks, pour an offering . . . Eumaeus, my farmer, he'll be herding stock down to the kitchen to be slaughtered for the feast. Five tables . . . no, ten, I'll invite everyone on the island. My crew as guests of honor, their families hanging on their necks. In years to come people will call them "The Fighters of Troy." And while the feast is preparing, I'll go up to the shrine and make an offering to the goddess to care for the soul of Laocoon.'"

Odysseus looked down at his hands suddenly. There was a silence. "So why's he just looking at me?" he said at last. "Looking without saying anything, his grim, white face with the bloodstain on his jaw. Then he opens his mouth. 'When you return to Ithaca, you'll be alone,' he says. 'You'll arrive in a strange ship. No one will know you. Your crew will be dead. Your home will be full of strangers. Your wealth will be gone. Your wife will be surrounded by admirers, and your son won't recognize you. He'll be sixteen years old, by the way. Not a baby, a man. Good luck, Odysseus.' And he's gone."

Odysseus swallowed. "Walked away, leaving me kneeling in the mud gasping. I don't know what to say. My mind won't grasp what he's told me. Then a voice brings me back to myself. I look up. It's my mother. I didn't know she was dead. 'Odysseus,' she says, and stretches out her hand to me. She takes the goat's blood and drinks. 'My boy.' She's crying. So am I. 'How did you die?' 'Of a broken heart,' she says, 'when you didn't come home.' Then I try to embrace her but it's like hugging fog, it's like the moment when you wake up and a dream slips away before you can clutch it. And she just looks at me. 'What's happening on Ithaca?' I ask. 'Go and find out.' 'Does Penelope still want me?' 'How can I tell?' 'What's my son like?' 'A fine boy,' she says. 'A fine boy. He'll be a fine man if they don't kill him first.' 'Who? Who will kill him?' But she's gone too. Now I'm looking around, and there are people pressing right up to me. Faces I know. Agamemnon, leader of the Greeks, my captain, standing there on the dead shore with his arms hanging useless by his sides, all the flesh melted off his face, the light gone from his eyes. 'By the gods, are you here too? But why?' I'm still kneeling in the mud. 'Who killed you? A fight on the way home?' He drinks the blood, then speaks. 'It wasn't the war,' he said. 'Nor the journey. It was the homecoming killed me. You think war's hard? Life's harder. My wife, Clytemnestra, and her lover slaughtered me in my bath. Slaughtered me like a pig,' he said. 'Blood overflowing the bath's rim, the last thing my living eyes saw was her face staring at me. The look in her eyes was harder to take than the knife's thrust.' 'What about my wife?' I asked. 'Penelope—what did you hear from Ithaca before you died?' But he shakes his head and turns away. Agamemnon, a dead soul. 'Is this where we all end up?' I shouted after him. No one shouted on that plain. My voice made the mist eddy, the ghosts with it. One of the crew puts his frightened face above the gunwale and calls, 'Come on, Chief, we have to leave.' When I stand up, though, they're pressing in on me. All the ghosts of all the dead. Hercules, Jason, Achilles . . . the stories don't make them immortal, I can tell you. Dead souls on a dark plain. I drew my sword. Its glitter was the only light in that dark place. They drew back just enough for me to leap on board. 'Cast off!' And we're drifting again across that misty ocean. Past the rock with the gull still on it. Out to sea, and the crew is staring at me. 'What did he say?' they ask. 'What's in store for us?' Eager faces, apprehensive. Doomed. I knew they'd never see home again. Laocoon told me.

"'We're going to make it,' I say. 'Home to Ithaca.' 'All of us?' 'All of us.' And they dip their oars and start to row.

"After a time I'm nodding off at the steering oar, and when I wake up . . ." He looked around at his audience. "When I wake up I'm back in Circe's house."

He sighed. There was a pause. Alcinous reached forward and filled Odysseus's cup, but Odysseus ignored it.

"We buried Elpenor, as he'd asked. Prepared meat for the journey, baked hard bread and filled barrels with water. It took three days to get ready. Meanwhile Circe was telling me all she knew about the islands nearby, warning me of a current here, a whirlpool there. She didn't know much. We left at night so I could steer by the polestar. 'Good luck,' she called. 'You'll need it.'"

Odysseus sighed. "I won't weary you with all the details of our voyage. Fog and storm, rocks and shoals. One island Circe had warned me of. An island of women. Sirens, she called them, with voices so sweet that any man who heard them would do anything on earth to reach them. Hurl himself overboard if need be. I heard them faintly one night, while the crew was sleeping. I knew what to do. Woke the crew, melted wax, and poured it in their ears. Then made them tie me to the mast. When dawn came we could see the island to the south. No sign of a house. You'd think it deserted if it wasn't for those voices floating across the water. If gold was a sound, if sunrise was a note, if good wine was something you could hear . . . that's how it was. Their song was like breath—you knew you'd die if you couldn't suck in another note, suffocate because you could no more survive without air than live a second without the sirens' song. The crew was rowing. I begged them to stop. They didn't hear a word, of course. I screamed at them, they tightened my ropes. Then set to their oars and rowed us away 'til the island had dropped below the horizon and the sound was lost in waves.

"Another island, we were trapped ashore a month, the waves flowing by outside the cove, a foul wind. The crew mutinied. 'Eleven years,' they said. And it was, by then. 'We've fought for you, died for you, followed you through thick and thin. Where does it end?' They'd never lost faith in me before. Some of them wanted to leave me stranded there and sail on without me. It took all my persuasion to bring them around. Then there were straits whose currents held us back a week. We nearly wrecked ourselves on some jagged rocks underwater, beached the ship to repair damage, sailed on. But not for long." He shook his head. "Not long before the final storm hit us. The gods know where we were. I didn't. Far out at sea, and the sky turns copper, the waves start to heave. We know there's something dirty coming, so we do what we can, double up rigging, tie down everything that moves. Braid up the sail tight and wait for it to hit." Odysseus looked at Alcinous. "It hit all right. Whistling across the water and laying us flat. Waves as tall as houses, solid as rock, slamming into us one by one. I saw men washed overboard, saw them clinging on, and the sea picking them off one by one, as if it hated men.

"It's the noise that shore people don't understand. That roaring that stops you thinking, and your eyes blinded by spray. Can't see, can't hear and the waves slamming into us. One tore away half the gunwale, and another knocked us down. I thought I was drowned then. I was underwater, rope twisted around one leg. When we came up I was clinging to the mast, so I started to climb. Clung to the masthead and looked down on the sea. The ship, what was left of it, submerged in foam. Not another soul left alive. I had a rope with me, strapped myself to the mast, two turns 'round my waist. I remember making the end fast, then feeling the mast crack under me, and that was the last thing I knew.

"I woke up lying on a beach. I don't know how long after. I don't know how I survived the storm. Waves sucking at my feet as if they were sorry they'd given me up. White sand, a fringe of palm trees, the ribs of a boat buried in sand, and two men standing over me in turbans. There were footprints in the sand all around me. People had been watching as I slept. One of the men stooped. 'The mistress said to take you to the house.' They were stronger than they looked. An arm 'round each shoulder, they dragged me to the trees, where they had a vehicle waiting, wheels like a cart and a wicker roof over it. They took the yoke themselves and pulled me up a well-paved road. Steeply up—the trees dropped down, I could see the sea stretching far away and then, high above, perched on a crag, her house . . ."

Odysseus paused, closing his eyes. "Calypso's house." It was a moment before he went on. "She was waiting on the terrace. As beautiful as Helen herself. They laid me on a couch and she was on her knees beside me. 'Poor man!' Tears in her eyes. Lifts a goblet to my lips, spiced wine, I drink. Her fingers supporting my head. 'All in one piece, I hope,' and she's feeling for broken bones. She bathed me herself, in a stone bath steaming with herbs. Massaged my back, my scalp. I wanted to get out, she splayed her fingers on my chest. 'No hurry!' she said. I'd already drunk her poison. She dressed me in silk. Back on the terrace there was a table laid, with candelabra, food, and the servants waiting. It was dark by then, the moon an arc of silver, a little wind tugging at the candle flames. 'Come and see my view,' she says, and takes me to the balustrade. I've never seen such a sight. The sea shining silver under the moonlight, islands studding it like jewels on a bracelet. 'It *is* special, isn't it?' she said. 'I knew you'd love it.' Five years." Odysseus closed his eyes. "Five years, I stayed there . . ."

"Five *years*?" Alcinous was frowning.

Arete said, "Did you never think of your wife? Your son?"

Odysseus opened his eyes, looking at her, then shook his head. "She drugged me. She was an enchantress, fooled me with a charmed life. Evenings on the terrace, mornings asleep. Picnics on the mountainside with the servants unpacking hampers. The house had courtyards with fountains in them, a room paneled with scented wood where we sat in winter around a little fire. Gardens, orchards . . . Five years rolled by like five days." He shook his head. "Then one day I fell sick; not bad, a fever. For a week I refused her wine. The last night I dreamed of Ithaca. Penelope was there, waving me good-bye. I wasn't on the ship, I seemed to be flying, but she grew smaller and smaller. When I woke up, my face was wet with tears. 'You had a nightmare,' Calypso said. 'Tell me what you dreamed and it won't come true.' I didn't tell her. I kept the thought of Penelope to myself even while her drugs fuddled my wits again. Clung to that figure waving me good-bye, and at night, when Calypso lay asleep beside me, I started to build Ithaca around it: the quayside on which Penelope stood, the harbor wall and town, the roofs of my house and the mountainside. My father, Laertes. There was an old man who looked after my pigs. I remembered his name, Eumaeus. The nurse . . . it took me a week to bring back her name, Eurycleia. And my son. I had no face for him—I never saw him. But I knew his name, *Telemachus.*

"Calypso knew I'd changed. She mixed her wine stronger. I left all I could, and when she was asleep, stuck my fingers down my throat to make myself sick. I started going for walks down to the beach. She had the servants follow me. I stood in the surf, staring at the horizon that surrounded Ithaca. Sometimes I thought, *I'll just swim out to sea. Maybe I'll reach Ithaca. Maybe I'll drown.* Eventually I went to Calypso. I told her about my wife, my child. I thought she'd scream at me." He shook his head. "Do you know what she said? Put a hand on my cheek, 'But of *course* you must go,' she said. 'Any time you like . . .'" He paused. "Not a boat on the island. As she knew. I was her prisoner as sure as if she'd locked me in chains. One day I found an old barrel sunk in the sand, swept overboard from some wreck. I thought, *I'll build a raft.* I began to gather driftwood, planks and old crates. Tore creeper from the trees to tie them together. Two rafts she burned, Calypso the enchantress. I hated her, by then. And feared her. And I couldn't . . . leave . . ."

Odysseus heaved a great sob and buried his face in his hands. No one spoke. At last he straightened himself up, wiping tears from his eyes. "But I did, though. In the end. Pushed out to sea and paddled away. I could see their torches through the palm trees as they hunted me, but there was no moon—I'd chosen that night carefully. The terrace blazing with lights that shone back at me from the inky water. And the current slowly took me away. When the sun came up I was alone on the sea, no land in sight." He sighed. "And there I drifted for sixteen days, sometimes paddling, sometimes not, sucking dew from my coat, trailing a line for fish. At night I lay on my back and stared at the stars. I wondered if people on Ithaca were watching the stars. That was all I thought about—that Ithaca I'd built in my head. In my mind, I wandered along every path, counted every stone in the wall of my house. I couldn't remember why I had ever left." He frowned like a puzzled child. "Why would anyone leave Penelope? How had I gotten there? To that raft on an empty sea? I lay on my back and watched the stars. The Hyades and Pleiades, Cassiopeia and the Bear. Days went by. Brine filled my mouth, soaked my beard. The sun burned my skin black. My food ran out, my water. I could feel my tongue filling my mouth, swollen as a rotten fruit. The raft started to come apart, ropes creaking under my back. It felt like my body was coming apart too, sinews stretched, skin decaying. I thought, *When the ropes give, I'll float on the waves like I'm a raft myself.* Flesh bloated and white like a dead fish. My face like a mask on the water, spray foaming through my eyes and mouth.

"Then, one night, I felt the raft lift to a wave, and knew the last storm had come. A raft of driftwood tied with creeper—I didn't have a chance. To be honest with you, I hardly cared by then. I lay on my back and watched the stars. Stars I'd seen from the mountaintop on Ithaca. Stars I'd watched from the camp at Troy . . ."

Odysseus didn't talk for a long time. Everyone watched him. Then he raised his head again. "But the storm didn't kill me," he said. "It landed me on your island. And here I am."

11

Arete tried not to worry too much about Nausicaa. Her daughter had fallen in love before—quite often, in fact. Arete had been bothered when Nausicaa had spent the entire day in the courtyard with the stranger. She didn't like the way he had allowed the girl to bring him trays of food and comb his hair—that, she thought, was irresponsible in a man his age. Although she didn't go as far as her husband in disapproving of fighting men, she shared his view that they were violent, self-centered, and destructive, and she certainly didn't want Nausicaa running off with one.

But she had faith in her daughter's essential good sense. Romantic she might have been, fond of stories, given to passionate enthusiasms and wintry sulks; but fundamentally she was a sensible Phaeacian girl growing up on a small island, princess of her little kingdom but utterly inexperienced in the world beyond its shores. That storm-tossed world—the world of fighters—was not for her, and deep down she knew it.

The arrival of that world, in the form of Odysseus, was troublesome. Like Alcinous, she had seen the stranger's charisma working on the inexperienced Phaeacians. His moody stare, his bunched shoulders and balled fists, the jut of his beard and tilt of his chin as he'd glowered around the hall: they had responded to them like small dogs when a wolf stalks into their kennel. He was bigger than anyone there. They knew it. He knew it. Alcinous, too, knew it, which was why he was so keen to get Odysseus off the island.

When he'd begun his tale—his wholly ridiculous story of witches, demons, giants, dead souls, and the rest—Arete had felt his charisma herself. Of course she knew it was all nonsense. She had seen enough of the world, before her marriage, to have come across fighters before, with their tales of gargantuan slaughter and impossible trials, storms that emptied the sea, battles that filled rivers with blood. Heroic exaggeration was their stock-in-trade. She had even heard the tale of irresistible singers—"sirens"—before, from a Hittite captain who'd sworn it had happened to his brother. Fighting men were all guilty of boasting. It was normal to them, a kind of game. Only the small-town Phaeacians fell for such yarns.

She didn't. She had felt the tug of Odysseus's voice, though. Felt the pull of those murmured words, words spoken so softly they might have been meant only for himself, except that they coiled around you and drew you in. That was how the magic worked. Suddenly you felt the salt spray on your cheek, the thump of fear in your own breast. Suddenly you were *there* with him, clinging to the raft, rigid with fear as the cold ghosts slipped past you. That was what a talking man could do, and the magic of his words had worked on her too.

At a certain moment, though, Arete had begun to feel something else, something more detached. She had become aware, as if she'd been standing beside herself, watching, of Nausicaa's spellbound awe, of her husband's frown of concentration. Odysseus's words had flowed on, rising and falling like breakers on sand. But Arete had suddenly understood what it was she really felt for him, beyond her suspicion of his kind and her fascination for his tale.

Pity.

Arete knew men. She had grown up with brothers, raised many sons. She knew all the captains and merchants, sailors and navigators who dined at their table, put up with their boasting, laughed at their jokes. She was something of a mother figure to them. So she knew that Odysseus, behind that scarred exterior, behind the tumble of his words, was horribly damaged. She had seen the spear he had thrown and the spilled wine spattering the wall. She had heard, too, the cry of pain his throw had torn from him. He was hurt, and not only in his body. Something, she sensed, was cracked in him. To Phaeacians he still looked like a fighter. But she wondered what other fighters would make of him. To them, everything was about status. Odysseus had lost his ships, his men, his home. Would they even recognize the hero who conquered Troy? Would they see him in this bowed man with grey hair and lined face, this old man hobbling across their courtyard with his puzzled eyes and the leg that couldn't carry his weight? His boastful, silly stories had made his lost years sound like an adventure. Read between the lines, though, and they told a story of disaster, of bungled raids and bad seamanship, of misfortune that had ripped away everything he cared for and left him, at the last, drifting naked on a raft, without company or possessions, broken.

Arete didn't much like their guest. But she did feel sorry for him.

He had finished talking, but no one spoke. Nausicaa had tears in her eyes. Alcinous looked thoughtful. It was left to her to reach out and take their guest's hand.

"I'm sorry," Arete said. "I'm so, so sorry."

The puzzled eyes turned toward her. He seemed more hunched than ever, as if, in retelling his tale, he had relived it physically as well. Odysseus clutched her hand and gave a sob. His hand was rough as sandpaper, calloused and warped, as if the sea had bleached all the softness from it. Arete was reminded of the salt fish the merchants dried for long voyages, hanging fillets in the sun until they looked like scraps of leather. His cheek felt the same when he pressed her hand against it. Once it must have been soft, she supposed, beneath Penelope's touch. No more. If he ever reached home, would his wife recognize him? And if she did, would she even want this wreck of the man who sailed away sixteen years before?

Arete hoped so. She wondered what she would have felt if Alcinous had disappeared and returned like this. Not, of course, that her husband would ever go off to war, or seek adventure—he was far too sensible. But she knew she would have wanted him back, whatever his state. She hoped Penelope was the same.

She felt dry, sore lips press against the back of her hand. Odysseus looked up at her, tears welling from his eyes.

"I've failed them," he said. It was as if he'd been speaking to her alone.

"Who?"

"Penelope. Telemachus."

"You've done what men do." She glanced at her husband. "Some men."

"It was wrong to leave them. Wrong to go to war. Wrong to spend so many years on the journey home."

"I thought bad fortune kept you away?"

He looked down. "I could have reached Ithaca if I'd tried. I'd have broken any enchantment. That's the truth. Now all I want is to go home."

He gripped her hand so hard Arete almost winced. "You can't be sure what you'll find there. Remember what Laocoon said." She didn't want to hurt him, but it was better he faced reality now. "Penelope may be with another man. Your son may have left home. He may be dead. You haven't been in Ithaca for sixteen years."

"It would be sensible . . ." Alcinous cleared his throat. ". . . to find out what's happening there before you go back."

Arete felt hot tears on her hand, and she reached up and touched Odysseus's face. "What will you do if you find her changed?"

It was a moment before he answered, and when he did, Arete could hear the depths of weariness in his voice. "I'll go in disguise, at first. If they've forgotten me, I'll travel on. I'm no coward. I can fight for some chief. I could be a sailor." He wiped his eyes with the back of one hand. "What does it matter what happens if Penelope doesn't want me? I'll live out my days fishing on some island. I'll dream about Telemachus, dream about Penelope. Or I'll become a servant and sweep the courtyard in a great man's house. In the evenings I'll crouch by the fire and hear them tell stories about Odysseus . . ."

The firelight flickered on the sides of the hearth. With infinite compassion, Arete watched it play over Odysseus's ravaged face, scour the furrows in his cheeks, burnish his silvered hair.

"I never deserved them," Odysseus whispered. "I see that now. My wife, my son. All I want is one more chance." He gripped her hand again, squeezing the fingers. "Please help me. Please help me to go home."

Arete glanced at her husband. He looked almost noble, she thought, in the firelight. The good, sensible man she had married.

Alcinous leaned forward and laid his hand on the fighter's shoulder. "Of course we'll help you," he said. "We're preparing a ship now. To take you home to Ithaca."

I n the great hall at Ithaca, Antinous took a draft of wine
and closed his eyes.

He was troubled. Not badly troubled—things were not
out of control. But badly enough to swear at a servant who
was trying to clear the table around him, and to follow up the
curse with a vicious slash of his table knife, which the servant
only just escaped.

It was annoying to have been up all night. It was annoying to
be unshaven—he hated being unshaven. It was annoying to be
in dirty clothes and feel limp, sweaty cloth, when he was used
to crisp linen. Most of all, it was annoying that Telemachus
had still not returned.

He should have been here by now. Antinous's breakfast should have been a celebration and a chance to plan next moves. Instead, getting rid of the woman's brat remained unfinished business.

Antinous stabbed moodily at his eggs. They weren't quite runny enough. Or maybe too firm, one or the other. Either way, they weren't as eggs should be. For a moment he considered running into the kitchen to beat Melanthius, which would have offered some pleasure. But somehow, Antinous knew, his irritation ran too deep to be assuaged by beating an old cook. He needed bigger prey.

"What are you staring at?" There was a young man crossing the hall. Antinous couldn't remember his name.

"I . . ." The young man looked around with a start. "I wasn't staring."

Antinous looked coldly at him. "You were staring."

"I wasn't, I . . ."

"Are you calling me a liar?"

"No!"

"Then you were staring."

"I wasn't . . ."

"So I'm a liar?"

"No!"

"So what," Antinous said, the words icy, "were you staring at?"

The young man looked around the hall. There were two or three others about, but all of them seemed occupied by something else. He swallowed.

"I didn't mean any offense."

Antinous pushed back his chair. He had worked himself into a fine rage now. A fine, cold, bloody rage. The young man had been staring. Insolently. It was about respect. He needed to be taught a lesson. Antinous felt a familiar thrill of excitement and cruelty swelling inside him as he stood up. This was power. This was control, again. This had the doubts in his mind scurrying back into the shadows, as scared of him as everybody else was.

He pressed right up to the young man's chest, breathing in the odor of fear. The young man took a step back. His eyes were wide and his lips moist, hanging slightly open. He was caught between two cruelties: the iron law that told him he mustn't retreat, and his terror of Antinous.

"I . . ."

Antinous grabbed the young man's chest, bunching his shirt in both fists, and threw him backward. He slammed against a column, his head snapping back against the stone. There was no fight in him. Antinous felt a moment almost of disappointment. Why wouldn't someone fight back? Why wouldn't they hurt him in turn? Now all he could do was stamp out his rage in blood. He pulled out his sword and swiped it sideways against his victim's lolling head. The young man gave a scream of agony, and blood spurted across the floor from his cheek. Antinous clutched at his hair and banged his head back against the column, again and again. He was so intent on what he was doing, so furious in his just rage, that he didn't realize, at first, that someone was pulling at his arm.

Antinous closed his eyes, trembling and quivering. Suddenly his hand hurt. His eyes filled with tears. It was so unfair.

"Antinous." He felt his arm shaken again and looked up. It was Eurymachus, the man he hated most in all the world, his rival. He looked down at the floor, where the young stranger's body lay hunched in a pool of blood.

"There's blood on my sleeve," he said wonderingly, looking at the fine silk spattered with dark spots. In a sudden rage he kicked the young man's body.

"Antinous." Eurymachus shook his arm again.

"I'm hungry."

"Have some bread." Eurymachus's voice was soothing, the way he'd talk to a dog he feared. Antinous liked that. It was a kind of respect. He sat down and took the bread Eurymachus held out.

"Too little salt," he said in his most unctuous voice. "If I've told Melanthius once, I've told him a hundred times. Seasoning is his greatest fault. The chicken last night . . ."

"Never mind that now." Eurymachus's handsome, doglike eyes were screwed up with concern.

"What's happened?" Antinous said in a more normal voice.

"Nothing's happened. Did he come?"

"No."

Eurymachus blew out a long, slow breath. "You're sure?"

"Of course I'm sure," Antinous snapped. But he had run out of anger. "We waited all night. Again."

"Are you sure this is the best way? Telemachus isn't a fool."

"He's a child." Antinous plucked moodily at his ruined gown. "We should have gotten rid of him before. Everyone knows we're waiting now. The island knows. The people. You know they hate us." Antinous brooded, his face lowered into the rolls of fat under his chin. "Ever since that meeting. They'd hang us from every damned tree if they had an excuse."

"Perhaps we should wait 'til after Telemachus comes back," Eurymachus said.

"No," Antinous said thickly, his head dangling. He was exhausted now, as he always was after violence. "It's better off the way we planned it. We wait on that island offshore . . ."

"Asteris."

"As soon as his ship appears, we seize it, night or day. Drown the crew. Kill Telemachus."

"Whatever you think best." Eurymachus was suddenly aware that Antinous was watching him, his piggy little eyes swiveled upward from his lowered face. He knew how dangerous

Antinous was, perhaps the most dangerous man he had ever met.

"And then?" Antinous said.

Eurymachus forced his own face into a bland smile. "And then," he said, "we discuss the future calmly and rationally. We give Penelope time to make her choice . . ." He listened to his own voice lilting blandly up and down. He would kill Antinous, he decided. Kill him first of all. It was too risky to leave him alive. Antinous was probably reaching the same decision about him. As Eurymachus calculated, he outlined councils, envoys, a sequence of meetings. "The important thing," he finished, "is not to fight among ourselves." He put his hand on Antinous's cold forearm and gave it a squeeze. "Friends?" he said.

A movement behind them made him look around. Medon, the old servant, was staring distrustfully at them.

"The mistress wants to see you."

Eurymachus glanced at the young man's body still splayed against the column. "Not here."

He dragged Antinous to his feet, and they hurried out into the hot courtyard. They met Penelope coming down the stairs. Eurymachus was astonished to see her outside her room—she hadn't left it since Telemachus's departure. Medon had slept across the threshold like a loyal dog.

Penelope was dressed in immaculate white, her hair bound up in a gold ribbon. She held her chin high, as if something was balanced on her head. She looked every inch a chief's wife—except that when he looked down, he saw that her feet were bare.

Eurycleia, the nurse, was behind her.

"I have something to say to you." Penelope's voice was clear and high, but suddenly it quavered, and she frowned like a little girl. "I can't remember it," she said.

Eurycleia leaned forward and whispered in her ear. Penelope blinked. "About my son, Telemachus," she resumed in the same clear voice, as if she was reciting a poem learned by heart. "You're waiting for him in a ship. You're going to kill my son. To kill him . . . to kill . . . him." Eurycleia put a soothing hand on Penelope's shoulder. Penelope clutched it and sobbed, her eyes filling with tears.

"*No!*" Eurymachus's voice throbbed. "Who told you this? I *love* Telemachus." Eurymachus glanced at Antinous, who was standing in a kind of stupor. So much the better—this was a chance for him. He advanced up the stairs toward Penelope and lowered his voice to a confidential murmur. "To me, Telemachus is like a brother. If anyone tried to hurt him, they'd have an enemy for life. *Kill* him? I'd hunt them down. Telemachus is my companion, my friend. He's the child . . ." He glanced over his shoulder and dropped his voice. "The child of the person I care for most in the world." He took Penelope's hand, but she snatched it away as if he'd bitten it.

"They want to kill him," she repeated. "They're waiting in a ship."

"Who told you this?"

"I know."

"Penelope." Eurymachus took her hand again and shook it. "Listen to me . . . I will never lay a finger on Telemachus." He stared into her eyes until they were caught. "That's a promise. Yes? You believe me?" His large, appealing eyes crinkled with emotion. Afterward, when Telemachus was dead, he would tell her Antinous was responsible. Things couldn't have worked out better. "I will—never—hurt—Telemachus," he said. "That's a promise." He raised her hands to his lips and kissed them.

From behind him, Eurymachus heard Antinous clear his throat. "A promise," he repeated solemnly.

F rom the fence above his pigpen, Eumaeus, the farmer, looked down on the roofs of Ithaca's big house and spat copiously into the mud.

The pigpen stood on a rise above the house. He could see into its courtyard. He could even smell whatever it was they were cooking. Meat, maybe even pork, but not one of his pigs— not likely. The day before, when two of the young visitors had come to take a porker, he had seen them off with dogs. The old man gathered saliva in his mouth and spat again, with some satisfaction. Spitting was the only way he could express his feelings about the big house and everyone in it.

The old sow came snuffling around the gob of spittle in the mud. Eumaeus reached over the fence to scratch her between the ears.

Not everyone in it. Not Penelope, of course. Nor Eurycleia, the nurse. Annoying old cow though she was—bossy, haughty, and disdainful of men with dirty hands and pig shit on their boots—she was still loyal to the mistress, and to Telemachus. Eumaeus sighed. He liked Telemachus and would do all he could, for the master's sake, but he had doubts enough to make him sigh. The boy was good-hearted; he was clever, maybe even cleverer than Odysseus—although that would be saying something. But he had been dealt a tough hand. Father gone, mother available, home overrun with phony guests, and no one to teach him how to fight. That was enough to overwhelm any young man. And besides all that, Eumaeus had a suspicion—a nagging worry—that Telemachus was soft.

He had done well in the town meeting, though. Eumaeus had to admit that. Stood up to them, fought his corner, blinked back the tears. He'd been proud of him then, given him his vote, of course, and smacked some young fools who bad-mouthed him in the tavern afterward. That was the worst thing about what was happening in Ithaca—he could feel the island turning bad. The rot in the big house was bound to spread. You could sense it even walking through the town, a growing discontent. Boys pushed ahead of you into the tavern, lounged on the harbor wall, didn't work. He saw old men going out to fish alone, their sons refusing to come. That had never happened in the old days. The old man sighed and spat again, with venom.

So Telemachus had sailed away, just as his father had, and not come back. And maybe wouldn't come back. He had heard, as most people had, what the young men in the big house were planning. There was always that sense of threat hanging over Ithaca now. Young men with swords, young men with spears.

A town boy had been killed just the week before. One day, Eumaeus supposed, they would come for him—they knew what he thought of them—but he was ready enough, ready with his dogs. Let them come. He was an old man, and angry, and he didn't care what happened to him now that Odysseus was gone.

Only the thought of Penelope gave him pause. Eumaeus loved Penelope. Loved her with utter devotion—would have thrust his hand into fire if she'd ordered it. With Laertes dead, Penelope was all that was left of the old times before his master sailed away. It broke Eumaeus's heart that she might end up married to one of the louts in the big house. And what would become of Ithaca then? Fighting, he was sure of that. A small party defending Telemachus's interests—they wouldn't last long. Rivalries between young fighters. Neighbors waiting to snap up Ithaca as soon as the fires began to burn. He knew what could happen. He had gone out into the world and seen fighting as a young man before he'd taken on the care of Odysseus's pigs. He still woke up at night, sometimes, remembering the things he'd seen: the broken gates and fallen roofs, the wrecked fishing boats strewn along the shore. He knew what happened when people stopped trusting each other, closed the shutters, unwrapped the rusting weapons their grandfathers had buried under the floor. He knew what a broken town looked like.

Eumaeus heard a sound from somewhere behind him. He turned heavily—he was no longer as mobile as he had once been. A stooped figure was making its way down the path from the mountain. Not many came from that direction, but he could guess where the man must be from. Early that morning he had walked the dogs up the mountain path, and from the top, looking down onto the west, the wilder side of the island, he had seen a Phaeacian ship beached in the cove. He knew she was Phaeacian by the purple sails the crew had hung in the sun to dry. He had wondered why she hadn't gone around to the harbor. This man had to be one of her sailors.

Eumaeus shielded his eyes against the morning glare and watched the man approach. He walked slowly, limping. An old man, then. Eumaeus could tell he was old from his hunched back. His face was lined as well, Eumaeus saw as he came closer, and his hair was a tangle of grey. A thick beard covered his face. Not a sailor, if he knew anything, and certainly not the ship's captain. He spat scornfully into the mud at his feet. More like a tramp.

One of the dogs at his feet gave a low, rumbling growl.

"Go on, boy," Eumaeus whispered.

The dogs were off: the big black dog, the bitch—smaller but nastier in temper—and the grey creature, half wolf, that he had found and reared. They surged around the tramp, who at least had the good sense not to run away. He stopped dead, waiting while the dogs snapped and snarled, nipping at the hem of his ragged coat. Eumaeus let them have their play for a moment before calling, "All right, then, let 'im come on."

He kicked playfully at the big black one as they slunk away, and he stooped to tug at the wiry grey fur of the half wolf. The tramp stepped slowly forward, his right leg trailing.

"What dus 'e want?"

"I am a stranger here. I ask for a guest's welcome." The tramp's eyes were startlingly blue.

"Dus 'e, now?" Eumaeus spat in the mud, contemplating the hunched figure in front of him. He sighed. "Then I s'pose 'e better come inside, 'asn't 'e? Which is 'ow soft I am."

He led the way across a muddy courtyard surrounded with prickly pear. Its deep ruts had hardened to a crust of mud. Broken barrows and pieces of fencing lay in piles, along with wagons that had lost their wheels, a dung heap under a cloud of flies, and a hayrick on a pole stuck drunkenly in the ground. The hut itself was low and misshapen, the two windows onto the courtyard uneven, the roof crooked. Inside, it was pitch dark after the hot sunlight. The back wall was cut from the living rock, with a hearth of rough stones on which smoked a fire of olive wood. There was a table down the middle, and the old man's bed, a pile of greasy sheepskin, lay in one corner. Hams and loops of sausages hung from the roof, and the hut smelled strongly of pig. Of dead pig, in fact—the carcass of a porker, throat gaping, hung from one of the beams over a wooden bucket brimming with bright crimson blood.

"I'll cook 'er for yer, seein' yer a guest. I gutted 'er already." Eumaeus snatched the porker down from its hook, skewered the pink carcass expertly on a long bronze spit, and set it on two metal cradles on either side of the fire. In a moment the skin began to blister and spit. Pig grease dripped into the flames, spluttering and filling the low hut with the stench of burned meat.

"Won't take more'n an hour. I'd have the boy turn it, but I sent 'im to town. Bit o' burn won't hurt." He gave the spit a deft quarter turn and the porker's feet swung upward toward the ceiling. "Nor will a bit o' wet. I 'spose you need a bit o' wet after yer journey." Eumaeus went to some shelves hacked crudely into the walls and pulled down an old goatskin worn shiny on both sides. He turned to see his visitor still standing in the doorway.

"Sit down, won't yer?" he blazed angrily. "Yer wants to be a guest, yer can be a flippin' guest. Sit down."

He banged two rough pottery cups onto the table, a blackened and filthy plank propped up on trestles in the center of the room, and filled them with wine from the neck of the skin. "'E won't like it," he commented, shoving one of the cups toward the guest. "I makes it myself."

The guest took the cup and drank. "It's good," he said.

"Then 'e's drunk some rank filth on 'is travels, is all I can say. Lived even rougher'n 'e looks. 'Ave some bread." Eumaeus pulled over the rump of a huge, stale loaf, more brown than white, wiped his bloodied slaughtering knife on a cloth, and hacked off two crooked slices. "Week old," he said proudly. "Yer needs all yer teeth to get through that. I'd give 'im oil to dip it in, but I ain't got much, and yer ain't worth it."

The stranger, too occupied in chewing the dry bread to speak, nodded his thanks.

"See?" Eumaeus said happily. "'E'll be a week on that slice."

The guest swallowed and coughed. "It's good," he said weakly.

"Good if 'e's a moth-eaten ol' tramp who don't see food more'n once a fortnight. Meat'll be ready in a while, an' I bet it's the first 'e's tasted in a year, which is 'ow soft I am." Reaching out one mud-caked boot, he kicked the spit around another quarter turn. The porker's ear flopped sideways, sizzling in the flames. "Who is 'e, then?" he asked. "Where's 'e come from? Tell us yer story."

The stranger took a deep breath. "I come from Crete," he said.

"Crete?"

"Crete. The island."

Eumaeus nodded. "Go on, then."

"I come from Crete," the stranger began again. "My father was rich, but I was not his true son . . ."

"Bastard, then," Eumaeus put in. "We calls a spade a spade, round 'ere."

The stranger looked at him through his puzzled old eyes. "A bastard," he agreed.

Eumaeus nodded happily and prodded the porker around another quarter turn. "Get on with it. We ain't got all day."

"I had no land of my own so I became a traveler, a soldier of fortune . . ."

"Mercenary," said Eumaeus, frowning. "Tricky buggers, mercenaries."

". . . which is how I reached Troy, fought in the war, and *then* . . ." said the stranger, speaking faster because he could see Eumaeus was about to interrupt again, "set off on my travels. I won't recount them all. I made a fortune in Egypt. I was shipwrecked . . . a lightning strike at sea, sail gone, mast gone, half the crew dead. I won't tire you with all the troubles I've seen, the miles I've tramped, the ports I've washed up in. A month ago I reached Kythera. I sailed from there on a Lastragonian ship."

"A Lastragonian ship." Eumaeus frowned. Suddenly he shoved back his bench and looked under the table at his visitor's feet. He gave them a long, hard stare, then straightened up, leaned forward with his hands on his knees, and stared unblinking into the guest's face.

His visitor pushed his chair uneasily back from the table. "That is my story," he said. "Now tell me about Ithaca. Who is the chief here?"

"Odysseus—everyone knows that. 'Cept 'e ain't 'ere. Everyone knows that too. 'E's missin'."

The visitor's eyes narrowed. "Do you have any news of him?"

The old man simply shook his head.

"What do you think happened to him?"

"I say 'e's dead," the old man growled. "What else would keep 'im away from 'is 'ome? Dead, like as not. Or dead near as can be, which is to say, 'e can't walk, or 'is back's broken, or 'e's captive in a dungeon somewhere, or they made 'im slave and sold 'im to the 'airy folk as live out east, either way 'e ain't 'ere, is 'e?" And Eumaeus looked around the hut as if to prove his point.

The old tramp's face was impassive. "What does his wife think?"

"Still waitin' for 'im, though I don't knows 'ow long. What is it? Cryin' now, is it? 'Ere."

He threw the bloodstained cloth at the stranger, who took it and pressed it to his face.

The stranger wiped his eyes, streaking the tears. "Does he have any children?"

"A boy. Telemachus."

"Tell me about him."

"'E's just a kid. Good 'eart. Clever, same as 'is dad. Soft, though. 'E never learnt to fight. No one to teach 'im, wiv his dad gone. Oh, don't start up again . . . what's wrong wiv 'im?" Eumaeus turned the spit angrily, and grease sizzled into the fire.

"What would happen," said the tramp, his voice trembling, "if Odysseus came back today?"

Eumaeus didn't answer for a moment. He leaned forward and prodded the porker with the tip of his knife, watching the juices run pink. Then he reached for the goatskin and filled their cups. The wine and the heat of the fire had turned his forehead scarlet.

"I don't know," he said slowly. "I used ter, once, but I don't knows anymore. I wish 'e ain't gone away, that's for sure. Then the big 'ouse wouldn't be full o' filthy buggers eatin' 'is pork, leastwise tryin' to eat it, what they comes 'ere, I tells 'em, 'Find yer own blasted pigs' . . . they don't likes it, but they don't like my dogs, neither. Sheep, though, they's barely a sheep left on the island. Oil, corn. Wine in the cellar, Medon tells me, 'One more month o' this, the chief comes 'ome, 'e'll be drinkin' water like a dirty beggar . . .'"

"Who are the men in the house?"

"Guests. Strangers. Flippin' vultures, I calls 'em. Arter Penelope, they is, to make 'er a new 'usband."

"Does she listen to them?"

"Not 'er. Not yet, anyways."

"Why don't the islanders stop them?"

"Why should they?" Sweat poured down the old man's craggy face. His voice was beginning to slur from the wine. "I thought they all loved Odysseus. Turns out I was wrong, don't it? Why should they love 'im wiv their 'usbands gone and their sons dead? I tells yer, I don't know nuthin' no more. I thought 'e was a good master, maybe I wuz wrong about that, too. I thinks about Odysseus now, all I remember is talk. I thinks, *'E leaves 'is wife, 'e leaves 'is son . . .*"

"He's sorry for that."

The old man stared at him, openmouthed. Then he suddenly blazed, "Oh, yer'd knows that, would yer? Yer'd knows what Odysseus thinks?"

"Eumaeus." The tramp rose to a crouch, clutching the old farmer's arm.

The old farmer snatched his arm away as if he had been burned. "'Ow does 'e know my name?"

"Because he told me about you. Eumaeus, I met Odysseus."

The pork sizzled on the fire. Hot, greasy smoke filled the hut. Eumaeus didn't react, to start with. He simply pushed the stranger away and nodded.

"Now we knows where we is, anyways," he said scornfully.

The stranger blinked. "Eumaeus?"

"D'yer know 'ow many types like you we 'as comin' 'ere to Ithaca?"

"What do you mean?" He sounded bewildered.

"'I bring a message from Odysseus' . . . any number o' those. 'I just seen 'im, 'e 'as a message for Penelope.' An' she swallers every word, fills their ragged little coats wiv gold. 'Stay as long as yer likes.' Easiest blasted story in the world, 'I saw Odysseus.'" Eumaeus snorted derisively and poured more wine from the skin. "Then we 'as Odysseus hisself, half a dozen on 'em. One even 'ad the scar on 'is thigh, cut it 'isself. 'I got it on my first boar 'unt,' 'e says. T'other one 'ad Odysseus's sword, 'e must 'a' nicked it. Gets 'is paws 'round Penelope, nearly fools all on us. 'E's 'alfway to 'er blasted bedroom, then I says, 'Since when did Odysseus 'ave a blasted Egyptian tattoo on 'is bum, greasy bugger.' We gets 'im, we toss 'im off the cliff behin' the big 'ouse, an' no doubts we'll end up doin' the same wiv youse."

The stranger stood up. "I'll go to Penelope myself. Now."

One of the dogs growled. "You ain't goin' nowheres," Eumaeus said quietly. "Yer'll stay 'ere where I can sees yer. Yer'll sleep in my corner wiv one dog on yer feet and t'other on yer blasted neck. Yer gets up in the night to take a leak, my dogs'll go wiv yer, an' if yer makes a run for it, they'll drag yer back by yer blasted little bangle." The old farmer's voice rose to a growl. "What I didn't ask for no guest but now yer 'ere, yer can stays 'til I knows 'oo the blazes yer are."

PART THREE

TELEMACHUS

14

I 've learned something about the timbers of a ship. They're not dead wood, like the planks of a table. You can feel the wind hum in them and the waves vibrate through them. Laying your hand on a gunwale or oar isn't like touching a door. It's more like placing your fingers against a pine tree quivering on a mountainside.

Right now I can feel the steering oar stiffen and relax beneath my hand. The sea, smooth and heavy as oil, barely ripples as we slip along. There's only just enough wind to sail by. The crew is asleep next to their oars. Above us, stars are unfurled across the sky like a field of night flowers. They're so bright I can see the sail's shape as a patch of starless sky, filling

179

and sagging above me. The rhythm of the deck under my feet has become second nature, like the creak of my own heart.

One day I'm going to learn the names of all the stars. I know the polestar, of course—I'm steering by it now, toward Ithaca. I know Orion and the Bear and Cassiopeia. Mentor taught me the sailors' stars, the Hyades and Pleiades. I know Andromeda, just below Cassiopeia, because Polycaste showed it to me two nights ago.

"Four bright stars in a row. Just above the horizon. And Perseus above her. Like a fork."

We both knew the legend. Andromeda boasted of her own beauty and was condemned by the sea god to be chained to a rock, where a monster would come and devour her. The fighter Perseus killed the monster and married her.

"Idiot," Polycaste said scornfully as we lay on the mountainside, the smell of pine resin mingling with the smoke of the fire on which we'd cooked our meal. It was the last night of our journey back from Sparta.

"Because she boasted about being beautiful?"

I heard the rustle of pine needles as she rolled over to look at me. "Because she needed help with the monster."

I miss Polycaste. Not just her scorn—although I miss that too. I miss her courage, her quick anger, her boldness. I'm going to need all of those on Ithaca. I miss her directness, her instant judgments and fierce opinions. I'm not like her. Me, I'm always putting myself in other people's shoes, seeing both sides of an argument, understanding people then making excuses for them. My instinct is to overthink, to put things into words, to rationalize . . . just like I'm doing now, because, of course, it isn't Polycaste's courage or directness I miss, it's just *her.*

When I lean my weight on the steering oar, the polestar swings back into view from behind the dark patch of sail. It's the scornful twist of her mouth I miss; the quick gesture with which she shakes back her hair; the ease with which, when she's washing her face in a mountain stream, she stoops to splash water up each bare arm. I miss the rustle of leaves as she turns over in her sleep. I miss her raucous, throaty laugh when something—usually some mistake on my part—amuses her.

She should be with me now, steering through the night. That's what we planned when we journeyed back from Sparta. But Nestor refused to let her go.

"We wish you good fortune in your return. I will give you a gold dish to place upon Odysseus's funeral pyre, as a mark of our old friendship . . . a *true* friendship—I cannot tell you how fond I was of your father, who hardly ever disagreed with my opinions. But then you must busy yourself with family matters . . . your mother . . . the government of Ithaca . . . decisions . . . Take it from one who has been making decisions for more decades than I choose to recall . . ."

But he did go on to recall them, of course—at length, burying the subject in mazy recollection, then pleading tiredness and going to bed. It wasn't hard to read between the lines. In Ithaca there's going to be a fight. He doesn't want his daughter caught up in it.

The morning I left, he came down to the beach to watch us board Mentor's ship. I took his hand as the waves hissed on the shingle behind us.

"You think I'm going to be killed," I said.

Nestor just looked at me, blinked his rheumy eyes, then nodded. "Yes," he said. "I do."

I didn't answer. After a moment Nestor went on, "You think me callous. I'm a hundred and ten years old—do you know how many men I've seen killed? Good men, kind men, friends. Soon I'll die myself. I long for it."

Polycaste raged on the terrace, but even she didn't dare disobey her father. For all that polish and old-world charm,

Nestor is quite as headstrong as his daughter. Polycaste and I said good-bye on the shore, alone, with a bear hug that slowly melted into something else. There's a kind of language in the way two bodies touch. A language in the squeeze of shoulder, chest and thigh, in the touch of fingers on each other's backs, in the strength of a grip that suddenly becomes soft and lasting. I felt a sudden heat beside me and knew Polycaste was crying. Then she pulled back, looking angrily away, like I'd done something wrong.

"You'll be fine," she said curtly. "Come and see me when it's over."

As I sailed out of the bay, I wondered if she was watching from the house. The empty space on the deck next to me felt more real than a presence. I could see the roof over the trees and the windows of the upper story. I nearly waved but stopped myself. If Polycaste was watching, she would have torn herself away from the window with a sneer.

I lean on the tiller again. A little wave clops against the hull. One of the sailors clears his throat and mutters in his sleep.

When I look back on it now, that short journey across the mountains feels like a lost paradise. If I'm killed—*when* I'm killed—at least I'll have had that. Nothing special was said or done, but we both felt a sense of freedom that seemed almost like an enchantment. The rest of the world—troubles, adults—might not have existed at all. Nothing existed except the two of us traveling through mountains that seemed to go on forever.

We left Sparta at dawn, with a faint mist still hanging over the little town and the mules stamping impatiently on the paved square outside the palace. Helen hadn't left her room since the day we arrived.

"Women's troubles," Menelaus said and gave me a greasy wink. I ignored him. Our last few days together, Menelaus had regained some of his bravado. He had taken us to see one of his vast warehouses, where rows of peasants were stacking harvested grain.

"My horses," he said, pointing to the stables on one side. "See? They are the fastest horses in Greece. One day perhaps you will have faster horses, but first you will have to kill me." He thought that was hilarious, slapped me on the back and roared with laughter.

On the day we left, though, he showed, just for a moment, a different side of himself—a glimpse of why the storytellers call Menelaus a great man.

"I've something for you," he said while Polycaste was adjusting her stirrups, then he tugged me by the sleeve. A servant was waiting under the trees with something wrapped in white linen. Menelaus pulled off the covers. Inside was a sword. Not one of those glittering swords studded with jewels that hung in racks in his armory. It was short and tarnished, with nicks on the blade and a row of holes in the handle where gems had been pried out.

"I was going to give you gold," Menelaus said, weighing the sword in his hand. He shrugged. "It impresses young people." He looked at me suddenly, and it was as if he'd taken off a mask. I saw the pain in his face and how tired he was, but something else too—the resolution that had taken Menelaus to Troy to win back the woman he loved. "I don't think you would have been impressed. Do you know what this is? It's more valuable than anything in my house. It was Hector's sword."

I couldn't hide my astonishment. Hector was the greatest of the Trojan fighters, perhaps the greatest of all fighters. He killed Achilles's friend Patroclus and was killed by Achilles in turn.

"We found it in his house in Troy. And we would never have captured Troy without your father. Here. Take it." He gave me a tight smile. "You're going to need it."

As we rode away, Polycaste said, "Well, at least we're done with that."

I didn't say anything. I was thinking how time changed people, wondering what Menelaus was like at my age, before Helen humiliated him by eloping with another man; before the war and his brother's death; before he went into that private hell where he and Helen poisoned each other every moment of every day. The sword pressed through my saddlebag as we rode away.

Even so it was a relief when we reached the frontier. The soldiers waved us through, and we trotted past the barrier onto the rough forest track that wound upward into the mountains. Soon our journey dropped into a natural rhythm. We got up early, before it became too hot, slept through the afternoon, and went on again when the heat of the day began to fade. Along the way we climbed ridges from where we could see forests folding away from us and the grey heads of mountains in the distance. We dropped into valleys filled with the splash of water. We paused at streams, stopped to explore forgotten little shrines and the ruins of foresters' huts. By the time we made camp in the evening, the shadows would be gathering under trees and in the hollows of rocks, and the pools we camped by were full of mysterious depths. We fished out fat little mountain trout and filled our gourds at waterfalls. Sometimes we talked for hours before dropping asleep.

We hardly noticed that we were traveling slower and slower—instinctively, neither of us saying anything—until a journey that should have taken five days had stretched to a week.

I give the steering oar a tug. The shadows on the horizon have resolved into the shape of Nirito, Ithaca's mountain. I can see the offshore islet of Asteris to one side of it. Soon I'll be home. I can already picture the big house—the courtyard where the young men lie snoring, the shattered hall and empty storerooms; my mother sleeping upstairs.

My mother is the reason I'm coming home.

"What's the matter?" Polycaste asked one evening while we were unrolling blankets on piles of dry leaves against the wall of an abandoned sheep pen.

"Nothing."

"Liar."

"I've been thinking about my mother."

"You're worried?" Polycaste stopped still, her blanket half-folded.

"She's alone with them. I should have gone home sooner."

"It's my fault."

"No, mine."

"We'll go quicker tomorrow." Polycaste gave the blanket a shake and gave a harsh laugh. "We'll get up early. After all, there's no point putting it off."

Putting it off. It's not like I ever forgot what was waiting for me in Ithaca. Every night I woke up after Polycaste had fallen asleep. I could hear the slow rise and fall of her breath. The Milky Way shimmered across the sky like a trail leading home. I knew that Ithaca meant the struggle with Antinous and the others. It meant a fight I couldn't win; it almost certainly meant death. I'd thought of not returning home. Even now, I can feel the temptation to throw my weight against the steering oar and turn the ship away from Ithaca. Perhaps Polycaste would come with me. I almost shook her awake, one night, to ask her. I could become a storyteller and tramp from tavern to tavern, house to house, telling stories about the war. I could go back to Sparta and ask to join Menelaus's retinue, or beg Nestor to let me stay in Pylos. Surely any chief would want Odysseus's son among his retainers? Or I could set off west, with Mentor and his crew, and found a colony. The sea's still full of empty islands. There are bays around its shores where no one lives but herdsmen and farmers, some of them still scratching the earth with stone tools. I could forget Ithaca and join that drift westward, in search of new lands, untouched territories.

I can't, though. People elsewhere might welcome me, but they'd sneer behind my back. Polycaste would sneer at me. I'd sneer at myself. The road to Ithaca is my fate, as inevitable as time. What's waiting for me at home is part of my story.

There's more to it than that, though. It isn't just duty that's driving me toward Nirito, or shame at what the world would say if I fled. It's anger.

I felt the anger on the first night of our journey, when I thought of Ithaca. Felt it burn and knew at once that anger wasn't a new arrival; it had been there all my life. Anger at my lost childhood, anger at my father. Rage at the young men who've destroyed my birthright, fury at what they've done to my mother. After that I waited for Polycaste to go to sleep, then I sat on the mountainside each night and felt my anger burn. Felt it—and recognized it as an old friend I'd never acknowledged, something as vital to me as breath. Something that's been inside me since my first conscious thought, often concealed but always present, flaring and guttering like the flame of life itself.

I felt my anger surge the last night Polycaste taught me how to fight. Felt it and was grateful to it.

"Get your weight forward. No, on the balls of your feet . . . knees apart. You look like a frog . . ." She couldn't stop laughing. "All right, we'll try again . . . weight *forward* . . . better—well, a bit better, anyway . . . hold the sword loosely . . . now lunge . . . sorry, have I cut you?"

I said, "It's nothing," and sucked my hand.

"What you did, you committed too far. Once you're moving, you can't turn, then you're a target. If we'd been really fighting, I would have disemboweled you."

"Good," I said and took up my stance again.

I tried to copy Polycaste, light on her feet, sword balanced loosely in one hand. She swayed. I thought she was lunging and leaped back. She laughed mockingly.

"Twitchy," she said. "Try again. The whole thing is to keep your opponent guessing." She flicked her sword out sideways and I jumped. This time she snorted with impatience. "Every time you jump, I could have you. Never commit until you know you've won. Never make a movement you can't control. *That's* better." I had taken advantage of her talking to lunge forward. She calmly stepped aside and thumped the butt of her weapon down on my wrist. I rubbed my numb hand as I stooped to pick up my sword.

"It was still stupid, but at least you were thinking," Polycaste said. "You committed again. Once you've thrown your weight for good and all, then you can't change direction. If your opponent's still on his feet, you're at his mercy. *Her* mercy. You have to *feint*. Go so far that your opponent thinks you're committed, but you aren't. They make their move, and that's when you twist and strike. Look, try again."

So we tried again—and again, circling and lunging while the shadows deepened under the trees. Hector's sword felt warm in my hand, and familiar, like the anger throbbing quietly inside me. I watched the tip of Polycaste's sword. Saw it move sideways, trying to tempt me into a lunge; saw it waver. I flicked my own sword. I knew she would underestimate me. Polycaste thought I had fallen into her trap and raised her own sword to strike. Instead of lunging toward her, I whipped my blade upward, catching her weapon just below the hilt. There was a grind of metal on metal and Polycaste's sword flew away into the undergrowth. In the same movement I launched my weight against her, raising my sword until the bronze was pressed against her woolen jacket.

For a moment we stood close. I was panting hard. If it hadn't been Polycaste, I know I would have killed her. I could see her skin up close, and the sweat beading on her cheeks. Her lower lip was caught between her teeth.

Then she shrugged unconcernedly and pushed me off. "You could be good, you know," she said. "You're quick and you think. You might end up better than me, one day."

That was praise, for her.

"What's it like in a real fight?" I asked as we packed the next morning. It was our last day of travel. The sea lay ahead.

Polycaste looked at me in astonishment, then laughed her raucous laugh. "How would I know?" she asked. "I've hardly ever left Pylos before. I'm a girl."

But we both found out the same evening.

As dusk fell, we dropped down into the little town by the shore where we'd originally planned to pick up a guide. Looking down from above, we could see a few lights winking among the dark rooftops, and smell fires. The sea spread out black toward the south.

"There's Pylos," Polycaste said, pointing. "We might as well stay in the town tonight. We can stay with that guide."

But the house where we'd asked for him before was closed up. We rattled the shutters and called, but no one answered, and there was no smoke from the chimney.

"There was that tavern," Polycaste said.

"Or we could go on and camp."

"What's the matter, are you scared?"

"No," I said.

We retraced our steps to the tavern. No one was sitting outside, but the alleyway was filled with the reek of grilled fish, and from behind the shutters we could hear a murmur of voices. Polycaste opened the door. Inside there was a fug of smoke from a charcoal brazier in one corner. Through it, we could just make out a table at the back and some upturned barrels with men sitting around them. The place stank of stale wine and the oily fish sizzling on the brazier. A man in a dirty apron stood by it, sweat pouring down his face as he prodded the fish with a fork.

Everyone stared at us as we came in. The conversation died away.

Polycaste walked confidently forward into the room. "We need somewhere to spend the night," she said in her loud, clear voice.

"I'll give you somewhere to spend the night," muttered one of the men. The others laughed. I put my hand on the hilt of my sword. Instinct. Straightaway I wished I hadn't—I knew what it meant to men like these.

Polycaste looked scornfully at them. "I'm Polycaste, the daughter of Nestor, chief of Pylos," she said.

"This isn't Pylos," said the man by the brazier, who I assumed was the tavern-keeper. "Nestor don't rule here."

Suddenly the atmosphere was wrong. The men were veterans. There were four of them. One had a splint strapped to his leg; another, a knotted sleeve where his left arm should have been; and a third, a coat made from the belt of a bear. I knew they were dangerous. They might have been less skillful at fighting than the young men at home on Ithaca, but they were just as savage. Their leader had a thick black beard. The left-hand side of his face was covered with a clumsy tattoo, a sea monster.

I stepped forward, letting go of my sword. "All we want is somewhere safe to spend the night," I said as reasonably as I could. I kept my eyes on the tavern-keeper. "Maybe you've got a stable at the back. We can sleep there."

"What's in the bag?" asked the tattooed man. He was talking to Polycaste, who had her saddlebag slung over her shoulder.

"Our things." She spoke bravely, but I could tell she was nervous.

"Open it up, then. Let's see what you've got." He glanced at his friends, who laughed.

"No." I had to draw a line, otherwise the men would push us back and back until we were helpless—I'd seen Antinous do that. I glanced around the room. The tavern-keeper had turned his back and was pretending to cook the fish. Two other men, in the far corner, had shuffled their stools around to look the other way. We were on our own.

I had to think fast. Our best chance was that the men would think us too-easy prey. They'd never expect a girl to fight. Four against one, they'd reckon, and me only a boy. They'd come for me first, thinking me the only threat, then have Polycaste to themselves. I don't know exactly what happened next. Fury frothed up in me. We were going to fight, and I *wanted* to fight. I'd had enough of negotiating, compromising, hiding. I wanted to hurt them.

Suddenly my mind left behind its first instinct of fear, almost as if it wasn't part of me, and began working smoothly, as if I could see how things were going to unfold. There was an alcove by the door, just enough room for me to take one step back. The saddlebag on my left arm masked my sword—*Hector's* sword—and the thought gave me a surge of confidence. I could swing the saddlebag into their faces and draw my sword in the same motion. Swing at them hard enough, and I could use the momentum to knock a second man off balance.

They had to move first. That had been Polycaste's lesson. Keep them guessing. Make them commit.

I took a step sideways. "Look," I said. "There's nothing valuable in the bags. We're travelers. We're asking for hospitality." Talking distracted them while I took up position. I weighed the saddlebag in my left hand. "If you want them, you'll have to take them," I said.

The men came at me in a rush. There was no science in it. As they surged forward, I swung the bag at the man on my right, sending him blundering into the man next to him. At the same time I pulled out Hector's sword. Instead of lunging, I let the third man, the leader, run onto it with his own weight. The shock jarred my arm. There was a sickening moment as I felt the sword enter his body, but I kept my arm steady. The man grunted in surprise. For a second I seemed to be holding him up. His breath stank, filling my nostrils. His face, the tattooed monster rippling across it, seemed pressed right against mine, with the brown eyes first surprised, then suddenly glazed. But I didn't have time to think about that. My mind was still working fast. I looked right, at the man with the empty sleeve, who was holding a short, bent dagger. Before he could strike at me, though, he twisted in shock and agony. Polycaste had stabbed him from the side, and in the stroke slashed at the second man, who was beginning to recover his balance. I shoved the leader's body at him and circled into the room, shoulder to shoulder with Polycaste. It was only then I registered the wrench as I'd pulled my sword from the body. When I glanced down at it, the first hand's breadth was glistening red.

There was a moment's shocked silence. The one-armed man was groaning on the floor, clutching his side. The other two, unharmed, stood with their backs to the door, panting. They looked down in shock at their leader's body, and then up at us. Then, with a glance at each other, they were gone. The door banged open. Their footsteps receded down the alleyway.

The tavern-keeper turned his fish, which hissed fat into the brazier. Only then did one of the men in the corner look around.

"They'll be back," he said without expression and turned back to his cards.

We led our mules quickly down the street. There was still enough light in the sky to see the beach, the flat, dark sea, and the distant promontory of Pylos. There were no lights in the town behind us. We followed the beach westward, then cut inland up a narrow gully choked with weeds and prickly pear. At the end of it we found a hollow under a rock face, where we tore out weeds to make space for a camp. We didn't light a fire.

"Are you all right?" Polycaste asked. They were the first words either of us had spoken since leaving the tavern.

"Yes."

"Sure?"

"Of course I'm all right," I snapped. "Why?"

"Because you're shaking."

"I'm not." I sat down on the hard ground and hugged myself. I didn't know what I was feeling. "I killed someone."

"He was going to kill you." Polycaste sat down next to me and put her arm around my shoulders. "You were brilliant. I didn't know what to do until the fighting started. You didn't stop thinking."

I shook my head. It was like I couldn't make my mind absorb what had happened. Even putting it into words didn't make it real. "It was the way he looked at me."

"The man you killed?"

"In the stories . . . in battles between fighters . . . they don't stop to think about killing . . . They just do it . . ." I was shivering. "He was a person," I said.

"A bad person."

"Does that make any difference?"

"I don't know."

There was a moment's silence, then Polycaste nudged me. "I'm sorry. I shouldn't have made us go in."

"It doesn't matter." It did. I just didn't want her to feel bad. "I said I needed to learn how to fight . . ." I could still see the man's startled eyes staring right into mine, then suddenly losing . . . what? Like a candle snuffed out, or the flame dying on a log; like the last edge of the sun vanishing behind the horizon; like the emptiness after a thunderclap. Gone.

"Anyway," Polycaste said more briskly, "you didn't have a choice." She stood up and went to the head of the gully. The bushes were just shadows now. The first stars were appearing overhead. "One of us ought to stay up and keep watch. We'll take it in turns."

I took the first watch. I knew I wouldn't sleep. I sat at the end of the track, wrapped in my blanket. Polycaste was soon asleep. To take my mind off it, I tried to picture Ithaca, my mother, Eurycleia, the nurse. But all I could think of was the man's dirty face with the tattoo of the sea monster on it and the sudden weight, so completely dead, as he slumped against me. Suddenly I found myself shaking, with tears pouring down my cheeks. I was ashamed of myself for crying. I hated what I'd done. I was confused. But at the same time, somehow, it felt as if I'd appeased that anger I'd discovered in myself, that sulky rage, like a stubborn and ill-tempered fire smoldering on an altar. I'd fed it, stilled it. I lived in a world where men fought. And I would fight too.

As I'll fight when I reach Ithaca, even though I know I've little hope of surviving. Not for the first time I wonder how the confrontation on Ithaca will start. I'll make a formal announcement of my father's death, and then what? I know what it will mean to Antinous and the others. No risk of the husband's return; no need to pretend Ithaca doesn't need a new chief because the old one's still alive. So—two prizes to snatch. One point in my favor: from the moment I declare my father dead, the young men are going to be at war with each other. But that's as far as the good news goes. Come tomorrow morning I'll be their rival for chief of Ithaca, and

I'll be in the way when it comes to snatching Penelope. Best dead, on both counts.

Factions will form. There's a fight brewing between Antinous and Eurymachus, although they've managed to work together until now. There's even a chance I can get Eurymachus to support me and eliminate Antinous. But only for a price: my support in marrying Penelope; my support in making him chief of Ithaca. I can pull that off if I want—Odysseus's son will still have some power in a town meeting—but I won't. My mother's freedom and the freedom of our island—they're the two things that matter most to me. I won't sacrifice them just to save my own life. That's why I'm steering through the night toward Ithaca, looking up at the stars and thinking I'll never know peace like this again. It was bred into me, the fight that's coming. The glory of the fighter's caste, and its end, crushed in one corner of the great hall with another man exulting over my body.

They'll attack me sooner rather than later. I'm guessing they won't want a public fight—people might run to help me. More likely an ambush somewhere quiet, or an accident, something that would cover their tracks from the charge of killing their host. A fall from the cliff, or a drowning at sea, the most common islander's death of all. A drowning at sea.

I peer ahead into the night. The dark masses of land ahead are starting to take shape. The deserted islet of Asteris, half a mile offshore, has pulled clear of Nirito's bulk. We're close enough to make out the wink of fires on shore. The light on the hillside must be from home, in the big house—maybe it's the brushwood brazier that keeps the guards warm at night. The light below must come from the little shack where fishermen smoke mullet and sardines on a beach littered with fish bones and sawn logs. For a moment, remembering childhood visits, I picture the gush of hot smoke when its rickety wooden door is opened and the fish hanging in silver rows inside. They had to build it under the cliff because everyone in town objected to the stench.

Over to the left there's another fire I can't place. It looks as if it's on the islet of Asteris, but no one's ever lived on Asteris, which is just a rocky mound with a few trees and enough sand to beach a ship. Perhaps a ship has pulled up there—but why would anyone land on Asteris with the harbor of Ithaca just around the point? Unless they were keeping a watch out to the south. But who would be looking out to the south? And why can't they keep watch from the house itself, which commands views all over the Ionian Sea? Unless they're trying to intercept a ship coming from the south. The only ships from the south, though, are merchants and traders.

And me.

Suddenly I'm wide awake, fingers tense on the steering oar. A ship from the south. A drowning at sea. I try to stop my mind racing ahead. I've nothing to go on but one fire on Asteris. The rest might be just imagination—fear, nights awake thinking through exactly this, even the delayed shock of the fight in the tavern. I make myself think calmly back through it all, trying to make allowance for the night, for being tired, for fear. Same result. There's a fire burning where I've never seen one in my life.

"Mentor!" I whisper his name, even though we're still a mile from shore. It takes a moment to rouse him. "There's a fire on Asteris."

"I don't see anything." His voice is still thick with sleep.

"Down by the water. There must be people there. A ship." My mind is moving fast now. "Wake the crew." I don't stop to think that Mentor's thirty years older than me, but I'm giving the orders. "Get them to the oars without making a noise. Get the sail down. Quickly."

"Maybe they're fishermen," Mentor says.

I could waste an hour telling the old man why they aren't fishermen. There isn't time. I'm already pulling the steering oar toward me, guiding the ship away from Asteris. The sail gives a great flap and the stars swing behind it. Grumbling, Mentor begins to kick the crew awake. I keep my eyes on the distant fire as they haul the sail down, get out oars, and, in silence, begin to pull away to the east. An oar splashes.

"Quietly."

Whether they're harmless fishermen, pirates, or men bent on murder, the only sensible thing to do is steer clear and swing out around the outlying rocks. Maybe that way we can slip into the harbor unseen.

"I can see it now." Mentor's voice.

"What do you think?"

"Fishermen."

"Why would they camp there?"

"Maybe they landed earlier and left a fire burning."

"Maybe."

There was a pause. "Better safe," Mentor agrees grudgingly. "Mind the rocks, though."

Everyone knows the rocks off Ithaca's harbor's mouth. I saw a ship wrecked on them when I was a child. Eurycleia took me up to the cliff, where a line of Ithacans were bracing themselves against the southerly gale, shielding their eyes from the sun. Looking down, I saw the remains of a trading ship splayed across the rocks like an insect crushed by a thumbnail against a windowsill. Breakers tugged at the wreckage, burying it in foam, then drawing back to reveal a broken mast, submerged gunwales, and the rock's teeth glistening through the smashed deck like the points of a knife. Tiny black figures clung to the mast's stump. From up on the cliff we could see them clearly, but there was nothing anyone could do to help—no fishing boat could go out in a storm like that. We watched the waves pluck figures off the deck one by one, until a massive breaker buried the whole wreck in foam and licked it clean.

"Ship," someone says. I look over my shoulder. I can't see anything at first, just darkness and the wink of the fire on Asteris. Then the fire is blocked out by something, reappears, vanishes again. There's something moving through the darkness between us and the islet.

"Comin' right for us," the sailor says.

I can hear the fear in his voice. That fear could kill us all if it turns into panic. "Probably nothing," I say as calmly as I can. "We'll make for the harbor anyway."

I can feel the men pulling harder. They can all sense the danger out there on the black sea. I try to calculate. The rocks are halfway between Asteris and the harbor point. We're better placed for the harbor, but they'll be faster than us— much faster—and it won't be dark for long. I glance eastward. The sky is beginning to turn pale. Dawn means light behind us, making us easy to spot. So no chance of making the harbor first.

If they catch me on board, they'll kill us all. Fishermen will find our ship wrecked on the rocks later this morning. No bodies, but everyone will know it's Mentor's ship. On the other hand, if they catch Mentor with no sign of me, they'll probably let him pass. So there's only one solution.

I touch Mentor on the arm. "I'm going to swim ashore."

"No, Telemachus!"

"I have to."

"It's too far. They'll see you getting into the water."

I don't answer for a moment. It's farther than I've ever swum before. But I'm not going to be drowned at sea like an unwanted puppy. The thought makes anger surge up in me again. "The rocks will hide me."

I kick off my sandals and tie them to my belt. Stooping, I pull my leather bag out from under one of the rowing thwarts and rummage in it, throwing out clothes until it holds nothing but Hector's sword.

"What are you doing?"

Instead of answering, I stare back into the blackness behind us. There's no sign of the pursuing ship. For a moment I wonder whether there even was a ship. Then, from somewhere well behind and to our left, I hear the splash of an oar. Everyone hears it. Someone in the bow mutters, and the sailors quicken their pace, trying to heave their ship's ungainly hull faster through the water.

"They're waiting for me," I tell Mentor quietly. "So long as they don't find me, you'll be safe. Make the harbor if you can. At least get close enough so people can hear you shout. Tell them I was never on board." I raise my voice. The whole crew has to hear this. "Tell them you left me behind in Pylos. Do you understand? If they don't find me, the rest of you will come to no harm."

"What are you going to *do*?" The old man's voice is shaking.

"Head for the rocks. We'll slip between them, and that's when I'll go overboard. I'll be all right." Easy to sound cheerful in the dark, when no one can see your face. "I'll swim to the cove below Eumaeus's hut."

"Rocks!"

I scramble forward across the rowing benches and cling to the bow, listening. The sea is pitch black; only the sky holds a little light. Then I hear the wash of a wave slapping against something solid and the suck of water as it falls away. I wish I could be more certain of the direction. These are the rocks sailors try to avoid at all costs, and we're steering right for them in complete darkness. Again I hear the pitch and hiss of waves. I look down to judge our speed, and suddenly I can see the darkness isn't quite so thick. There are ripples spreading out from our stem. When I look up, the land ahead is starting to take shape. Suddenly I see the rock, not where I expected but almost abreast of us.

"Sharp left!" But Mentor is already heaving on the steering oar to drag the ship around. Glancing astern, I see a black shape emerging from the night, a warship, sleek and low, its oars, like the legs of a water insect, lifting it smoothly toward us. There must be twenty men on board. I look the other way. The channel between the rocks is no wider than a ship's length, but enough for us to pass through.

"Don't forget, I was never on board. Let Mentor do the talking." For a moment I wonder whether it's right to leave them behind. But they're safer without me—far safer. I clasp Mentor's hand, glance at the warship, oars rising and falling in unison, and then, as the rock's wicked crown hides it from view, I slip into the water.

It's cold. Paralyzingly cold in the deep Ionian, as if the cold wants to hug me and drag me down. For a moment I can't think. The weight of my bag tugs at my shoulders. I have to force myself to kick out toward the rock, a sharp outline across the brightening sky, but when I reach it there doesn't seem anywhere to hold on. A low wave lifts me closer. I kick hard on stone and gasp with pain. Blood warms my foot, and suddenly I think of sharks. The black depths of the sea spread out around me. There's no point giving in to such thoughts. Fear will kill me more surely than any shark. I reach out one hand, grip a pinnacle of slippery rock, and look around.

Mentor's ship is already curving eastward beyond the rocks. Daylight is coming on fast—I can see the old man crouching at the oar. And here's the warship already. Deciding against the passage through the rocks, its helmsman has chosen to cut his prey off on the far side. Twelve oars rise and fall in unison—a trained crew. And in the stern, braced against the oar, is the unmistakable, burly figure of Antinous.

Antinous, who goaded me, ridiculed me, filled my dreams with fear. Whatever happens in the hours and days ahead, I'll do all I can to settle my account with Antinous.

Oily seawater washes around me. Looking up, I see the stars vanishing one by one as the day gathers strength. Perseus is gone, and then Cassiopeia. For a moment longer I think I can see Andromeda winking at me; then the sky stretches blankly overhead.

I let go of the rock and begin to swim.

W hen I was a child, we called Eumaeus's house the farm, but it's not much more than a hut, really, built against a bank, with a dirty yard sprawling around it and pigpens on the far side.

I know Eumaeus is in by the smoke from the chimney. I don't knock, though. Instead, I go up to the single window and listen for a moment, which is how I learn Eumaeus has a prisoner.

"Yer ain't goin' anywhere." The farmer's unmistakable, gruff voice. Peering in, I can see his visitor sitting disconsolately on a stool by the fire. An old man. The dogs are on either side of him, neck muscles tensed.

"I need . . ."

"Yer already took a bleedin' leak, yer been leakin' like a bleedin' pipe. If yer can't hold it in, yer can piss in yer bleedin' shoes."

The stranger whimpers.

"Or a bucket," Eumaeus adds, "but yer can wash it out yerself."

"I assure you . . ." the stranger begins. Well-spoken.

"Oh, 'e assures me all right, 'e assures me all 'e likes, but I ain't assured, am I? I don't trust yer . . . I don't trust yer no more'n I trust the pig with black ears as ate Spot's puppy."

"I'm not a Trojan spy," the stranger says solemnly.

From the window I can see the look of triumph on Eumaeus's face. He leans forward and shakes a finger in the stranger's face. "What is jus' what you would say," he breathes cunningly, "if you *was* a Trojan spy."

Time to go in. One of the dogs stands up. The other barks.

"Someone comin'," Eumaeus says, and gives an oath as I open the door.

"Telemachus!" he exclaims, limping over and clutching both my hands, shaking them like he wants to pull them off, then raising each in turn to his lips. "I ain't expectin' yer. No one ain't expectin' yer. Yer taller."

"I've only been away three weeks."

"Then yer bigger. Yer something. Yer looks different." He frowns. "Yer wet, anyways. Come in."

"Who's your guest, Eumaeus?"

"Guest?" Eumaeus looks contemptuously at his visitor and spits on the floor. "What 'e's only a bleedin' tramp as talks bollocks, an' now . . ." He raises his voice angrily. "Now looks at 'im bubberin' and snivellin', what's wrong wiv 'im now?"

It's true, the guest is weeping as he looks at me, hunched over on his stool, rubbing his eyes with the sleeve of his gown.

I take a closer look at him. A powerful man—or powerful once—and probably good-looking with it. But it seems like life has been hard on him. His back is bent, and his face is scarred and weather-beaten, his hair streaked with grey. A traveler or sailor, maybe a mercenary. A dangerous man once, perhaps, but not anymore.

The stranger wipes his eyes again and looks at me, still without standing. His eyes are fiercely blue and somehow distant. "You're Telemachus?" he asks in a hoarse voice.

"I am. And your name?"

"'E's a blasted liar's what 'e is," Eumaeus puts in fiercely. "What 'e comes 'ere, askin' to be took in, an' it's all lies."

"How do you know he's a liar?"

"'Cause I got eyes in my 'ead, an' ears to hear wiv. 'I tramps many miles,' 'e says. Look at them shoes, 'e ain't tramped many mile in them. 'I comes in a Lastragonian ship,' 'e says. Well, I seed the ship'e come in, it were Phaeacian, what I seed their pink sail, greasy buggers. Bollocks, every word of it, an' 'e sits there eatin' my pork," the old man finished indignantly.

I take another look at the visitor. Unarmed. Not threatening. "Who are you?"

"That's what I wants to know," Eumaeus interrupts. "'Oo the blazes is'e, an' 'oo sends 'im? One o' them, ain't 'e? 'I met Odysseus. I got a message from Odysseus.'"

I shouldn't be so shocked, but nonetheless I feel a surge of anger. I don't need this. Not now, not ever. My father's dead. I don't need any more games.

"Get me some wine," I tell Eumaeus. I try to keep my voice calm.

While he draws it from his old goatskin, I sit down slowly on the stool, recovering strength. I don't look at the stranger. For some reason I'm feeling a mad, enraged urge to pull out Hector's sword and kill him now. Instead, I ignore him.

"I went to Sparta," I tell Eumaeus. "There was no news. I made a decision."

"What's that?" Eumaeus has pulled the spit from the fire and started slicing thick hunks of pork.

"Odysseus is dead." I hear the clatter as Eumaeus drops his knife. "No one has any news of him. No one's seen him since the day he left Troy. Tonight I'll declare Odysseus dead. Tomorrow we'll raise a pyre and read the funeral rites."

Saying it out loud is harder than I expected. I've slammed the door shut on sixteen years of dreaming my father will return. I'm not a child anymore. Eumaeus comes slowly over to the table and sits down next to me. He covers my hand with his huge, calloused paw. Neither of us speaks.

"*No . . .*" The stranger's voice is a low moan.

Eumaeus reaches across and slaps him hard, backhand, across the face. The stranger cringes, hiding his face behind his hands. "'E says 'is father's dead," Eumaeus growls. "'E don't needs none o' yourn bollocks now."

I bite into the thick slab of bread Eumaeus has handed me. It's dry as dust, impossible to chew. "Is my mother safe?"

"She'll be better now you're 'ome. What are you doin' 'ere, Telemachus? Why didn't you come in the 'arbor?"

"They were waiting to ambush me on Asteris, Antinous and twenty others. I had to swim for it. Mentor took the ship in."

"Yer can 'ide 'ere if yer needs."

"No. I have to see Penelope. I have to tell her about Odysseus."

"*Odysseus*," the stranger whispers.

I spin around in fury, but something stops me from striking him. I can see the red mark where Eumaeus hit him.

He gets up, stooped. Comes over and stands in front of me, standing too close so I can see the deep blue in his eyes, smell the stink of his breath.

"Telemachus."

"What do you want?"

"Telemachus." He repeats my name as if it were a kind of prayer. "What would you say . . ." His voice is stronger than I would expect. "What would you say, Telemachus, if I told you that I *am* Odysseus."

Eumaeus lets out an oath. I push the old beggar away. How many imposters have we had over the years? All of them confident they can prove it. Perhaps they'll have met someone who sailed with Odysseus and now hold a nugget of information "that only Odysseus could have known"—the scar on his thigh, usually. *A scar right here, right up my thigh.* Best to get it over quick.

I draw a deep breath. "Odysseus has a scar on his body. Where?"

"Many scars," the stranger whispers. "Many scars." The wrong answer.

"What do you know about Penelope?"

"I did her wrong."

That's not what I expected. I pause. "What color are her eyes?"

"Green."

"How does she weave?"

"With her left hand."

"What does she wear around her neck?"

"The locket I gave her the day I left."

I'm a bit surprised, I admit. Others have given the right answers before, but there's something unusual in the way this stranger replies. Not thinking, not striving to impress—just telling me what he knows with an odd air of bewilderment.

I go on. "There's a shrine to the goddess on Ithaca. Where?"

"On the mountainside above the house, past the gate in the orchard."

"Odysseus left four offerings there. What were they?"

None of the imposters could ever answer this.

The stranger pauses, his eyes fixed on me. "A boar's tusk," he says huskily. "The tusk that ripped my thigh. A sprig of laurel. I cut it with Penelope in the woods above her home. My sword. I dedicated it the day before I left for war."

My attention is fully on him. And it's then I'm struck by the way he's looking at me. Inspecting me . . . no, *devouring* me, with a greedy, all-encompassing fascination.

I shiver, take too long a pull on Eumaeus's harsh wine, cough.

"The fourth." For some reason my voice is hoarse.

"A wooden owl." The stranger's blue eyes close. "I left it at dawn the day we sailed."

A tusk. A sprig of laurel and a sword. A carved owl. I shiver. Perhaps the sea's chill has gotten to me. Anyone could go to the shrine; anyone could bribe the priest. It proves nothing.

Eumaeus gets up angrily and twists the skewers of pork on the fire. "Look at 'is ugly ol' face. Odysseus was strong as a tree, quick as an eagle. My master were a fighter, not some blasted ol' tramp. If this is Odysseus, then we's all buggered."

As he sits down again, I feel his rough hand briefly gripping my shoulder. Support.

I can't take my eyes off the stranger, though. "Who made the owl?"

"I did."

I. Not "Odysseus." *I.* But this isn't Odysseus, I know that. Odysseus is young, strong, a fighter. Odysseus is dead.

"I made two," the stranger says before I even ask him. His eyes are locked on mine. This isn't possible—I know it isn't. No one knows about the second owl, the one my father carved for his daughter in the town.

"Where is the second?" My voice sounds unsteady in my own ears. I can feel it now, the second owl, pressing against

206

my belt. Only we know about it. The girl and her mother. I. Odysseus. Suddenly I'm no longer aware of the hut, or of Eumaeus watching spellbound from the fire. It's as if no one else in the world exists; as if there's no other moment but this one, this second in which my question hangs unanswered between us.

"I gave it to my daughter," he says.

Eumaeus swears coarsely. "Odysseus ain't got no daughter!"

The man on the stool ignores him. "I lied about her," he says, directing his words to me alone. "I lied to Penelope. I lied to everybody." He pauses and swallows, then goes on with a wrench, as if the truth is something, an arrow, he has to pull out of his own body. "I had a daughter with a woman in town. The night before I left, I carved an offering for each of you, to keep you safe. Yours I dedicated at the shrine, but I couldn't leave hers there. She has it, Telemachus."

How many days, how many nights? Days I'd walk up to the clifftop and pretend I saw a sail. Nights I lay awake, imagining that at any moment I'd hear the great gate slam, voices, a commotion. When I was young enough I convinced myself, more than once, that those footsteps were real. My eyes filled with tears as I lay in bed. I actually got up and ran downstairs to greet my father.

And found the hall empty, the guards asleep. Nothing.

How many different scenes did I play out in my head? The fleet sailing back into the harbor at dawn. Doors opening, children running out. The scrunch of keels on the sand, men jumping down, taking women in their arms while the sails billowed and the oars were stowed for the last time. Eurycleia shaking me awake in the middle of the night. And a hundred times—a thousand times—my father striding into the hall while the young men feasted, his face grim and his sword drawn.

But it was never like this: an old man hunched on a stool in a pig farmer's hut. No ships. No men. And *old*. Why did I never realize my father would grow old? That he would be scarred, broken—that eight years of war and eight of travel would wither his muscles and twist his legs, fill those blue eyes with that look of helpless pleading? As if he were a son looking for his father's blessing. As if he isn't a returning chief but a fugitive begging for help.

I don't take the hand he's holding out to me. I sit down and hold out my cup for Eumaeus to refill.

"Telemachus?" My father's voice trembles. He can feel the hostility. He can feel my anger like heat from a fire. I don't even know why I'm angry. Perhaps it's because I've found my father just when I'd stopped looking for him. Or because he isn't the hero I've pictured for sixteen years; he's a tired old man, an imposter.

Or perhaps because I've always been angry with him, every day of my life. My father: the first stranger I ever hated.

"What's 'appenin'?" Eumaeus's gruff old voice is trembling. He looks at the stranger. Gets up, goes to him, and peers at his shoulders, his face, his chest, the way he might inspect a pig he was thinking of buying at market.

"Eumaeus." Is that a note of half-forgotten command in my father's voice? The old farmer can hear it too. And perhaps he hears in it, at last, the echo of remembered tones; a voice faded and hollowed out by time; a voice he never expected to hear again. Suddenly Eumaeus is weeping, gripping my father's shoulders and weeping like a child who wants to be forgiven.

The sound of Eumaeus's tears breaks me. I have the sense of a void filling, a circle closing. *Odysseus*, who was missing for so long. I go to him myself then, and let my father take my hand. His touch is odd, harsh, tanned by salt—so dry and cold I can hardly sense any human warmth in it. I look into his eyes and suddenly, there, I see something I recognize as my own, a shard of mirror in a vast darkness. I may hate him, but I can't ignore my own father. And all at once I'm overwhelmed, not with love but with pity—pity for this poor, scarred old man quivering inside the name of Odysseus, pity for the wanderer who's come home alone, to find his house ruined and his fortune gone.

I always thought I needed a father. It isn't like that, I realize. Odysseus needs me.

H ours later I'm watching the big house from the
shadow of the olive grove.

    I knew a man in town once who broke his leg. It
mended slowly and crooked. It took time for the bone to
knit, time for the hurt to heal, time for it to stiffen enough
to carry his weight. Even then it didn't grow straight. He had to
learn to walk again. We watched him hobble across the town
square, treading gingerly on his twisted leg as if he wasn't sure
whether or not it would hold. It's going to be like that for my
father and me. It will take time for us to meld together, father
and son, time for scar tissue to form and the bones slowly to
unite. We'll have to learn how to walk on this crooked, tender

thing, our bond, test its strength little by little. Learn what it is to be part of each other.

Only we don't have any time.

We talked for hours this morning, but not about the things we should have shared—my childhood, his journey. There was no time for that. Instead, we talked about the battle that awaits us here on Ithaca in the next two days. About Penelope, imprisoned in the big house. About Odysseus's return.

Neither of us has any illusions about how complicated this is going to be. I came back to Ithaca expecting a fight. I'm still expecting one.

A few years ago, Odysseus might have returned home to Ithaca in triumph and been welcomed as a returning chief, but it's different now. Ithaca's changed—I saw that at the town meeting. Odysseus could stand up under the plane tree, he could tell them, *"I'm back, but your sons, your husbands, you're never going to see them again."* Five hundred men. Would anyone leap up to acclaim him? I don't think so.

He didn't want to hear that. "They love me," he kept saying, shaking his grey head. "They love me. They'd follow me to the ends of the earth."

If Odysseus had come back a few years ago, the young men in the house might have packed their things, paid homage, and left. He's lost that opportunity too. The ruined courtyard and empty cellars, the feasts, the destruction—those are the work of invaders, not guests. The men in the house will expect Odysseus's vengeance. They'll kill him first.

That was when the discussion got difficult. Odysseus wanted to charge down to the house, sword in hand, and take them on. He and I, with the goddess to give us strength. It took all my tact to argue him out of that. How to tell your own father he's no longer the fighter who conquered Troy? That he's old and weak? That his son has only ever fought a single fight, and his enemies are stronger than he is?

Odysseus sat on his stool, brooding. "Who are they?" he said at last, so I listed them, and my father nodded at each name. Most were children when he left for Troy. Now they're in their prime, stronger than he is.

"Antinous is the worst," I finished. "He's vicious. And Eurymachus, Polybus's son."

"No." Odysseus shook his head decisively.

"You've never met him."

"I knew his father. There's good blood in that family. His father was a good man. Count Eurymachus a friend."

Commanding me, like it wasn't open for discussion. I didn't want to argue with my father on our first day together—perhaps our last day—so I forced myself to think impartially. Eurymachus had spoken for me at the town meeting. He'd given me money for my journey to Pylos. Had he been trying to ingratiate himself with Penelope? Maybe. But he'd shown me other kindnesses over the years. Grudgingly I was forced to admit my father could be right.

"He'll help us," he decreed. "Four against thirty. Maybe more than four. We'll have supporters in the town."

Eventually Odysseus accepted he couldn't just march into the big house and take possession. We needed to buy time. And it was in this acceptance, this talking through options, that I finally undersood this really was Odysseus sitting here in the hut—Odysseus, the great strategist, the trickster, the man who dreamed up the wooden horse. His mind moved like lightning. He was always two steps ahead, dismissing plans before we'd even described them, weighing pros and cons, conjuring up schemes. And I began to feel *proud* this was Odysseus, proud to be his son—which only added to my confusion. Proud, angry, resentful. How could I not be confused? For a moment

I found myself missing those hours last night when it was just me, sailing across a starlit sea alone.

At last Odysseus said, "Do what you planned yourself. Tell them I'm dead. Announce my funeral. They won't attack you until it's over. Meanwhile we must get me into the palace, disguised."

We needed to get Odysseus into the palace. We needed to get Eurymachus on our side, but we agreed that could only happen at the last minute. We needed to divide our enemies into smaller groups—Odysseus had a plan for that as well. Talking about Penelope was the hardest of all. Odysseus listened in anguish as we decribed her hesitant, distant voice, the days without eating, the looms full of empty pictures. I was against telling Penelope of Odysseus's return, because I wasn't sure she could take the strain, let alone keep the secret. To my surprise, Odysseus accepted that without hesitation.

"Better not," he said gruffly. "She won't recognize me now. Better she doesn't know."

It was late by the time we finished planning and I made my way down to the big house under cover of the olive grove. From where I am now, crouched under the trees, I can see the whole forecourt. The ground outside the big house is full of debris—broken cart wheels and chariots awaiting repair, smashed furniture, abandoned mattresses. Old cooking pots have been thrown out of windows and messes swept out through doorways. Flocks of sheep and goats have left piles of dung drying in the heat. Now, at high noon, the rough ground outside the gate is chalk white in the sun, so blinding it hurts to look at. Stray dogs lie panting in the thin line of shadow under the wall. The guards are slumped apathetically against the doorposts, while the beggars have taken shelter under the covered well a few yards away.

I've known this courtyard all my life. Smoke rises from the kitchen chimneys the way it always has. I've known the two guards—one whittling a stick, the other scraping mud from his sandal—since I was born. But today the smoke smells different—bitter, somehow—and the guards look like strangers. I'm noticing it all because, for the first time ever, this scene I know so well no longer feels like home. I'm on a foreign island, and this is a doorway I've never passed through before.

I leave the shade and walk quickly across the baking earth to the gate. Startled, the guards pull themselves upright in an untidy salute. Speed is everything, Odysseus said. Don't give them time to think. I stride briskly into the courtyard. Melanthius, the cook, is standing under the balcony, talking to one of the young men.

"Melanthius! Call everyone to the hall. I have an announcement to make."

Heads appear from the tents. None of them can hide their astonishment. They expected me to be dead by now. I ignore them and stride into the hall, snapping my fingers as if that's going to keep things moving. Can I trust Melanthius? I guess not. That's one of the risks we have to run. There are servants who like the young men being here. The cook is close to several of them, not least Antinous, whom he worships despite the fighter's rudeness. Maids like Melantho have had affairs with them. Village boys have gotten rich on tips. Whom can we trust? I've known these people all my life. Now I have to work out whose side they're on.

I climb up on the hearth and feel the heat of the fire on the backs of my legs. The young men are crowding into the hall as word spreads through the house that I'm back. Eurycleia appears on the stair landing, mouth open in wonder. I know she'll run up to Penelope as soon as she hears what I have to say, and for a moment I wish I'd gone to my mother first. But that wouldn't have worked—we agreed in Eumaeus's hut. Cooks spill in from the kitchen, wiping their hands on aprons. Antinous, face impassive, takes a seat at the front. Eurymachus leans against a column, looking troubled. These are the men I'll be fighting tomorrow. The thought brings a simultaneous rush of terror and exultation.

"There's something I need to share with you." No introduction. No apology for calling them in or explanation of my return. Go straight into it. "I went to Pylos for news of my father. Nestor received me there as a friend. He spoke of the ties that link him and Odysseus. If ever I need help, he told me, he will come to my aid with Pylos's ships and men. Next I went to Sparta, to the court of Menelaus and Helen." A murmur runs around the room. No one there has met Helen of Troy. In their world, that's status, something I badly need. "He gave me Hector's sword as a gift. He told me he will never forget the service my father did him in the war. If he ever heard of trouble in Ithaca, he told me, he would come here to help."

The smart ones—Antinous, Eurymachus—will know there isn't the faintest chance Menelaus or Nestor will send an armed expedition to rescue the sixteen-year-old son of Odysseus. Antinous is scornfully picking his nails, his chair half turned away from the hearth. But some of the others, at least, are looking thoughtful. Above all the heads I can see Odysseus's armor on the walls, its dull bronze winking in the light from the door.

"Neither of them could give me news of my father, so I have come to a decision. Tomorrow I will declare Odysseus dead. I will raise a pyre on the shore and say the funeral rites for my father."

There's a gasp from Eurycleia. From the corner of my eye, I see her fleeing upstairs to tell my mother. The young men have broken out into an instant hubbub. Antinous is frowning. That's something gained, in any case—I've thrown him off balance.

I raise one hand. "I want you to respect Odysseus's memory. Medon?" The old servant is waiting by the kitchen door. "Take down all the armor from the walls and lock it in the armory. I'll polish it for the ceremony, as a gesture of respect." My father's hunting bow catches my eye. Its horns are yellowed, and the quiver of arrows next to it has mildewed. It's hung there all my life, and I can't bear to see it moved. "Leave the bow. That will always hang there in Odysseus's memory."

I step down from the hearth into a sea of urgent talk. Young men pluck at my sleeve, asking questions, but I ignore them. It's worked. The plan is in motion.

Eurymachus appears in front of me. "Come with me. Quickly."

He pulls me out into the kitchen corridor. It's deserted. "That was brave," he says briefly.

"It was necessary."

"That isn't what I asked you here for." His handsome face is serious. "Listen, Telemachus, there's something going on. You've got to be careful."

Now I'm the one who's thrown off balance.

"There was a ship waiting for you. Off Asteris, I think. Antinous tried to ambush you on your way home. I don't know how you got past. Twenty of them. They were going to kill you, Telemachus. They want you dead."

He shakes my arm as if he's trying to wake me up. I pull my sleeve away and he winces, as if I've hurt him. "This is serious, Telemachus. I don't expect you to like me, but please trust me. *Please*. They want to kill you. You've got to take care."

One more squeeze of the arm and he's gone, leaving me staring down the corridor.

Perhaps my father was right about him after all. I'm still thinking about Eurymachus as I climb the stairs to my mother's room. But it's Penelope who needs my attention. Eurycleia will have reported my return by now, and my announcement. And I'm about to do something I've never done before—lie to my mother.

If it weren't for Eurymachus, I would have noticed the silence before going in. Penelope isn't sitting at her loom. Instead, she's over by the window, gripping the sill as if she can no longer hold herself upright.

"It isn't true!" she shouts.

"Mother . . ."

"He's *alive!*" She's across the room, gripping me by the arms. "It isn't true!" Tears streak her face, trickling black makeup down her cheeks.

"Mother, I've decided . . ."

"He isn't dead. Do you have proof he's dead?" She shakes me. Penelope's eyes are more focused than I've seen them in months.

"No, but . . ."

"Then he isn't. I know he isn't. You can't tell people otherwise." Penelope wipes angrily at her cheeks with the hem of her dress, staining it black. She scowls at the marks and goes to sit at the stool by her loom.

"How do you know?" I ask.

"I had a dream." Penelope sniffs. Her anger has vanished suddenly, leaving her limp. "The goddess sent me a dream. Odysseus came back to Ithaca. He was poor. He killed all these men. He . . ." She looks down, blushing. "He made me his wife again." She shivers suddenly and hugs herself.

"It was just a dream."

"Dreams tell the future."

"They're not real."

"The goddess sent it to me. Can you prove it isn't true?"

"No, but . . ."

"So there you are—he's coming back! He's coming back," she repeats, looking idly at the cloth on her loom. She reaches out one hand to touch it. "See what a stupid picture," she says. "It doesn't show anything."

"I think it's very beautiful," I say dutifully.

"Do you?" Penelope shrugs and looks down at her hands. "You must tell them he's coming back. Tell them about my dream."

"Mother . . ."

"They tried to kill you." Suddenly Penelope's eyes fill with tears. She looks up at me, blinking. "They tried to kill you. There was a ship waiting. I couldn't do anything about it. I spoke to Medon, he just shrugged. He said, 'It's more than my life's worth.' What does that mean?" She shakes her head, bewildered. "I put my oil lamp in my window to warn you. I knew you wouldn't be able to see it, but I did it anyway. Now they'll try to kill you again. You've got to go away . . ." She lays one hand on my arm. It's the longest speech I've heard from my mother in a year. "Do you understand? You've got to get away before they kill you. Take a boat. Take this . . ." She fumbles around her neck, unclasping the gold pendant that always hangs there. "I've got jewels too, a box. Take it and go. Leave the island today. Go to my father's house, or back to Pylos. Go . . ." She stops with a sob, hands crushing the pendant.

"Mother . . ."

"Go!"

"I'm not going anywhere," I say gently.

Penelope seems to collapse then, like a puppet whose strings have been cut. For a moment she sits with her face in her hands, then looks up. I thought she was crying, but her eyes are dry.

"Then they'll kill you," she says coldly. "I've lost my husband. Now I'll lose my son as well. I'll put you on the same pyre you build for Odysseus. I'll put ashes in my hair and scratch my face until it's bloody." She looks curiously down at her own fingernails, as if checking how sharply they could rip flesh.

"We did it when my grandfather died. We howled so long we were hoarse for weeks. The women at Troy must have buried husbands and sons every day, then worn black and waited for the grave to open for them. That's what women do, isn't it? It's what I'll do. I won't let them marry me. I'll be a widow. I'll go to the shrine every morning until my legs get too fat to carry me. I'll mutter to myself and everyone will start to avoid me. They'll say I've gone mad."

"You won't go mad." Out of habit I'm trying to make my voice light and cheerful. "No one's going to hurt me. Everything's going to be all right."

My mother looks at me without smiling, almost without love. "Go away," she says at last. "I'm not going to make it worse by pleading. Go away."

I've never been dismissed like that before. I bow stiffly and close the door behind me. For a while I just stand there, back against the door. Should I go back in and tell Penelope that Odysseus has returned? Tell her my announcement was just part of a trick? I don't dare. We agreed it was better to keep Penelope in the dark. I have to stick to that.

A sudden noise from below breaks through my thoughts. I hurry down the stairs and stop dead on the landing, looking down into the hall.

Odysseus is sitting on the ground against a column. He's slumped like a beggar, shoulders rounded. His hair is covered in dust, and his clothes are rags. He holds a beggar's bowl loosely in one hand and has an old leather satchel draped over one shoulder. His head is lolling on his shoulders like he's drunk.

Beggars are allowed into the great hall—that's custom. It brings luck to give them food and drink. In return they joke and poke fun at the fighters in a way no one else is allowed. Quite often, there's one beggar who takes up residence and becomes a kind of jester. At Ithaca, his name's Irus.

Irus is circling around Odysseus now. He's angry, and you can see why—there's another man on his patch. I guess beggars are as touchy as fighters, in their way. They have their territory, they have their pride. Odysseus is on Irus's territory, and he's not happy about it.

The men in the hall love that.

Antinous is in the middle of them, slumped in a chair with a cup of wine in one hand. His face wears a cruel little smile. You can see what's on his mind.

"Send him away," Irus whines. "This is *my* place, *my* hall."

I never liked Irus much. He's a big, bragging man with the kind of belly you shouldn't see on a beggar. Beggars often have twisted legs or some other deformity, but there's nothing wrong with Irus, he's just too lazy to work.

He's carrying a staff, as he always does, and takes a vicious cut at Odysseus's legs. Odysseus rolls clumsily out of the way, and the young men roar with laughter.

"Why did you let him in?" whines Irus.

Antinous says, "Because we're bored." He puts one hand over his mouth and screws up his eyes as if he's thinking. He keeps pretending to think until he has the hall's full attention, until all the young men are looking eagerly at their leader, waiting to see what he has up his sleeve. Then Antinous takes his hand away from his mouth and says quietly, "Fight."

They all take up the chant as they prod Odysseus to his feet, thrust a stick into his hands, and drag chairs into a rough circle to act as a ring. From the landing above, I watch bets being made. Odysseus stands stupidly in the middle of the ring, holding his stick as if he doesn't know what to do with it. Irus stops whining and drops into a crouch, gripping his staff in both hands. Odysseus watches him dully, like a bear tracked by a dog. His hurt leg is slightly crooked. He turns himself with slow, shuffling steps as Irus dances around him, his stick trailing in one hand.

"He's going to drop it," someone jeers. There are whistles, catcalls.

And then suddenly it's over.

It ends so fast I have to blink and play it back in my head to see what happened. Irus lunged forward, aiming a vicious blow at Odysseus's head. It never landed. Faster than you could think, Odysseus stepped aside and whipped his own stick across Irus's belly with such force that in a second the beggar was coughing and retching on the ground. That's all I see: Irus kneeling in agony. Then the hall erupts. It's like Irus's pain triggers something in them. Young men swarm over the chairs and engulf the beggar like hounds bringing down a boar. Irus tries to crawl toward the door, covering his face with his arms, but he can't shake them off. I can't even see him as the men rain down blows, fighting among themselves to reach their victim. He gets halfway to the door but no farther. Someone kicks him onto his side, and I see a chair raised to smash down on his head. There's a shriek of laughter as Irus screams.

I can't watch after that. They aren't men. They're animals—animals singling out the loser, who becomes the target, becomes prey. A bird with a broken wing, a dog with a hurt leg. Weakness triggers something that belongs not to people's rational minds but to those crueler and darker instincts that relish blood, forget danger, crave violence. For a moment, as he lies under the blows, Irus's terrified eyes catch mine, and I shy away from their contact.

Because I know I can't help? Or because I can see myself there if things go wrong tomorrow—myself twitching under the same mob, a deer brought down by wolves.

I look at my father instead. Odysseus has sunk to the ground, holding his leg as if he's been hurt. I'm thinking, *He made it too easy; he should have spun the fight out.* Then I notice Antinous watching him too. Alone among the young men he hasn't gone after Irus.

"He hurt me," Odysseus quavers.

"He didn't touch you," Antinous says contemptuously, and cocks his head. "You know how to fight."

"I fought in the war."

"Who with?"

"Nestor."

"What's your name?"

"Aethon."

"Why do you beg if you can fight like that?"

"My leg. I was wounded in the war."

"Your leg." Antinous looks away. I think he's going to ask more questions, but suddenly he seems bored. "You can stay for the evening," he announces, like it's up to him. "Someone lay him a place. It's time we ate. Other people fighting makes me hungry."

The second part of our plan is accomplished: Odysseus is inside the palace. Tables are set in order. Melanthius leads cooks in from the kitchen, carrying wooden trays of meat and bowls of olives. Cups are filled. Irus is still lying in the corner of the hall, his face unrecognizable under a mask of blood. He's still alive, twitching, so I send two of the servants to do what they can for him. Then I see my father go up to Antinous.

I catch something odd in his expression. I can't place it at first. Then I get it: his eyes are gleaming with mischief.

He sits down and takes a roll from a basket. Antinous frowns.

"Did you ever meet Odysseus?"

My mouth is dry. This wasn't part of any plan.

"Once," Antinous says shortly.

"Did you fight him?"

"I was a child. He gave me a toy dagger."

"Did you thank him?"

Antinous doesn't answer. My father leans forward and—to my astonishment—prods Antinous with the tip of his staff. "You should have thanked him."

Antinous looks around again, his eyes narrowing. Then he looks back at his plate. "Don't push your luck, beggar man," he says in a low voice.

I can't stand any more. I clap my hands and get the feast under way, but I don't let it last long. I send them away early, and for once they listen to me. There's no chance to speak to my father. When the torches are out, I climb the stairs to my room and close the door. In the corner there's a trapdoor leading to the roof, and I clamber onto the clothes chest and thrust it open.

A shaft of moonlight strikes me full in the face. When I haul myself up to the roof and stand up, Ithaca lies spread out around me, bathed in moonlight. There isn't a breath of wind. Above, Nirito towers into the air. Its valleys drop toward the sea in thick clefts of shadow. I can see the roofs of the town, glinting silver, and beyond them, the flat expanse of the sea, waveless and bright as a polished mirror. I don't think I've ever seen Ithaca so still. The hot night air feels as if it's welded to the land, as if the whole scene, mountain and sea, would ripple were a gust of wind to blow through it. The cicadas are silent. Shadows hang like sleeping bats around the cypress trees.

The island's asleep, its people and creatures sleeping with it. Suddenly I feel something wet on my cheek. I didn't even know I was crying. But this is my home and I'm not ready to leave it yet. I look up at the familiar stars: the Bear, Cassiopeia, Andromeda. I want to show Ithaca to Polycaste. I don't want to die in a brawl in the great hall.

There's no point giving in to hopelessness. I'm not going to die, I tell myself. We'll make a fight of it, however hard the odds. I feel the anger still burning steadily within me, and that gives me some comfort. I settle down to wait. Gradually the courtyard falls silent and the sentry makes his last rounds. I can see the flicker of flames on the courtyard wall and watch it grow dim. An owl hoots softly from the olive groves. Only when the palace is silent do I get up to go.

There are trapdoors all over the roof, above staircases and corridors. On the far side, there's one that reaches the stair where Eurycleia stood to listen to my speech this morning, and where I watched the beggars fight. From there I can get to the armory, where I had all the weapons taken this morning. I'm going to take weapons for the three of us—me, Odysseus, Eumaeus—and hide them in the hall. The rest will be locked up to stop anyone from using them in the fight tomorrow. The visitors will have the weapons they always carry, but nothing else.

Crouching, I hurry across the roof, staying well away from the parapet above the courtyard. Beyond it I pull open the trapdoor and lower myself down, scrabbling with my feet until I touch the rung of a ladder.

That's when I hear voices.

They're coming from below. One person on the landing where I was standing earlier, the other in the hall. The voice in the hall is too faint to make out, but the one on the landing I recognize straightaway. My mother.

I ease myself down the stair until I can hear properly, with my mother's voice close below me.

"Sixteen years," she's saying. "He left sixteen years ago."

"Sixteen years," a man's voice echoes, and suddenly I'm gripping the balustrade, because it's my father talking.

I peer down into the hall. Odysseus, still in his beggar's rags, is sitting in dark shadow under one of the columns. His face is out of sight—I guess that means Penelope can't see him either. I can just make out his legs sprawled in the glow of firelight and the open satchel next to them.

"Did you ever meet Odysseus?" Penelope asks.

"Yes." His voice sounds low and grating. Can't she recognize him? Did Odysseus look so different, sound so different, sixteen years ago? All at once I realize that I'm never going to know my father. This beggar, this old man, maybe. But I'll never find the Odysseus—young, strong—who left Ithaca for Troy.

"I fought alongside him," he says.

"Tell me a story about him."

My father clears his throat. "We were making a night attack. Waiting in a ditch near Troy, the walls in front of us. It was cold, frost on the ground, frost on the bushes. Our cloaks were thin. I thought we'd die of cold even if the Trojans didn't get us. Odysseus kept thinking about Penelope . . ."

"How do you know?" my mother laughs. "How could you tell what he was thinking? You're just saying what I want to hear."

Odysseus doesn't answer.

"Whenever strangers come here," Penelope says, and I notice how normal—how sane—her voice is. "Whenever ships come into port, I always ask them, 'Have you seen Odysseus?' 'Did you meet Odysseus?' You'd be surprised how many did. So many men fought in the war. So many had stories about him. Tell me more."

No answer from the hall.

"Was he clever?" Penelope prompts.

It's a moment before I hear Odysseus's voice from the shadows. "Always."

"Brave?"

"Mostly."

"Was he honest?"

For a long time there's no answer. "No," Odysseus says at last, and I hear him sigh. "He told lies."

Penelope laughs, a shrill sound from close below me. "People always said that about him. I told them, 'They're just stories.' I pay no attention."

"He needed to be loved," Odysseus says. "He wanted everyone to hang on his every word, and they did. It was the look in their eyes, the way he could hold them when he talked. He sat outside his tent, on the shore at Troy, he started talking, a crowd would gather. He'd see their eyes in the firelight, the way they listened. His voice was like the crackle of flames. His stories warmed them. It didn't matter whether they were true or not . . ." His voice breaks suddenly. "But they weren't. Or weren't always."

"I knew that."

"He told me . . ." There's a deep sigh from the shadows in the hall. "He told me he betrayed his wife and son."

I listen until the silence seems so tense it might almost crack.

"He kept a woman in the town," Odysseus goes on. "He had a child."

"I know about that too." Penelope's voice is suddenly cold.

"Didn't you mind?"

"Of course I minded."

"Did you think of leaving him?"

"If he'd stayed, I would have left him." She pauses. "When I had the whole of Odysseus, losing half of him seemed like the end of the world. When he was gone, half seemed better than nothing."

"How could you still love him?"

"People can't decide that." Her voice mocks him. "You can make yourself like someone or respect them. But you can't make yourself love or not love."

"Would you still want him if he did come back?" Odysseus's voice is hoarse now. "Let me tell you, I met him again. After Troy, I was traveling. We were on an island. You should have seen him then. He was broken. Strength gone, courage gone, he was a shell. He couldn't talk, even, just sat by the fire, watching it burn. Would you want Odysseus if he came home like that?"

226

"*No!*"

Penelope hisses it so furiously I can barely hide my gasp. For what seems an age, silence creaks around us, the trickle of time flowing past something, a stone in the current, that can never be unsaid. No sound comes from my father.

It's a long time before she goes on. "But my son tells me he won't come back. Thank you for talking to me." Her voice has become distant—the chief's wife talking to the beggar in the hall. "I'm going to my room now. Good night."

I hear her footsteps rustling away down the corridor. I almost run down to my father, but something stops me. I'm thinking, all those years, Penelope knew what Odysseus was like, knew about his deception as well as his bravery, knew his brilliance, knew his lies. To me, she always described Odysseus the way the storytellers did—as a fighter, a hero. That was the father she wanted me to have, but she knew the other side of Odysseus as well. Sixteen years of waiting, sixteen years of love, but now I know there were other feelings woven into that patient vigil: anger, bitterness, sorrow. What does she want now? What will Penelope do when she recognizes Odysseus, the man who betrayed her? Odysseus is her unfinished business, the thread still left in her hand with the tapestry incomplete. All this time I've been wrong about my mother. It isn't only for love that she's sat at her loom for sixteen years. She's been waiting for an ending.

I don't go down to my father. Only he can decide what to make of what he's heard. This is between him and Penelope. Instead, I stay leaning against the balustrade, watching the hearth and listening to his breath rasp in and out, until the flames burn low and the sound mingles with the slow breathing of dogs around the fire.

I don't sleep. I'm exhausted, but there's too much on my mind. Just before dawn I fumble my way down to the armory, pick three swords and three spears, wrap them in sacking, and carry them to the hall, where I hide them beneath the woodpile. My father appears to be asleep, and I don't wake him. I lock the rest of the weapons in the armory and hide the key under a stone.

By then it's almost daylight, and from below I can hear the first noises of the town waking up. There's a streak of light coloring the sky behind the mountain. I set off downhill, making for the shore. The road's still dark, overhung by thick trees. I hear bleating ahead, smell the hot reek of sheep, and step onto the grass to let the flock flow past me, its shepherd too weary to greet me with more than a nod. The sheep are being driven to the big house to be slaughtered for the funeral feast. They'll be dead by noon. I walk on through the rutted mud they've left behind. The town's first cottages are silent, but as I pass, a shutter swings open. A woman comes out onto the porch in her nightgown, yawning and stretching. I can almost smell the fusty warmth of her sleep. She greets me with a smile and stoops to lift a bucket of water, splashing it over her arms. For a moment I imagine Polycaste again, washing her arms in the mountain streams where we camped on the way back from Sparta. By the time I reach the square there's enough light to see the tavern-keeper hooking his shutters against the wall. Cats slink along the roadway, searching for breakfast. A dog lifts its head to look at me, then lowers it, trembling, to the ground. I stand under the spreading branches of the plane tree. There are birds twittering among the leaves, a bright, harsh sound. One drops to the ground, cocks its head at me, then flutters back to its perch.

I remember the debate here, when I begged the townspeople for a boat. I'd do it better now. With more skill and experience, I might have kept the town on Odysseus's side, turned them against the visitors in the big house and somehow forged a force to defeat them. But it's too late now. With the toe of my sandal I turn over a drift of last year's leaves, which are crumbling into the dry earth. They break at my touch. A man and woman come into sight, pushing a wagon piled high with onions. I walk on past the quiet buildings to the beach, and stoop to touch the water. A ripple turns itself over, slapping the back of my hand. When I put my tongue to it, I taste salt. I look out across the sea. A single cloud hangs in the sky, bruised and dark, above the distant mainland. Elsewhere it's clear, with the clean, fresh brilliance of early morning. I can smell resin from the pines behind the beach. Slowly I walk along the sand with my sandals dangling from one hand. Fishing boats are drawn up along the shore, and between them I can see the furrows carved by the keels of boats that have already put out.

The creak of oars reaches me across the sea. Looking out, I can see half a dozen boats rowing slowly toward the point. Their wake shows briefly in the water, then fades from view. It's almost cold. I stoop and pluck at an abandoned anchor whose bronze flukes have stained the sand copper-blue. I walk onto the rocks and climb to the flat point where men, yesterday, began building my father's pyre. Neat piles of wood, shorn of their twigs, have been stacked around the base of the pyre, where logs are placed crosswise, leaving gaps for the flames to flow. A great heap of kindling and twigs stands to one side. When it's finished, the pyre will be taller than I am.

At my grandfather's funeral we needed ladders to lift the old man's body to the top. I can still remember its limp, soft weight in my hands, the cold feel of it through the layers of winding shroud. This will become my own pyre if things go badly. Hands will lift me onto the heaped wood this very afternoon. There'll be a speech from Antinous. They'll call me mad to have turned on my own guests. "A sudden madness sent by an angry god"—that's the sort of thing people say. And the flames will ripple and flare in the afternoon wind, trailing smoke across the harbor and filling the courtyard of the big house with the smell of fire.

Time to go back. I take the quick way along the beach, greeting the fishermen who, one by one, are preparing their boats for sea or sliding them down into the friendly water. A boy, no more than seven or eight, is paddling thigh-deep. Two others have splashed farther out, their brown bodies glistening. For a moment I feel an urge to pull off my shirt and wade out into the sea myself. A last swim, out to the harbor mouth, where I can turn and float, feeling the lift of the salt water and looking back at Ithaca, my home.

Mentor is sitting on rocks at the end of the beach. He's by himself, hunched over. He doesn't answer when I say his name. There's a vicious purple bruise on his cheek. Antinous.

I sit down next to him at the water's edge. "Did they catch you?"

He doesn't anwer, just sits there, staring at the sea.

"Did they hurt you?" I reach up and touch the bruise on his cheek. He winces.

"I'm sorry," I say. "I'm sorry."

His lips are trembling. "It had to be." So quiet I can hardly hear. When Mentor turns to look at me, there's a kind of film over his eyes, as if he can't focus properly. "It wasn't the pain. It was the things they said."

"Tell me."

He can't. He bows his head and sobs, then gets it under control. "Dreadful things. Threats. My wife, my sons . . . what they'd do to them . . . and me. How can men say things like that? What kind of men must they be?"

I put an arm around the old man's shoulders. When we left for Pylos he wasn't an old man, but he is now. I can feel him shaking.

"I didn't give you away," he says.

"Thank you."

"Not because I was brave." He shrugs my arm off. "Because I knew it would make no difference. They'd go on beating us anyway. What kind of men can do that and feel nothing?" He looks bewildered. "Do you think the war was like that? All of them brutal? Even Odysseus?"

I nod. I don't know whether he can see me or not.

"You've got to go away, Telemachus." Mentor fumbles for my hand. His is cold and weak, shaking. "Go away. Find somewhere else. There are places you can go. Islands, colonies. I'll come with you. My sons, others. There must be another way. You mustn't . . ." His face dissolves. He's crying. "You mustn't become like them."

I could go now. There are fishing boats on the beach. I could leave Ithaca, leave Odysseus, leave this death that's waiting for me. Find Polycaste at Pylos and a new life, an island, peace. The sea glistens at the mouth of the bay. A long row to the mainland, where the forests will hide me. I'm tempted—I can't pretend I'm not. But it's too late for that now. I reach across and touch the bruise on the old man's cheek. I can feel all the slights of my childhood in that bruise, all its pain, all its humiliations. Just for a moment I'm tempted to ask Mentor for help. But he and his sons have done enough already. I can't ask them to die with us as well. I squeeze the old man's hand and turn away. Briskly I climb the track to the back of the house, stopping only when I reach the kitchen yard. There's an odd noise coming from a shed against the kitchen wall. Inside, twelve women kneel in rows, grinding grain in stone bowls. The women scrape stones steadily around the bowls, making a rhythmic sound like the noise waves make, grinding rocks into sand. One of them, with a strip of colored cloth tied around her head, stops suddenly, stretches, yawns. "I wish they'd all leave," she says to the other women. "These guests. Then maybe we'd have some rest."

Does this ordinary scene happen every morning? I wish I'd risen early before to watch the big house come to life. What else have I missed? Ordinary things—the things people don't notice but are actually what life's made of. I turn and cross the yard to the kitchen door. Outside, a man is chopping wood from a heap of logs stacked against the wall. I want to go over and count the orange and buff rings in the sawn trunks, to see how old the trees were when they were felled. The man leans on his axe for a moment. Wood chips litter the earth around his feet. As I reach the kitchen door, a boy comes out, yawning, with an empty bucket to fill at the stream. From the doorway beyond I can smell the reek of burned charcoal. I wonder what's happened to the sheep I passed on the road earlier.

The kitchen is too crowded. I don't want to talk. So instead, I pass along the corridor to the great hall to find my father.

Odysseus isn't there.

His satchel is still lying against the column where he slept, but there's no sign of him. I run to the courtyard but it's empty too, the young men still sleeping in their tents. Perhaps my father has slipped out through the side door. In the orchard I hear a heavy droning from the darkness under the trees. A shadow ripples the air near the trunk of an ancient olive tree—a swarm of bees. But there's no sign of Odysseus.

Panic surges up inside me. I hurry back to the kitchen, where Melanthius, the cook, is lifting sheep hocks from a cauldron with a slotted spoon.

"The tramp who was sleeping in the hall last night . . . Have you seen him?"

The cook shakes his head. He's a burly man with a white beard, once, it's said, a priest. "He was gone when I stoked the fire this morning at dawn."

Just after I went down to the village, then. Perhaps Odysseus was only feigning sleep when I looked into the hall earlier.

"He's a tramp," the cook shrugs. "He'll have taken off. They do. Best count the silver dishes." Laughter.

Has Odysseus really left? I heard what Penelope told him last night. Maybe he's scared she might not want him anymore; or scared by the odds against him. Even now he might be begging berths from the ships in the harbor, or rowing out to sea, one man against the waves, with the sun on his neck and the weight of the ocean against his oars. Returned and fled, the burden of sixteen years' absence too great for him to bear.

I run upstairs, but all the doors are closed along the corridor, and there's no sound from behind them. Downstairs, I cross the courtyard to the main gate and find Eumaeus herding three hogs out of the olive trees with a thin birch stick.

"My father's gone." I glance over my shoulder to make sure no one can hear. I can hear the panic in my own voice.

Eumaeus snorts. "No, 'e ain't. I seed him go up the mountain early. Took the cliff path."

Eumaeus points with his wand, and suddenly I understand. The path to the shrine. My father's gone to the shrine. I set off after him, feet slipping on loose stones. Lizards snap away into cracks in the rock. It's beginning to get hotter. When I glance over my shoulder, I see the bruised orange cloud I noticed on the beach spreading along the horizon like water flooding through a breached dam. There'll be a storm later. The air is still. Grasshoppers flick from the path in front of me. To either side the olive trees shrill with cicadas.

I lift the sacking over the shrine's door and peer into the rancid fug inside. In the flicker of oil lamps I can see Odysseus kneeling in front of the altar.

The priest's sarcastic laugh breaks in on me. "See who's here?" he cackles. "See who's come back?" He points at the kneeling man. "Your father."

Odysseus looks up at me. As my eyes grow used to the murk I can see his cheeks are wet with tears.

"He told me he was a tramp. Said his name was Aethon. *I* saw through him straightaway. You can't tell lies in here. We see everything. *She* sees everything . . ." The priest gestures to the blackened statue on the altar, whose white enameled eyes glitter in the candlelight. "Odysseus of Ithaca, after sixteen years. What's left of him, anyway. See? I gave him his offerings. Like a child playing with its toys."

The tray lies in Odysseus's lap. He holds the little carved owl in one hand. In the other he's slowly crushing the dried bay leaves from the mountain where Penelope grew up.

"Leave us." The priest looks like he wants to protest, but he obeys grudgingly, letting the sacking fall in place behind him. He'll listen at the door, but I no longer care.

"Did you sleep well?" I ask gently. The same voice I use with my mother.

Odysseus shakes his head. "I dreamed . . ." He breaks off, and his beard sinks onto his chest. For a moment he doesn't speak. "I dreamed of Penelope," he goes on at last, then looks at me. "Why did I stay away?"

"Only you can answer that."

"Maybe it would be better if I leave again."

"You can't go." I crouch down next to my father. "You *can't.*" I hold my father's soft, bewildered eyes.

Slowly Odysseus shakes his head. "No." He picks up the boar's tusk and lays it down again, picks up the blade he dedicated the day he announced he was leaving for Troy and weighs it in his hand. "How much can you fight?"

"A little. No one taught me. I killed someone."

"Were you scared?"

"Not at the time. Afterward, I was."

"Always afterward." Odysseus nods. "I went to the town yesterday. I saw my daughter."

"Did you speak to her?"

"I didn't dare."

"How did you know her?"

"She was with her mother. *She* hasn't changed."

"Has Penelope?"

Odysseus shakes his head and lets the dust of the bay leaves pour out between the fingers of his left hand.

"She loves you."

"How can she?"

I take my father by the arm. Through his cloak's rough sacking I can feel a fighter's hard muscle. "You're Odysseus," I say. "You led the Ithacans. You conquered Troy. The men we'll fight today are empty. You understand? You're worth all of them together."

A curious smile twists Odysseus's scarred face. He raises one hand and taps his forehead with two hard fingers. "Sham," he whispers.

"No!" I clutch my father's hand, pulling it down, but Odysseus only shakes his head.

"Leave me now," he says in a more normal voice. "I want to speak to the goddess."

"*Speak* to her?"

Odysseus nods as if that's the most normal thing in the world. "Alone."

I don't know what to think as I skid down the path back to the house. Is my father mad? Is he in any state to fight a room full of murderous young men, trained fighters half his age? Will his tired body break first, or his weary mind? I pass a sloughed-off snakeskin on the track, crusted and old. Above, in the clear sky, I see an eagle wheeling. It turns, suddenly, and drops, faster than sight, to snatch a pigeon from the air and flap away on slow wings, a small, black burden hunched in its talons. As I reach the gate, a single rumble of thunder sounds from the east. A cold breath of air touches my neck. The olive trees toss. There's a storm coming. Outside the gate, a flock of goats is kicking up clouds of dust, the stray dogs barking at them and the goatherd slashing at them with his switch. Eumaeus leans against the wall.

"Find 'im?"

"He'll be down soon. Wait here."

I need to see my mother. As I cross the courtyard I pass young men rising, yawning and readying themselves for the day. They stand in a line, bare-chested, at the water butt in the corner. They're stretching and loosening the sleep from their shoulders, confident in their muscled, fighters' bodies. One is shaving over a dish of steaming water, peering at his own reflection in a burnished shield held by a servant.

The upper floor is silent, but when I knock at Penelope's door, her voice answers. She's sitting on her unmade bed, hair loose and feet bare, frowning.

"Are you all right?"

She nods but doesn't speak.

"I'm sorry we argued yesterday." I need to say that before the day begins.

"Did we?" She shrugs. "It doesn't matter."

"I love you."

"And I love you." She looks up at me, puzzled.

I come and sit on the bed next to her. "What's the matter?"

"I had another dream. Of Odysseus. He was here." She looks down at the bed. "He was right here with me. He was *old*." She shudders suddenly. Through her nightdress, I can see how thin my mother is. In the morning light she looks ill.

"It was a dream."

"He said . . . he said, 'Why did you wait for me?' I didn't know how to answer. He was sick, I think. His poor face all scarred, and he had a limp. It was Odysseus, though. I know it was him, and I woke in a sweat." She shivers, hugging herself. "Maybe he's dead, that's what the dream's telling me. On an island somewhere. Or in Egypt."

"No!"

She looks bitterly at me. "You were the one who told me he's dead."

I say, "There's something I must tell you. Odysseus isn't dead. He's here . . ."

"No!" The violence in her voice startles me. She lifts one small hand and presses it hard against my mouth. "No!" And she goes on, spitting out each small, hard word separately. "I—don't—want—to—hear." Slowly she releases the pressure from my mouth.

"Mother . . ."

"People say these things. They'll say anything. 'I saw him in Crete.' 'He's on a ship.' And then you say, 'He's dead,' and now, 'He's alive.' I—don't—want—to hear any more. It's just stories, stories. Everyone uses his name for themselves. 'I saw Odysseus. I want money.' He isn't here." She shakes her head, her hair flying wildly. "I saw Odysseus leave. I know him. He hasn't come back."

"Mother, please, you have to listen."

"No!" Penelope squeezes her hands over her ears and shuts her eyes tight, folding herself into a ball like a child frightened of the dark. I put one hand on her neck. I can feel it tense. With her eyes still closed, she says, "Today I'll choose a man. A new husband. It's time."

"No!" She doesn't respond. I shake her arm. "You mustn't. *Please.*"

No answer. I plead with her, but she won't speak again. It's no use. For a moment Penelope saw the world as it was, but the shadows are pressing around her again. I leave her in the end, but before I go I stoop to kiss the top of her head. There are grey hairs among the black, I notice. My mother is growing old.

Full of foreboding, I close the door and make my way down to the hall. It's full. The young men have dressed for Odysseus's funeral. Their hair is oiled. They wear brightly colored shirts, sashes bound around their waists, and leather cloaks with embroidered hems. Some have ornamental daggers thrust into their sashes, others, swords in richly-embroidered scabbards.

I beckon to a servant. "You'll find Eumaeus waiting by the main gate. Tell him to come in."

I nod to Eurymachus, who's wearing a green silk shirt studded with bronze medallions. A moment later Eumaeus sidles into the hall and makes his way to the corner. There's still no sign of Odysseus. Antinous, in crimson, is inspecting the jewels that encrust his fingers, with a knot of admiring men around him. Some are studying the table already set out for the feast, piled with wine jars and trays of bread. Others are slouched on the benches or leaning restlessly against the tables, drumming their fingers, playing with sleeves and tassels. Peacocks. Or prize-fighting cocks. Show birds dressed for display, strutting, preening, always eyeing one another for the fight. I'm thinking, *It's what Odysseus must have been once. It's what I was born for.* I see Odysseus come in at last, wearily pausing on the threshold to look at the brilliantly dressed young men assembled for his own funeral. His head is down. Slowly he makes his way around the walls to a column and settles beneath it, his beggar's satchel on his knees. He doesn't look up at me.

My mouth's dry, and I beckon over a servant with a pitcher of water. I remember how high, how young my voice sounded when I addressed the town meeting. That mustn't happen.

I swallow the cup of water gratefully and climb on a bench. "Guests!" It takes a moment to silence the hall, but at last I have their attention. "I would ask you to show respect for my father today." Faces look up at me, skeptical, bored, a few assuming the solemn expression they think appropriate for a burial. "Today we will light a pyre in memory of Odysseus. You all know how hard this will be for my mother, Penelope, so I have decided there will be no grand procession down to the beach. We would rather divide the procession into small groups. Antinous, we would be grateful"—I stress the *we*—"if you would lead the first party down there. I will come later, with my mother and the remaining guests."

It sounds reasonable enough, doesn't it? A couple of the men nod. But Antinous is frowning. "Why?" he says in a loud, harsh voice. "Odysseus was chief of Ithaca. He deserves a show. We should go together."

"This is as my mother wishes it." My mouth is dry.

Voices start to break out. I glance at my father, but Odysseus is staring at the ground like he's in a trance.

"Please!"

I have to persuade them, I *have* to. This was the best plan we could come up with. If things go well, we have a chance of overcoming half of them before the others figure out something's wrong. But already it's coming unstuck.

"No!" Antinous is snarling, in a rough bark quite unlike his usual voice. There's something wrong with him. He's pale, and his whole body is quivering. Does he suspect something? "We'll stay together." His small, sharp eyes dart around the hall.

"Please . . ." I'm trying to speak above the hubbub, but another voice stills all of us.

"No one's going to the shore."

The silence is immediate. I look around. Penelope is standing on the stair landing. Is it her words that have hushed everyone, or her appearance? I expected her to come prepared for a funeral, wearing black, with her face whitened and ashes in her hair.

Instead, Penelope is dressed as a bride.

Her gown is white. There's a twine of bay leaves in her hair. A thin gold chain hangs around her neck.

"No one's going to the shore," she repeats, her voice clear and determined. Suddenly she points at the wall. I don't know what she means, to start with. Then I realize she's pointing at Odysseus's great bow. "Bring that to me."

A servant unhooks it, and the bow is passed from hand to hand across the hall. As it reaches Penelope, the bright sunlight in the doorway shivers, and the square of sky above the hearth dims suddenly. Everyone feels the cold breath of air flowing into the hall. Servants hurry to light torches in the brackets around the wall.

Penelope takes the bow, taller than she is, and turns it over in her hands. Its wood is dark, the ivory horns at either end yellowed with age and smoke. The string hangs loose between them.

"Today," she says, "I'll choose the man I'll live with." Her hands caress the smooth wood of the bow. "I'll marry the man who can string this bow."

A murmur of surprise and confusion fills the room. I look for Eumaeus but can't see him. Penelope speaks above the commotion. "Odysseus could string this bow. I won't take a lesser man than him. If no one can string it, I'll die alone." As she speaks the words, she looks straight at the tramp by the woodpile.

And that's when I realize she knows. She knows it's Odysseus; she's known all along. This is the ending Penelope needs. We made our plans, but it's hers we'll follow. The ending that will close sixteen years of pain.

A test not for the others but for Odysseus.

"Give it to me."

Antinous strides across the hall, the other young men parting for him. No one questions his right to try the bow first. He seizes it from Penelope, his face set, and weighs it in his hand. Suddenly he gives an odd little giggle and rolls up his sleeves. He plants one foot firmly in front of him, sets the lower horn against it, and curls the fingers of his left hand around the grip.

For a moment he stands, rocking on his toes. The torches around the walls flicker in the cold gusts that steal through the door. No one speaks. Delicately Antinous untwists the string with his right hand and, still holding it, sets his hand halfway up the bow's haft. He lowers his face, rocking farther and more slowly, as if he's trying to recruit strength from deep within his bulk. A growl emerges from somewhere inside him, rising in pitch until it becomes a high wailing, almost like a woman's lament. Suddenly his body hardens and convulses. The bow whips and gives a great creak as he bends it back, hand drawing the string to the top of the shaft. I can hardly watch. He's done it, I think. He's strung the bow. Antinous's face is purple. The tendons on his arm stand out like ropes. His fingers scrabble for the horn at the top of the bow, trying to hook the string over it. But there's something despairing now in his shriek. His right foot stamps the floor, seeking a better purchase, and as it does, the bow gives a great kick. Like an animal wriggling from a hunter's grasp, it leaps into the air. Antinous's voice becomes a wail and dies. He staggers back against the wall as the bow clatters to the ground, unstrung.

Before anyone can move, Antinous lunges forward again. His fingers scrabble at his belt. Suddenly he has an axe in his hands. He raises it high over his head, but just as he's about to bring it down on the bow, Eurymachus grasps his wrist.

"Stop." His voice is cold and calm.

Antinous glares at him. The two men's faces are only a hand's breadth apart.

"Others can try this test."

A mutter of angry agreement runs around the hall. Slowly, still glaring at Eurymachus, Antinous relaxes, lowers his arms, takes a step back. Eurymachus picks up the bow. He keeps his eyes on Antinous as he takes up his stance, left foot braced against the lower horn. He bends the bow a couple of times before trying to string it, grimacing as he senses the hardness in the wood. Old wood, stiff as the tree from which it was cut, unyielding.

The torches flicker again. A cold breath sweeps through the hall like the tongue of death. Penelope shivers. Some of the young men draw their cloaks around them as a few fat drops of rain fall into the hearth, making the fire hiss. But Eurymachus seems unaware of the sudden chill. He fixes his eyes somewhere in the distance, to the left of where Antinous still stands. A frown of concentration creases his handsome face. He dips his body to the right as he scoops up the string, as if he's dancing with the bow, coaxing it, seducing it. There's no preliminary posturing. Suddenly he tenses, and the string slips easily up the bow's polished shaft. Eurymachus's hips swivel as he brings it close to his face. For a moment I think he's going to kiss the yellowed horn as the string drops into place.

But the string stops dead two fingers short of the notch. It's as if, having curved the bow so far to his will, Eurymachus has suddenly hit resistant metal beneath the pliant wood. He straightens his back, yielding nothing, and urges the string another finger's breadth toward its goal. He's muttering to himself now. His eyes are closed; his narrow shoulders begin to rise. Then suddenly, carelessly, he throws the bow aside and walks away. The crowd parts for him. Eurymachus goes to the door and stands with his back to the hall, looking out.

No one speaks.

After a moment another man steps forward. It's Agelaus, the brute who was in a knife fight over Melantho the day Mentes arrived. I don't know much about him except that he comes from one of the islands in the east of Greece and is said to be rich. A black beard covers the lower part of his face. His rounded shoulders curve into arms as thick as branches, ending in red, jointless hands that grip whole bones of lamb when he eats. I know he's a wrestler. Once, when they were all wrestling on the beaten earth to the side of the house, I saw him take on all comers, one by one, and fight them to a standstill. He didn't want to let the last man go but threw him again and again, expressionless, until the other man's face was a mask of blood, one eye was gone, and his arm hung broken at his side.

Jerkily, Agelaus unhooks his cloak and drops it on the floor. Wiry black hair covers his arms and shoulders. He picks up the bow and shakes it, like he's punishing a puppy he wants to train, then wriggles his shoulders, sets the bow's horn against his foot, and begins to heave. I catch the puzzled look in his face the moment he realizes the bow's stronger than he is. Maybe he never fought anything stronger than himself. He strains. The bow gives nothing back. Instead of bending, it starts to bend Agelaus, sliding his fingers back down the haft until the bow rises straight and Agelaus bows before it, hands on his knees, panting and groaning with the effort.

Penelope is still standing on the stair. Her back is straight, her expression calm.

"Isn't there anyone else?" she asks contemptuously.

The young men are beginning to sidle back. None of them is stronger than Agelaus. None of them can string the bow if Antinous and Eurymachus have failed—and they know it.

"What about the beggar?" Penelope asks. She's looking straight at Odysseus.

"He's a tramp," Antinous says thickly. They're the first words he's uttered since failing to string the bow.

"He's a man," Penelope says.

I don't know what to do. Once, Odysseus could string that bow. But that was sixteen years ago—before Troy, before his journey, before fortune took him in its fingers, bowed his back and greyed his hair, crushed his strength, clouded his eyes.

But there's nothing I can do—nothing any of us can do. I watch Odysseus shuffle to his feet. Someone laughs.

"Give him a chance," Eurymachus says. He turns from the door. His voice has resumed its usual lighthearted tone, as if nothing bad has happened. "Go on. What harm can it do?"

Grudgingly Antinous stands back as the tramp limps to the space under the landing. When he reaches it, though, he stands stupidly, staring at the bow on the ground without picking it up. He looks up at Penelope, then at me, his expression puzzled, as if he doesn't even know who I am.

Suddenly thunder rolls directly overhead. Some of the young men look up, muttering charms. There's a tossing of branches outside, a hissing sound, and a clapping of canvas from the tents in the courtyard. Rain closes the doorway, as if drawn across by a grey curtain. It drums on the roof, darkens the sky, pours suddenly down onto the hearth, dousing the fire and filling the hall with the smell of wet ash. A trickle of dusty water, dark as blood, curls through the doorway, finding crevices in the beaten earth until it puddles at Odysseus's feet.

He stoops and picks up the bow. His face is bent so low I can't see his expression anymore. I'm trying to focus on a plan. What happens next? When Odysseus has failed, do I call for the funeral to carry on? Or is that the end of my father's homecoming? I just don't know. My mind is slipping on the facts, failing to grip them. Numbly I watch Odysseus pluck at the string. His fingers seem too clumsy to hold it. As if he's playing for time, he picks up the quiver in his free hand. It swings sideways on its strap, and arrows cascade out onto the floor. Everyone laughs as Odysseus goes down on his hands and knees, scrabbling to gather them up.

"Get *on* with it," Antinous snaps.

Odysseus bobs his head, trying to collect arrows and hold the bow at the same time. When he stands up, the bow is dangling in his left hand, an arrow in his right.

"Get on with it!"

Odysseus sniffs, sets the bow against his foot, and grasps the string. The arrow is still dangling from the little fingers of his right hand. He bends suddenly, but it's a false start. Like a horse shying at a hedge, he stands up again. I can see his legs trembling.

"Maybe . . ." Eurymachus begins.

But he never finishes the sentence. Suddenly Odysseus stoops. His hand grips the bow, crushing the hard wood. As his weight comes on it, the bow curves like a tree caught in a forest gale. It bows, uncomplaining, as Odysseus grasps the upper horn and twists it back. I hear Penelope gasp. In a single, smooth movement, Odysseus slips the string into the notch, swings his arrow to the string, and bends back the bow. It gives a deep creak, almost like the growl of an animal, then booms as he releases the string.

His arrow catches Agelaus full in the throat. It drives through his neck, snapping his head back. Agelaus's fingers claw wildly at a beard that's suddenly saturated in flowing, thick blood. One of the servants screams. Odysseus is already reloading. His second arrow drives into Agelaus's chest, its force tumbling him backward over a table. Merciless, Odysseus fires again, hands finding the arrows without his even looking, eyes picking his next target as soon as each arrow is gone. I vault the balustrade to be at his side, but Odysseus pays no attention to me. The young men tumble backward to escape arrows that seem to have invaded the hall like a swarm of hornets. I see one man caught full in the back, a dark stain spreading around the shaft that has suddenly appeared, antlerlike, between his shoulder blades. I see another hit in the eye, hands clawing his face as he goes down, and another desperately trying to pluck a shaft from his trailing leg. Blood flows over the hearth, mingling with spilled wine on the floor. There's a crash as the table of food goes over, smashing wine jars and plates against the wall.

It can't last. There are too many men, too few arrows. I sense the flow slacken. From the corner of my eye I see Antinous, still unharmed, pulling his dagger from his belt. Odysseus steps back. When I glance at him, my father is breathing hard, nostrils wide and forehead filmed with sweat despite the cold in the hall. The bow trails in his left hand. His right hand is empty. The arrows are finished.

I'm thinking, *We have to get to the woodpile, reach the weapons I hid last night.* I pluck at my father's sleeve, but Odysseus isn't seeing me. An odd whimpering sound comes from deep in his chest. Giving up, I race over the hearth to the woodpile. As I reach it, I turn in time to see Antinous lunge at my father with his dagger held in both hands. Odysseus screams. Letting the bow fall, he scrambles desperately back over upturned tables and benches, shoving men aside. At the corner of the hall, he turns, at bay. Antinous is coming after him. From somewhere he's swept up a short bronze spear, whose tip winks dully in the light from the torches. His face is cold, intent, murderous. There's no time for me to do anything. Heart stopped, I watch Odysseus slide down the wall, hands pathetically trying to cover his face. From behind them he shoots me a desperate, pleading look. Our eyes lock.

And in that moment I don't see a hero or fighter. I don't see the conqueror of Troy, the man I dreamed of all through my childhood. I see only one thing: fear.

19

I never reach my father, but someone else does. Everything seems to be moving at half speed. I see Antinous draw back the spear. I see his teeth bare in a snarl. But the blow doesn't fall. Eurymachus has crossed the hall. Cool, expressionless, he drives his sword up beneath Antinous's ribs. I watch the bronze disappear into Antinous's soft body, as if Eurymachus has wrapped it in a curtain. For a moment there isn't even any blood. Antinous just stands there, like a statue of a man holding a spear. Then he drops the spear and goes over sideways, blood spurting as Eurymachus wrenches out his sword.

I shout my father's name. Pull the hidden swords from their sacking, race across the hall. Rage is welling up inside me, elbowing fear aside. Eumaeus is by my father already, swinging a footstool to drive off the men who are already starting to press in.

"Take this."

Eumaeus grips the sword I pass him, and, swapping his stool to the other hand, slashes at a man in blue who's charging Odysseus with his sword at arm's length. The man screams, clutching his severed arm, and goes down on his knees as Eumaeus crushes the stool down on his head. Eurymachus is already stabbing and parrying. My father is still whimpering on the ground. I drop a sword at his feet and turn to face our enemies. Four of us against a horde of men who are moving toward the corner like sharks, sensing blood in the water.

"All right?" Eurymachus touches my shoulder and grins briefly.

No time to answer. A man charges me, eyes squinting in vicious concentration. I let his weight carry him on, step back, and thrust my blade into his belly. There's no time to think about what I've just done. Another man is already feinting at me. Watch their feet, Polycaste said. I see the man's weight roll forward onto his toes—the blow's coming. As it arrives, I twist aside and bring my blade down on the attacker's neck. I'm not scared anymore. This morning, yes. Right now, though, I'm feeling cold, pure exhilaration—the exhilaration of a battle that's been waiting for me all my life. I can do this. I can fight and survive, kill and turn to face whatever danger comes next.

Peisander, one of Antinous's friends, hurls himself at me, lifting his sword in both hands. He was one of the men who dressed me as a girl and made me sing to them. I dodge the swinging sword and stab him sharply in the groin. Peisander screams, and as he goes down, I kick out at his face, feeling my foot jar against bone. Then I'm feinting again as someone else slashes at me. I parry and slash back, but miss. Eurymachus's sword cuts in from one side, though, and blood flowers from the man's ear. I step back, take a deep breath, then dance forward again as a spear flickers past me. I don't even see who's holding it but bring the hilt of my sword down hard on someone's hand and kick out again. Suddenly the exhilaration is draining out of me. This is hard. My thoughts were surfing ahead of each danger in the beginning, but now the threats are coming thick and fast, from every direction. I *can't* foresee them all. And my sword's getting heavier. How can I keep lifting it? Suddenly I'm tired, and know it. I start noticing other things, stupid things. A swallow darting into the hall through the open doorway, circling the beams in a flash of red and blue and disappearing through the opening above the hearth. I lower my sword.

Luckily I'm not the only one who's tired. There's a general lull in the fighting, as if by agreement. Eurymachus rests his hands on his knees, panting. The others stand back, forming a ring around us. For the moment we just watch each other, chests heaving. It isn't the usual exchange of glances, though—it's the gaze of men who intend to kill one another. I become aware of rain still drumming down on the courtyard and hearth, as if the heavens are unburdening themselves of all their fury. It feels like the end of the world. A deluge to drown everything. Skies melting until water laps over the harbor wall, creeps up streets and alleys, reclaims the mountainside and washes over the peak of Nirito. My mother's loom will float upon the waves. Her pictures weren't meaningless after all. They showed this: chaos.

A man slashes at me, and dully I hit back. The battle starts again, but untidily. I can feel the heaviness in my arm. When another man thrusts a spear at my side, I'm too slow in responding and feel a burning pain along my rib. How much longer can I go on? I can sense Eumaeus's weariness as well. The old man is grunting as he fights, his breath coming in hoarse, rasping pants. Eurymachus's hair is black with sweat, and there's a crimson bloodstain on his shoulder. He was fighting with sword and dagger to start with, one in each hand, but now he's holding his dagger awkwardly.

Like water built up behind a dam, the men in front of us seem aware of their own weight, their power to overwhelm. They thrust forward, pressing us back. Eurymachus gives a sudden gasp of pain but keeps on fighting. All of a sudden I'm treading on something soft. I'm standing right over my father. There's nowhere farther to retreat.

Odysseus moves.

I feel him move beneath my feet. At first I think he's simply cowering farther back and step over him. When my father moves again, it makes me angry, for some reason. All I want is to fight, now—fight until some blade slips through my guard and it's finished. The sooner the better, so I can drop this weight in my hand, lie down, and quietly sleep. When my father pushes me to one side, I push back furiously, and it's only then I realize that I'm shoving against an immovable strength.

Odysseus has risen to his feet, like a bear uncoiling itself from winter sleep. A spear jabs at him. He grabs its hilt and tears it out of the fighter's hands. I hear a roar. Somehow Odysseus has a sword in his hands. He grips me by the shoulder and shoves me aside, pushing me against the wall so hard that for a moment I'm winded. Pressed against the wall, I hear Odysseus howl again. And watch my father move across the hall. *Move*—he doesn't walk or stride; he just *moves*. The sword blade flickers around him like lightning around a tall pine tree. With great sweeps of the weapon he clears a path before him. Men clutch at him, screaming, and he tosses them aside. Blood drips from his wrist. His progress becomes a dance. He rocks from side to side, yelling and slashing, as if he's cutting not men's bodies but nets that seek to ensnare him, cutting himself free, turning with a roar to scatter the cowering men around him.

I do what I can to keep up. I'm still winded, but I follow Odysseus with Eurymachus and Eumaeus at my side. Sweat fills my eyes. The others are beaten now and know it. Most are going down on their knees, begging for mercy, but Odysseus ignores them. The fighting lust has taken hold of him. Melanthius, the cook, is pushed against him, babbling a plea for forgiveness. Odysseus slashes his throat with a single movement. Only when they realize they have no hope of mercy do the last men stand to fight. Odysseus crushes them as he moves forward. They retreat against the hearth with the rain wetting their backs, a dozen of them standing on the bloodstained bodies of their friends. Odysseus closes in for the kill.

As he moves in, I sense something's wrong. Why does Eurymachus push me aside to take my place at Odysseus's elbow? I'm too out of breath to complain, but when I look at Eurymachus, there's something odd in his pose. My mind's too tired to work out what. Eurymachus is still jabbing at our enemies, but he keeps glancing at Odysseus, to his right.

Watch their feet, Polycaste taught me. Watch their feet, and you'll know where they're going to stab next. Mechanically I look down at Eurymachus's feet. Twisted to one side, weight on the toes, ready for the kill. But to kill whom?

Then I know. Eurymachus doesn't even draw back his sword. The blow's disguised; no one in the hall will ever see who dealt it. But I know what Eurymachus is planning to do. "A good family," my father said. "You can trust Eurymachus." But I never did, despite all that friendliness, all the good humor. I knew all along Eurymachus was false.

As Eurymachus's knife sweeps upward toward Odysseus's heart, I throw myself in front of my father. I feel a blow against my side but stay on my feet. Clutching Eurymachus by the throat, I bring my sword up, through soft clothing and flesh, and feel blood flow hotly over my hand.

Suddenly Eurymachus and I aren't standing together. I'm carrying him, supporting his weight. He smiles at me. His smile is as charming as ever. He's still smiling as the sense melts from his gaze and he slides down my chest to his knees.

I'm kneeling too. I'm not sure why. The edge of the hearth touches my cheek, and I put my hand on it. The stone's wet with rain. I'm clutching my own side. I see Eumaeus's face and feel the old man tug at my hand, but I don't let him pull it away. I don't want to, though I can't remember why it's so important to keep it there. Eumaeus turns me over, and I sit back against the hearth, looking up at the roof. Suddenly the roof seems too far away, or maybe too close—I'm not sure which. I can see my father now, sitting on the ground. There's no one else in the hall—no one alive.

"Easy." I see Eumaeus's lips move before I hear the words—or perhaps I just imagined that. The lips move again.

"You're hurt." There's a pain in my side. I stop resisting Eumaeus and let him drag my hand away. There doesn't seem to be anything else to do. I watch Odysseus drop his sword and pass a hand over his face like he's washing it. When he takes his hand away, his face is smeared with blood. That makes me want to laugh. I want to tell my father to wash his face, but the words seem too big for my mouth and my tongue's too dry, so I just nod, hoping he'll understand what I mean.

Then I see my mother, and the sight of her brings another wave of pain to my side, along with a wash of confused noise: women screaming in the distance and the drumming of rain on the roof. I'd forgotten it was raining. Penelope's wearing white. But as she walks slowly across the hall, the hem of her gown, trailing on the floor, becomes soaked in crimson, as if it's drawing blood up from the earth.

She doesn't seem to notice. I watch her drop to a crouch, not beside me but next to Odysseus. She takes his face in both hands. I watch my father's eyes slowly come into focus as he looks up at her. I don't see her lips move, but I can hear the words she whispers to him.

"My husband," she says softly. "My husband."

20

The sky is clear, the rain is gone, the heat has returned, scorching the houses of the town and plunging the benches under the plane tree into deep shadow. Sitting back in the chair they've made for me, I can feel my eyes closing. My father told me I'd feel faint. I'm no longer in danger, but I'll be sick and faint for a week, at least, from loss of blood.

My father's talking now. It feels like he's been talking forever. He's winning the town over, steering them toward him—and he's loving every moment of it.

So are they. If I half open my eyes, I can see them lining the benches, eyes fixed on Odysseus as he tells his tales. Such tales. A one-eyed giant who ate sailors. A monster called Scylla who plucked men from the deck and devoured them. The witch Calypso, who kept him captive in her palace for five years.

I've learned a lot more about my father in the last twenty-four hours.

The morning after the fight, I woke in my bedroom to the smell of burning. They were fumigating the big house, purging it, and cleaning out the smell of death. When I lifted my head to look through the open door, I could see a brazier burning on the landing. Servants went from room to room, scattering dried lavender. Smoke billowed from the courtyard, where they were burning the tents. In the afternoon they carried me out to the garden. A pall of smoke hung over the harbor. They'd fired the pyre built for Odysseus and were burning the bodies of the young men. The smoke hung over the town in the windless air, choking the streets and dropping oily black soot on the sand.

That wasn't all Odysseus did to purify his house. He killed the servants who had helped the intruders. I watched a group of boys, dressed only in their shirts, led out to the orchard with wrists bound. I wasn't strong enough to protest. Later I watched Melantho, my mother's maid, killed in the courtyard. She'd slept with two or three of the young men, Agelaus and Eurymachus among them. Odysseus ordered a rope to be slung between the galleries, and Melantho was brought out. She was struggling, and kept struggling as they looped the rope around her neck and tautened it. She went on struggling, toes scribbling frenzied messages in the dust, until her body sagged suddenly and Odysseus let the rope fall slack.

I can still smell dead fire as I lie under the plane tree. It's a rottenness in the air like the sour smell of old meat. I wonder how long it'll take to wash away. I wonder how long it'll be before anything feels normal again. But perhaps I'm too tired to wonder anything. I feel soaked in exhaustion, like a rag dipped in water. I let my head drop back against the chair and look up into the canopy of leaves.

This morning I watched Odysseus bargain with the parents of the young men who died—those parents who live on the island, that is. Others will arrive from the mainland in the next few weeks. The parents demanded blood money, threatened feuds. Odysseus was as masterful as a lawyer, arguing, persuading, cajoling, until hands were shaken, backs slapped, and the threat of an island riven by blood feuds was lifted. When the other families arrive, he'll deal with them just as skillfuly. He can do that, just like he can lead, and fight, and tell stories.

Which he's doing now. He's describing Troy, its walls rising sheer from the plain like cliffs, and the Greek camp on the beach. Listening to him, you can almost hear the blare of the Trojan trumpets, see the banners fluttering as the soldiers come out to fight. He describes the wooden horse and Troy's last night. When he talks of their departure for home, he chokes up, and Penelope has to reach out a hand to comfort him.

Before the meeting, the villagers came into the square hesitantly. I saw knots of them gathering outside the tavern, talking in hushed voices. But as soon as Odysseus began to speak, they were his. Leaning forward in their chairs as he talked. Women covering their mouths as he described the men he had led and lost. It was as if he cast a spell over them. One thing I can see—he needs them more than they need him. Odysseus doesn't just want a majority to support him as chief. He needs them to leap to their feet, to pledge him everything. He needs them to love him—and they will.

I close my eyes. My head's aching, as if it's carrying an odd weight. I managed to walk most of the way down to the square, but Eumaeus and Eurycleia had to help me the last few steps and maneuver me into this cushion-lined chair under the tree. Eurymachus's sword cut deep—another inch and I wouldn't be here now. The night after the fight, I woke up screaming. When I came to myself, Eurycleia was sitting over me, moistening my forehead with a cool cloth. She dipped the cloth in a bowl of water and wrung it out. The dribble of water in the bowl reminded me of when my mother cooled me during hot nights when I was a child.

I watch my mother stroke Odysseus's hand. I've barely seen her since the fight, but I've heard her laughter coiling along the corridor like a girl's. It's been years since I heard my mother laugh. I've seen her holding Odysseus's hand as we dine together, and the shy smile she gives him when he drains his cup and leads her upstairs. Penelope has her husband back, and I've never seen her look so young, or so alive.

Am I jealous? I suppose so. The truth is, my father's come home and my mother doesn't need me anymore. And it's not just her I've lost. It's my home. My father's voice fills the hall now. His laugh echoes along the corridors. The house isn't mine anymore. Odysseus has returned to Ithaca, and suddenly this island I call home has become too small.

Odysseus has visited me often. He sits on the end of my bed, hands on his knees, talking about my future.

"You fought well. You must see some proper fighting now. A brawl around the hearth is nothing to boast of. I'll send a message to Menelaus. He'll find an army for you to fight in. You'll travel to Egypt or to Crete. You must feel the quiver of a chariot under your legs and the pull on the reins as horses charge into a line of archers. You must see ships landing on a beach and a town in flames."

When I don't say anything, he looks down at me, frowning, puzzled. "You need to rest," he says. "You'll be better after a week's rest."

I've spent most of the time thinking about Polycaste. About our journey across the mountains—the owls hooting in the twilight as our fire burned low, the cold sheen of dew as we woke to morning mists. I've thought of how we talked as we sat by mountain streams, watching the spray flick up from rocks and the rainbows fanned by the sunlight. There is another way. Polycaste and I both know that.

I can go on learning to fight, but I don't want to. I could choose my father's world if I wanted, but I don't want it. There was a flame of anger inside me, but the anger's burned out.

Yesterday morning, I had them carry me down to Mentor's house. He was sitting outside with his sons, eyes closed in the sunlight. His sons welcomed me. Their wives ran indoors for jugs of wine and trays of bread while Mentor's wife piled cushions on a soft chair.

"He hasn't been the same since they beat him," she whispers. "He's tired. Don't make him talk too long."

I put my hand on Mentor's, and he opened his eyes. "I'm going to leave."

He nodded, tongue moistening his dry lips. "Good . . . good."

"Will you come with me?"

"Where will you go?"

"Somewhere in the west. We'll find an island, start a colony. Others have done it."

Mentor nodded again and closed his eyes. "Good," he repeated. "Good."

His sons helped me gather the rest of our crew. Together, painfully, we went from house to house. I wasn't sure they'd accept me as leader, but no one objected. Eumaeus is coming—I was surprised by that. But he's had enough of fighting, enough of war. He wants a quiet place where he can raise his pigs in peace and watch the sun set over the sea each evening. We've got half the crew who sailed with us to Pylos. My half sister's coming, and her mother too. They were never accepted in the town; they want a new home. There are farmers from the mountain who've pledged to sign up, and boys with too many brothers who want new seas to fish.

We'll sail to Pylos first. I hope Polycaste will join us. Then we'll sail west until we find an unsettled island. Mountains full of game, seas where no one has fished. An empty island with untouched forests, some pasture where we can graze our sheep, a beach with headlands that jut out to protect us from the winter storms. We'll make decisions together, sitting on the hillside in the evening. We'll grow old together.

My mother cried. "One comes home, the other leaves." What else could she say? She clutched my hands, and I watched the tears coursing down her cheeks, streaking them with her eyeliner, just as my death would have furrowed them with ashes.

My father tried to stop me from going. "Your place is here, with me. You'll become chief in your turn. You'll make a name for yourself as a fighter, just as I did."

When I shook my head, he looked as if he was about to say something, then simply shrugged. He knows he can't command me.

This morning he woke me at dawn with a knock on my door.

"I've got something for you." A charm—a little boar carved from olive wood. "You should leave an offering before you go. We could go to the shrine together."

"No."

"The gods watch over you."

"Did they watch over you all those years you were wandering?"

Odysseus smiled—that mocking look I can't endure, and that almost makes me love him. "Haven't you heard the owl hoot outside your window? An eagle falling from the sky to snatch a dove from the air? The prophet in Sparta told you I was alive. He was right, wasn't he? Didn't you see a swallow in the hall during the fight? The goddess's messenger, bringing me courage in battle. You're clever, Telemachus, cleverer than I am, but sometimes I think you're a fool." He laughed and pressed the little boar into my hand. "For luck!"

Odysseus is finishing his speech now. I glance over my shoulder. The beach is strewn with driftwood and seaweed, as it always is after a storm. In the distance I can see the mainland through air as sharp and clean as mountain water. Beyond the horizon I'll find Pylos. I feel my black mood lifting, shredding like sea fog to leave my mind clear. I look around at the familiar little houses, at the faces I know so well, at the mountain towering over the rooftops. It isn't that I've lost Ithaca. I've grown out of it. Perhaps it's because there's less space for me now that Odysseus has returned. But maybe I would have had to leave anyway. There's nothing new on Ithaca. Life is how it's always been. Blood deserves blood. A fighter's status grows with the nicks on his sword and the plundered gold on his arms. Men brag and boast, snarling and fighting their way to fame. A brave death, their name in the stories—that's the only glory they know, the only glory my father knows.

I know that world too. I know it, and I'm sick of it. I don't want to live by fighting. I don't want war. I don't need a Troy of my own.

Applause breaks out in the square, scattered cheers, a drumming of feet on the beaten earth. Penelope stands up to put her arm around her husband's waist. Odysseus has come home. I lie back in my chair and close my eyes, content.

The next morning we climb on board our ship to leave.

I haven't slept. Most of last night I heard my mother weeping in her room. She spent yesterday evening pleading with me, begging, cajoling. She clutched me the way she hugged me when I was a child.

"You'll come back when I die," Odysseus said.

"Before, I hope."

"Perhaps."

He's gripping the gunwale of our ship now, as Mentor's sons stow sacks of seed under the benches. Their wives look frightened, unused to the sea. The boys who are coming with us are playing around the mast. It feels like a game to them. Beyond them, on the beach, town boys are splashing each other in the water, swapping jokes with their friends who are leaving. Mentor is solemnly counting barrels of water. Eumaeus's pigs are squealing in the makeshift pen he's knocked together in the bow. Behind it, chickens are trussed up in netting stapled to the keel. It's hardly a war galley.

"The man who brought me home," my father says, "tried to live the way you want. He sold dye made from seashells on an island in the west. A dull man with a dried-up wife and a foolish daughter. Is that what you want?"

Our stern dips as a wave rolls under it and on up the shore. There's a stiff wind blowing. It rustles sand across the beach and blows the smoke from the big house out sideways over the olive groves. I can see two forlorn white figures standing up there, on the terrace: my mother, with Eurycleia beside her. My father's talked a lot about the Phaeacians, always scornfully. I want to find them—Alcinous, Arete, and Nausicaa. To find them and trade with them. I want to ask them about the islands even farther west, where we might settle, plant our crops, and build our town.

Odysseus's hands tense on the bleached wood. He's up to his knees, wading out, not wanting to let us go.

"We're men," he says. "We fight. No one can change that. There's no easy home for you to find. Why do you think it took me so long to come home? Because storms blow you off course and journeys never end. Men are born wanderers. There's always another island for you to find."

He has to let us go then. The water's too deep. Looking back, I see the islanders thronging the beach. Their fishing boats line the sand. Behind them I can see Nirito, the big house, the ashes of the pyre. My father, thigh-deep in waves, with one hand raised in farewell.

But I don't look back for long. Sun sparkles on the water, and the wind tugs urgently at our sail. Polycaste is somewhere beyond the horizon. I grip the steering oar and turn my face to the open sea.

ACKNOWLEDGMENTS

With thanks to my agents Andrew Lownie and David Haviland, who were instrumental in helping shape the book; to Maia Larson and the brilliant team at Pegasus, who have done a wonderful job in editing it to final form; and to my old Greek teacher, Martin Hammond, who first pointed out to me that *The Odyssey* is as much about Telemachus as Odysseus.